Coastal Lights Legacy – Book Two

# REVEALING LIGHT

## Marilyn Turk

Published by Forget Me Not Romances, an imprint of Winged Publications

ISBN-13: 978-1-946939-83-8
ISBN-10: 1-946939-83-8

# Chapter One

Spring 1883, Fernandina, Florida

A woman's scream pierced the air, stilling the conversations of the people on deck. Sally Rose McFarlane jerked away from the guard rail toward the rear of the ship.

She exchanged fearful glances with the elderly couple beside her.

"What on earth...?" the woman said.

Commotion broke out among the passengers as running feet pounded the wooden deck, forcing people to make way for someone shoving through the crowd. The elderly woman fell onto Sally Rose, nearly knocking her down.

Sally Rose threw one arm out to grab the railing while clasping her hand over her new hat. Then a man with a valise tucked under his arm ran past, bumping her into another passenger. "Oh, I'm so sorry, sir," she said to the elderly man.

Voices called out.

"Thief!"

"Stop that man!"

"He stole that lady's valuables!"

Passengers pointed fingers toward the culprit. A woman nearby swooned.

Sally Rose steadied herself as the steamboat bumped into the dock below. The thief rushed down the stairs to the lowering gangplank.

No sooner had she regained her composure than she was propelled against another passenger as a tall, dark-haired man rushed past, stepping on her toe in the process.

"Ouch!"

He glanced over his shoulder in her direction, and their eyes locked, pinning her in place. A hint of apology passed over his handsome features, and she quickly forgave the offense.

What depth those eyes conveyed in that brief glance. She buried that thought as the scene unfolded down below. Leaning into the railing, Sally Rose craned her neck along with the other passengers who jostled for position to watch the chase. Her heart pounded while she sought a glimpse of the action.

The first man jumped to the dock. His feet thudded against the wooden planks, then he dashed off again, clutching a brown valise. The second man sprinted after him, closed the distance, and tackled the thief to the ground.

Cheers erupted from the ship's audience.

"Good job!"

"Well done!"

"That'll teach him!"

Sally Rose kept her eyes fixed on the hero as she rode the wave of passengers disembarking the ship. A throng of excited people gathered on shore around the gallant gentleman and his captive. Several men clapped the man on the back, calling him a hero and congratulating him on his feat. He said nothing in return, just sat astride his prisoner.

His hat had been knocked off in the scuffle, revealing thick black hair curling over the edge of his collar. High cheekbones chiseled the handsome face, the cleft in his chin emphasizing his serious expression. His brown jacket stretched taut across broad shoulders. The thief was certainly no match for this man.

A well-rounded woman in a burgundy traveling suit stood beside Sally Rose, holding her parasol aloft. Eying the men, she mused aloud, "I wonder who our hero is."

"Who?" Sally Rose feigned ignorance.

The woman smiled knowingly at Sally Rose, then nodded in the direction of the man. "Don't tell me you haven't been admiring the scenery too."

"Why, I-I was just observing the drama, like everyone else."

Lifting her eyebrows, the woman smirked. "Um hmm. Who wouldn't want a man like that to come to her rescue? Maybe *I* should scream."

Sally Rose jerked her head toward the woman. "You wouldn't...."

The woman chuckled. "Don't worry; I won't. I'll have to find another way to get his attention." She nodded to Sally Rose and with a bemused grin, sauntered closer to the scene.

Sally Rose gaped at the woman's brazen attitude. Well, Mr. Hero had gotten all the attention he needed, including her own. She had more important business to attend to.

The town marshal elbowed his way through the crowd, barking orders, so she lingered to watch as he took custody of the thief. Mr. Hero picked up the valise along with his hat. He put his hat back on and turned his attention to a wealthy-looking matron just reaching the end of the dock, aided by a man and a woman on each side of her. The hero strode over and handed the valise to the matron.

Her face crumpled into tears as she grasped her bag. "Oh, thank you, sir. These are my most precious family heirlooms. I thought I'd never see them again."

He tipped his hat, then turned on his heel and walked away.

"Sir!" the woman's acquaintance called after him.

The hero looked back.

"Sir, how can we repay you? We want to reward you for your efforts."

A hint of a smile crossed the man's face as he shook his head, touched the brim of his hat, and continued on his way.

When he passed the crowd still standing affixed to the spot, his gaze connected with Sally Rose again. Her face heated, but she couldn't keep herself from being drawn into those eyes and was unable to make herself look elsewhere. Abruptly, he looked away, and she released a breath. *Sally Rose MccFarlane, why on earth are you staring at that man?*

Even so, his demeanor made her curious. Surely he enjoyed getting so much attention, yet something told her that hadn't been his motive. One thing was certain—he was incredibly handsome. However, she needn't give him another thought. She had more important things to do and a new position waiting for her.

She straightened the long, fitted basque of her dark blue walking suit. The most expensive clothing she'd ever owned, it was made with the finest satin she could afford. Hoping she'd smoothed out the wrinkles from traveling, she sighed, then adjusted her hat and stiffened. She'd wasted enough time. Lifting her skirts to keep them from snagging, she stepped across the railroad tracks to the red brick station on the other side. A sign with bold black letters boasted "Fernandina Depot." Sally Rose paused to take in the quaint building with wrought iron grates and finials flanking the green arched windows. She studied the much-erased chalkboard on the wall that listed the day's arrivals. The heavy door groaned on its hinges when she pushed it open and made her way to the ticket counter.

"Excuse me, sir," she said to the ticket agent. "When does the next train leave for Cedar Key?"

The man behind the bars on the window continued to scribble numbers in a ledger without lifting his bald head to look at her. "Nine o'clock," he grunted. "How many tickets do you need?"

"Just one."

His busy pencil halted in the middle of his task, and his head jerked up, the lopsided spectacles nearly falling off his nose. He peered in every direction, his eyes searching around her as if looking for someone else. "You alone, young lady?"

"Yes, sir. I'll be traveling unaccompanied."

Shaking his head, the attendant returned his attention to the tickets. "I see."

Sally Rose slid her money under the bars and took her ticket in return, noting she was assigned to the White Only rail car.

She cleared her throat. "Sir?"

The agent looked up. "Yes? Did you need something else?"

She started to explain, but as the hero from the ship approached the window, she didn't know what to say.

"I..no, That's all. Thank you." Did she need to explain to him? She looked White because she was part White, but she was also

4

part Negro. What difference did it make if he knew or not? A stab of guilt pierced her conscience. What would her parents say about her silence? She stifled the thought and quickly stepped away, glancing briefly at the man who took her place in front of the counter. Could he tell she was hiding the truth?

She scanned the waiting room area of the depot. With two hours before the next train arrived, the wooden benches didn't look inviting, especially since she'd be sitting for the next nine hours. Hopefully, the train to Cedar Key wouldn't be as crowded as the one she'd taken from Cleveland to New York before sailing south.

With plenty of time until the train arrived, the lovely spring day beckoned her outside. The fresh air was invigorating. She inhaled as deeply as she could, despite the constrictions of a tight corset, enjoying the scent of flowers in the air. Her legs still felt the motion of the sea after the long boat trip, and she resisted the urge to stagger as she walked along the sidewalk. How long would it take before she became accustomed to being back on land again?

The warm, sunny weather was welcome after the cold, dark winter she'd left behind in Cleveland. Sally Rose admired the beauty of Fernadina as she strolled down Main Street away from the busy waterfront where ships waited to load or unload cargo. Colorful azalea blossoms adorned bushes in yards down the side streets. As she walked along the boardwalk, she regarded the displays in the store windows. Once when she glanced up, she almost nodded to the person staring back at her before she realized she was gazing at her own reflection. Who was this refined woman in the window? Could that really be Sally Rose McFarlane?

A subtle smile crossed her face. Yes, that was her. She was a woman of importance now. She was on her way to achieve her dream.

~

After purchasing his train ticket, Bryce Hernandez strode toward town, anxious to distance himself from curious onlookers. Why was he still acting like he worked with the Pinkerton Agency? It was no longer his job to pursue and capture criminals, yet here he was, barely a month out of his former position, jumping into affairs that were not his business. The last thing he'd wanted to do was call attention to himself. But he just couldn't stand there and do nothing while a thief made off with an elderly woman's valuables. Someone had to stop him and no one else had attempted. Too many people stood by and watched when wrong was being done. Perhaps it was his legal training or his desire for justice. Whatever it was, his days of being actively involved in law-keeping were over.

Spotting a hotel ahead, he decided to grab a bite to eat in the establishment's dining room. He was famished and knew it would be hours before his train reached its destination. He eyed a table in the corner and headed toward it. The waitress came over and served him a cup of coffee. Bryce ordered bacon and eggs, then sat back against the wall and stared out the side window.

Before long, he'd be starting a new life, a quiet, peaceful life—a life he desired after leaving the recent turmoil of union riots as a Pinkerton. For a while, his work had been a welcome distraction from his grief. But not anymore. He'd had enough of the big city, the constant chaos. He was ready for a slower pace, but he wasn't ready to go home to Cuba quite yet. Too many memories were there. At least in Cedar Key, he was close enough to visit, even if he never went home to stay.

~

Sally Rose saw a familiar group standing on the boardwalk ahead. The elderly couple from the ship waved her over. They had introduced themselves as Mr. and Mrs. Barnes, along with their companion Mildred. Sally Rose breathed a sigh of relief, thankful for their company.

"There you are, dear. We lost sight of you in all that dreadful mess." Mrs. Barnes patted a wisp of gray hair back into place. "You must join us for breakfast."

"Thank you, but ..." Sally Rose couldn't think of an excuse before the woman grabbed her arm. "I have to catch the next train to Cedar Key."

"You have plenty of time to eat. I believe that train doesn't leave until nine," Mildred said, her forehead straining against the pull of her bun.

"That's right, and I noticed you didn't eat much of anything this morning on the ship. Surely, you're hungry," Mrs. Barnes said. "I'm starving to death."

One look at the plump old woman with round cheeks revealed that remark wasn't quite accurate. Sally Rose couldn't ignore the rumblings in her own stomach. True, she hadn't felt like eating aboard ship, whether from anxiety or fear of seasickness, she didn't know.

"Come along, dear. We're staying at the Egmont Hotel just around the corner. I hear they have a wonderful restaurant."

Sally Rose was tugged along by Mrs. Barnes's firm grip while Mildred assisted Mr. Barnes. Once they entered the hotel dining room, the elderly gentleman shuffled to the table with his cane as he followed the waitress, then pulled out a chair and motioned for Sally Rose to sit. She accepted his gesture, appreciating his gracious effort. He then drew out his wife's chair before their companion helped him into his.

As breakfast proceeded, the couple wanted to know where she was going, why she was alone, and where she had come from, repeating the questions several times. Sally Rose answered each question with patience, remembering the time she too had taken care of an elderly person.

"I'm on my way to Cedar Key, where I'll be a governess for the Powell family. I grew up on a farm in Ohio, but for the past two years, I've been employed at Miss Middleton's School for Young Ladies in Cleveland as companion to the headmistress's mother."

"Do you have an escort meeting you at the train? A pretty girl like you shouldn't be alone." He glanced at his wife and leaned forward. "Why, if Mrs. Barnes didn't need me, I'd escort you myself!" The old gentleman winked at Sally Rose.

"Mr. Barnes! Will you please behave yourself? You're embarrassing our guest." His wife slapped him lightly on the arm. "I'm sorry, miss. He shouldn't be sticking his nose in your business."

Sally Rose couldn't help but smile at the playful behavior of the couple, reminding her of her own parents. A twinge of sadness twisted her heart as she pictured them together. Mama and Papa were just like that—before Papa passed. She fought tears from the void she still felt from his death, then quickly pushed her memories back where they belonged.

"No offense taken. But to answer your question, sir, no, I do not have an escort."

Mrs. Barnes pointed her spoon at Sally Rose. "After that business on the ship today, I must agree with my husband. You should have an escort to protect you. You never know what kind of scoundrel is looking to take advantage of a lady."

Sally Rose bit her tongue and tried not to show her ire at the woman's comment. Why did she need a man's protection? She had survived in the city of Cleveland, which had plenty of unsavory characters. Surely, Florida was safer.

"I'm sure I'll be fine. God looked after me on my train ride from Cleveland to New York, then I met you good people on the ship. I promise, I'll be careful."

As she spoke, she noticed a Negro couple being refused admittance to the restaurant, with the manager pointing to a sign by the door which read "White Only." The woman's shoulders drooped, then her husband slid an arm around her and guided her out of the restaurant.

Sally Rose shuddered. She could've been refused admittance too. She'd never seen such signs back home in Cleveland.

"Are you all right, dear?" Mrs. Barnes tapped her on the hand. "You look like something frightened you."

Jerking back to face Mrs. Barnes, Sally Rose raised her napkin to her lips, patting the moisture above them, then blotted her forehead. "I believe I'm just adjusting to this climate. It's a bit more humid here than in Cleveland."

Mr. Barnes chuckled. "That's for certain, but I prefer this to the snow. It may be warm, but the sunshine and sea breeze make it pleasant. You can expect the same kind of weather in Cedar Key, from what I hear."

"I'd much prefer the warmth too," said Sally Rose.

Mildred leaned forward and whispered to Sally Rose. "Say, isn't that the man who caught the thief?" Her bun nodded as she inclined her head toward a man sitting alone.

Sally Rose glanced to a table in the far corner of the restaurant where, indeed, the silent hero sat. He caught her gaze and met it. She gasped. Oh dear, what if he thought she was staring at him? Averting her eyes, she reached for a glass of water and took a quick drink. Too quick, for she choked on it; sputtering, she began to cough. She grabbed her napkin and covered her mouth as heat rushed to her face, then scanned the room looking for an exit.

"My goodness! Are you certain you're all right, dear?" Mrs. Barnes asked.

Sally Rose nodded, trying to repress the urge to cough again. "I'm afraid I swallowed too quickly." She took a few deep breaths. "But I believe I better return to the station now. I wouldn't want to miss my boarding time."

"Yes, indeed, you'd better run along. I do wish we could escort you, but we'd just slow you down," Mr. Barnes said. "You be sure and write to us when you get settled, and let us know how you like your new position. Just send it to Mr. Harold Barnes at the Egmont Hotel in Fernandina. We'll be here until it gets too hot in June."

"I will, and thank you for your hospitality." Sally Rose pulled on her gloves, then pushed back from the table and stood. "It was very nice to meet you all."

"I hope there's no trouble on the train like there was on the ship. I pray you'll have a safe trip," Mrs. Barnes added.

Sally Rose nodded and smiled, then left the restaurant, hurrying to get to the train. She scurried down the boardwalk past shop windows on her way back to the depot. The thought of Mr. Hero sitting alone eating his solitary meal troubled her, yet she had no idea why. She peered up at the courthouse clock to see how much time she had left. Across the street, her heart tugged at the scene of a small Negro boy shining a white gentleman's shoes. The boy looked so much like her little brother Toby. She returned to the depot, found a bench to sit on and smoothed back the wisps of hair that had escaped her bonnet.

"All aboard!" the conductor soon announced.

Sally Rose made her way through the crowd of passengers and those sending them off. She climbed the steps to the railcar and chose a seat next to the window. This land was the place of her birth, and she wanted to get a good look at it. Other passengers filed into the car, settling into their seats. She watched them, wondering who would be joining her during this trip on the facing bench.

Her breath stuck in her chest when she recognized Mr. Hero coming down the aisle. Would he sit with her? She tossed her valise on the opposite seat, hoping it'd look taken. He gazed in her direction and hesitated as if considering the option. Then he turned away and continued toward the other end of the car. She exhaled slowly, relieved. Well, at least she didn't have to spend the next nine hours with him. So why did she feel just a bit disappointed?

# Chapter Two

"So I said to Mr. Jones, 'Frances, we need to go to Florida. Why, there are steamboat rides and beaches and what-all down there.' Mr. Jones was hard to convince, thinking he couldn't possibly leave the business for that long. But here we are!" The buxom woman gave her head a defiant jerk, forcing the large flower on her hat to agree.

Mrs. Jones sat across from Sally Rose and had chattered incessantly since the train left Fernandina an hour before. A tow-headed little boy, with his finger up his nose, snuggled beside her, staring at Sally Rose. Mr. Jones gazed out the window, helpless to get a word in the conversation, and obviously resigned to silence.

Sally Rose smiled and nodded, occasionally stealing a glance out the window while trying not to be rude. Finally, the little boy fell asleep across his mother's lap, and the woman began to doze as well, rocked to sleep by the steady jostling of the train. The father's head had fallen back against the seat long before.

The train tracks soon left the banks of the Amelia River and headed southwest. Alone with her thoughts, Sally Rose tried to envision the family for whom she would be working. The advertisement had said there were three girls and a boy. What would they be like? Were they like her brothers and sisters back home? Although she had spent the past two years caring for an elderly woman, she was just as familiar with taking care of children. The oldest in the family, she was always the one in charge of not only her siblings, but also Aunt Kate and Uncle Joshua's children as well. She recalled Papa's words, "Sally Rose, you do a good job takin' care of other folks. But don't forget to take care of yourself too."

Bittersweet memories moistened her eyes. When would she see her family again? Cedar Key was a long way from Ohio. She had already been traveling for days and still had hours to go before she reached her destination. She closed her eyes and pictured Mama's face, her brow etched with worry and her pursed lips a sure sign that tears threatened. Despite her disapproval, however, Mama hadn't begged her to stay. A tiny needle of regret pricked her.

"Sally Rose, I don't like you goin so far away, but you got a strong will, so you gonna do what you gonna do. Just don't let that strong will keep you from rememberin' Who's in charge!" She could still see Mama's eyes looking deeply into her own, trying to search inside her soul.

"Yes, Mama. I know God's in charge, but I believe He wants me to do this."

At least that's what she'd told Mama, but was she right? Was this idea to be a governess God's will or her own? Deep within, she had a craving to be somebody, to prove that she could be successful, that she could make a name for herself. Papa understood her. He was the only one who ever did. She still missed him so. Oh, how she wished she could have told him about her new opportunity! He would have shared her excitement, would have realized her need to strike out on her own.

"Rosie, you can do whatever you makes up yo' mine ta do. I knows you'll do well, whatever that is." She could hear Papa's voice.

With Papa's support, she had the courage to take the job in Cleveland as Mrs. Middleton's companion. She remembered the bear hug he'd given her the day she left the farm, and how he'd patted her shoulder, assuring her the other children would be there to help him and Mama.

She sniffed and removed her handkerchief from her sleeve to pat the moisture gathered in the corners of her eyes. The train entered a dense swamp, plunging the car into a shadowy, primeval world. Unusual vegetation caught her attention as she stared at the tropical scenery of tall palm trees and spiky bushes below. Mr. Jones, sitting across from her, coughed and awakened, peering out the window at the landscape.

A large reptile slid into the water as the train rumbled past.

"Oh!" Sally Rose gasped.

"Alligator," the man said. "You ever see one before?"

Sally Rose shook her head. "Only in pictures. I had no idea they were so large." And fearsome.

"They get bigger than that. They'll eat small animals—pigs, dogs, whatever. Even hear they'll eat children if they get close enough." The man's thin mustache turned up into a wry smile.

"Oh, my!" Was she expected to protect her charges against alligator attacks? She shuddered.

"Don't worry. I don't expect they'll be crawling through town. Cedar Key is a bit more civilized than that."

"Thank God."

"Didn't hear you say your reason for going. You have relatives in the area?"

"No. I'm going there to take a position as governess for the Powell family."

"Traveling alone?" The man's eyebrows lifted. "So will you be staying in a hotel? We'll be at the Bettelini. It's the largest."

The man's line of questioning sent a slither up her spine, and she resisted the urge to squirm. She straightened. "I'll be living with the Powell family, my employers."

"You're going a long way to take care of someone else's children. Don't they have a mother?"

The man was getting under her skin. "Of course they do. However, I'll be their teacher."

"They don't have a school?" Mr. Jones raised his eyebrows as if he questioned the necessity of her position.

"I don't know. If they do, I doubt it teaches more than reading, writing, and arithmetic."

"What more do you need to know?"

Sally Rose tried to sound polite, even though Mr. Jones wasn't. "Music, French, geography, Latin, to name a few subjects I will teach them."

"That so? And you know all that, do you?"

"Yes, I am familiar with the subjects."

"The family must have some means, then, to bring you all this way for that."

Sally Rose pursed her lips. She'd already shared more personal information than she intended. The man's rudeness was appalling. She turned her attention back to the scenes outside the window and gestured to some unusual plants with sharp pointed leaves growing densely together beneath the pine trees.

"I wonder what type of bushes those are."

"Palmetto. They'll cut you if you get close."

Goodness. Did the man ever have anything positive to say? She didn't know which was worse—his wife's prattle or his prying and inappropriate questions.

The train began to slow down as the conductor entered the car and called out, "Next stop, Albion! If you're continuing on and need to leave the train for necessaries, be back on board in thirty minutes or the train departs without you."

Mrs. Jones and her son awoke.

"Mommy, I need to go to the privy!"

The woman sat upright and looked around. "Where are we?"

"Albion. It's just the first stop." Her husband nodded toward the youngster. "Better take the boy to the outhouse."

"And will you accompany us, Mr. Jones?" his wife asked.

Mr. Jones frowned. "I might as well stretch my legs a bit too."

As the train stopped, Mrs. Jones took Junior and disembarked. Mr. Jones stood behind her, acting as though he were leaving too. But instead of getting off, he returned to his seat, grinning at Sally Rose as if he'd pulled off an amazing feat. His gaze raked up and down her body as his lips pulled into a lecherous sneer. Her heart thumped an alarm and she recalled Mrs. Barnes's warning. Sally Rose gritted her teeth at the man's audacity. Who did this man think he was, anyway? Well, she wasn't going to give him something to ogle. Abruptly, she stood and lifted her chin.

"Excuse me, please. I believe I must disembark as well." She straightened her dress, giving herself some breathing room from her tight stays, then pulled up her gloves and adjusted her hat, avoiding eye contact with Mr. Jones. She had no idea where she'd go, as long as it was away from him. Poor Mrs. Jones had an unfaithful husband, of that Sally Rose was certain. She left the train and walked toward the depot, hoping Mr. Jones wouldn't follow. She breathed a sigh of relief when he didn't.

Seeking shade from the bright sunlight, she strolled to an area covered by the small depot's roof. She inhaled the fresh air, respite from the train's smoke and studied the people around her, a habit she always enjoyed. She must have gotten that habit from Mama, who used to make up entertaining stories about people they saw when they went to town. Sally Rose and her siblings learned to join in the story-telling, laughing at each other's creative tales. She smiled at the memory. What a brilliant way to prevent any unruliness from the bunch of youngsters. Sally Rose planned to use that exercise with the children she taught.

A feeling of being watched prickled her neck. Startled back to the present, Sally Rose glanced around, afraid Mr. Jones had followed her after all. Instead, she saw Mr. Hero, leaning against a tree trunk some twenty feet away. Heat rushed to her face, and she raised her fan to dry the sweat beads forming on her upper lip and hairline. Trying to divert her gaze, she used the fan as a shield, but not before she saw his slight nod at her.

Her heart leaped. Should she smile back and acknowledge him? Why, she didn't even know who he was. She'd seen him disembark and assumed he was getting off at this stop to stay. But he appeared to be waiting too. She certainly didn't mean to encourage advances from a stranger, nor did she want to rejoin Mr. Jones on the train. Glancing around her, she felt trapped, uncertain which way to turn.

# Chapter Three

It was the woman from the ship. He'd seen her across the restaurant sitting with some other people. But he hadn't seen the others on the train. Could she possibly be traveling alone?

Bryce Hernandez wanted nothing more than a bit of exercise when he disembarked the train, grateful for the opportunity to move his legs. But he hadn't planned on encountering the lovely young lady he'd noticed earlier. She was stunning, impossible to ignore. The chestnut brown hair that framed her face so elegantly was swept into a mass of curls in the back, topped by a small, dark blue felt hat adorned with a single pheasant feather. Her tasteful walking suit fit her trim, shapely figure perfectly. She had an exotic air about her. Maybe it was her light olive skin that reminded him of his half-sisters back in Cuba—or maybe it was the way she carried herself. Why would such an attractive woman be alone? Her husband must be waiting her arrival at the end of the rail line. Yet her demeanor conveyed a certain type of independence.

She turned and faced him, then averted her eyes and glanced back and forth, as if looking for a way of escape. He nodded and smiled, but she hid behind her fluttering fan. He hadn't meant to frighten her by staring. Why hadn't she smiled back at him? Surely she didn't think he was flirting. He'd only meant to be polite. The last thing he needed was a woman's attention.

The conductor's voice rang out. "All aboard!"

The woman picked up her skirts and practically fled toward the train. After giving her a chance to put some distance between them, Bryce sauntered back as well. His thoughts returned to the day's events when he'd reacted as if he still worked with the Pinkerton Agency.

When he got to Cedar Key, he'd be a law partner again in a small town where he could relax and enjoy some peace and quiet. Mr. Powell's letter assured him of that. He looked forward to settling in as an obscure lawyer in a new place.

He waited for the other passengers to board the train, and then boarded himself. Making his way to his former seat, he was surprised to find it occupied by a new passenger. He shouldn't have waited so long to get on. No matter; he'd find another. He moved back through the railcar, looking for an open seat. Seeing one up ahead, he strode toward it. He pulled up short when he reached the compartment. The seat was next to the woman he'd been admiring.

"Is this seat taken?" Bryce looked at the other occupants of the berth, noting a husband, wife, and child across from the woman.

She appeared surprised, her eyes widening at his question.

"Sit yourself down," the wife said. "Junior was supposed to sit there, but he's afraid of trains and has to sit next to his mama." She peered down at the boy huddled up against her.

Her husband shrugged as if he had no interest in the matter. Bryce looked back at the woman next to the empty seat, who gave a quick nod, moving her valise closer to her feet as he sat down.

Directly across from him, the mother wasted no time as she jumped into introducing herself and her family, then proceeded to tell him the story of her life … or so it seemed.

He removed his hat and placed it on his lap, trying to act interested in what she was saying. At least her incessant talk saved him from having to talk about himself. But his mind was actually focused on the lovely woman next to him, now gazing out the window. Who was she, and where was she going? She still hadn't given him a smile. Apparently, she was just unfriendly. Then again, why should he care about her business anyway?

~

Sally Rose tried to breathe normally. The proximity to the handsome man made her heart thump. Could he hear it?

Of all people, why was *he* the one who took the seat next to her? Was it intentional? He'd not sat there before. She tried to concentrate on the scenery outside the train, thankful the other woman's chatter prevented uncomfortable conversation with the man.

The landscape changed from verdant green forest to wide open spaces, stretching on and on. She'd not expected this type of hilly scenery, which reminded her of the country back in Ohio. The biggest difference was the sandy white ground that showed through the greenery. And, of course, the sporadic stands of palm trees and palmetto that dotted the hills.

A loud snore erupted nearby. She jumped and exchanged glances with the man next to her, whose hint of a smile and nod toward the woman across from them made her cover her mouth to stifle a giggle. Once more, the family had fallen asleep. Sally Rose was thankful for respite from Mrs. Jones's talking. But her heart resumed its erratic beating now that the woman no longer provided a distraction.

She grabbed her fan and waved the air to cool off. He, too, fanned himself with his hat.

"It's a bit stuffy in here, isn't it?" He whispered, no doubt to not awaken the others.

Sally Rose faced him and nodded, once again drawn in by his eyes, those deep pools of mystery that begged understanding. What was it about him that was so disarming, yet strangely familiar?

He leaned toward her and spoke in low tones. "Frankly, I'm enjoying the quiet."

She couldn't help smiling. At least they had one thing in common besides sharing a train ride. "Me too," she whispered.

"My name is Bryce Hernandez."

Finally, she could stop referring to him as Mr. Hero. "Sally Rose McFarlane."

His eyebrow lifted.

Sally Rose frowned. "Is something wrong?"

He shook his head. "No, nothing."

And just like that, the spell was broken. His expression turned serious again. The weight on his shoulders seemed to reappear. For a brief moment, she thought she had been wrong about his droll attitude. The hint of light that flickered momentarily in his eyes extinguished. What on earth caused his moods to change so swiftly? She turned her attention back to the scenery.

~

Sally Rose McFarlane. What a lovely name. She did indeed remind him of a lovely flower, but not a soft pink one—a rich, deep, scarlet one. But McFarlane? That name out of his past, from a time he barely remembered. He never would have guessed this young woman had a Scottish name, especially the same family name he used to have.

She'd finally smiled at him though. And melted his insides right down to his toes. As if she weren't beautiful enough. But her smile lit up the area around them before she turned away once again. Just as well. As long as they were quiet, the others slept. Despite the silent warning his heart gave him to keep his distance, he wanted to know more about her. However, once they went their separate ways, he'd never see her again. A cloud of sadness returned to darken his mood.

~

"Next stop, Cedar Key!"

Sally Rose had never been so happy to hear those words in her life. Once Mrs. Jones had awakened, she'd resumed her drivel for the rest of the train ride, while her husband stared out the window or glared at Mr. Hernandez. Was it possible Mr. Jones was jealous that Mr. Hernandez had taken a seat beside her? There had been little conversation between them the remainder of the trip.

As Sally Rose looked out the window, she saw water on either side of the train. She gasped, her hand over her chest.

Both men asked at once, "What is it?" They exchanged warning glances.

"I didn't realize we were going over water. Where is the land?"

Mr. Jones answered with authority. "Cedar Key is an island. You didn't know that?"

"Well, I did, but I assumed there would be a bridge."

"Not a big bridge. Just a bunch of small bridges that connect little islands across the marsh until you get to the main island of Cedar Key."

"I see." Sally Rose disliked the derisive tone in Mr. Jones's voice. She focused on the sights outside, praying the trestle was strong enough to carry them as the train rocked and swayed over the water. How long before they'd be on dry land again?

Soon the swampy area, dotted with clumps of reeds and mud, disappeared as the train found solid ground. The train whistle blew its arrival and white buildings came into view while they slowed to a stop. A putrid smell wafted through the window, and Sally Rose covered her nose with her gloved hand.

"You're smelling marsh mud." Mr. Hernandez leaned forward to speak so she could hear above the din of screeching train wheels.

She hoped the whole town didn't have that odor. When the train finally stopped, the Jones family stood and gathered their things. Sally Rose waited for them to depart before she followed suit. They said their farewells, and Sally Rose wished them a nice stay. As she smiled at the little boy, he spoke to her for the first time. "You're real purty."

Heat rushed to her face. "Thank you."

Just before Mr. Jones left, he turned and said, "He's right," and winked.

Sally Rose shuddered. She was quite relieved to see him leave. Mr. Hernandez scowled after the man, then stood and put on his hat. "Can I help you with anything?"

"No, thank you. I'm sure my trunk will be waiting outside."

"Well, good day, Mrs. McFarlane. It was a pleasure to meet you."

Mrs? He thought she was married. Well, it didn't matter what he thought after all, did it? Sally Rose straightened her bodice, attempting to settle the fluttering in her stomach. She swallowed to moisten her dry throat. "Thank you, Mr. Hernandez."

He stepped down from the train first then turned to offer his hand to her. She took it, the warmth of his touch surprising her. They nodded goodbye and separated to look for their parties.

She watched as a tall man with gray-tinged black hair approached Mr. Hernandez. The men shook hands and began to walk away.

Sally Rose heard children's voices coming from her right. "There she is! She said she'd be wearing a blue suit! Miss McFarlane! Over here!"

Turning in the direction of the voices, she saw three little girls and a boy waving their hands at her. The children broke loose from their mother's grasp and ran to her.

"Wait, children!" the anxious woman called out, trying to catch up with the youngsters. When she reached the group, she gave an apologetic glance to Sally Rose. "Please forgive their manners. Miss McFarlane. I'm Ellen Powell. Welcome to Cedar Key." Mrs. Powell, a pleasant-looking woman who emanated warmth from kind, brown eyes, placed her hand on the shoulder of the tallest girl. "This is Adele, the oldest." She moved down the row, patting each child on the head. "This is Lucy; little Frank, whom we call Benjamin, his middle name; and this is Tilly, our youngest."

The three girls with their beribboned hair and white pinafores lined up like stair steps and demonstrated their best curtsies. The oldest girl held her chin high, clearly proclaiming her independence and rank among the others, while the youngest child clung to her mother's skirts. The little boy with the white blouse and suspendered brown short pants bowed, encouraged by a gentle push on the back from his mother.

"I'm so happy to meet you all." Sally Rose smiled at the children. Her heart swelled at their cheerful faces. *What delightful children! Yes, this is where I'm supposed to be.*

"We'll get Mr. Powell to help with your trunk. There he is. Frank!" Mrs. Powell waved at the tall man on the edge of the platform, the one speaking to Mr. Hernandez.

He came over, with Mr. Hernandez following behind. "Miss McFarlane, I presume? Frank Powell. It's very nice to meet you."

Sally Rose tried to speak but felt tongue-tied as Mr. Hernandez approached.

"It's very nice to meet you, sir." She nodded and gave a slight curtsy.

Mr. Powell turned to Mr. Hernandez.

"Allow me to introduce my new law partner, Mr. Bryce Hernandez. Mr. Hernandez, this is Miss Sally Rose McFarlane, our new governess."

# Chapter Four

Sally Rose and Mr. Hernandez stared at each other in uncomfortable silence until he spoke. "We've already met."

Frank and Ellen Powell exchanged confused glances.

Mr. Hernandez stayed focused on Sally Rose, making her insides squirm. "We met on the train," he said.

"Of course!" Mr. Powell said, breaking the tension. "Well, I'm glad you're already acquainted." He motioned toward a horse-drawn carriage parked beside the station. "Let's get you two settled. Since Miss McFarlane is going to be living with us, she can ride in the buggy with Mrs. Powell and the children. You and I can walk to the Schlemmer House Hotel where you'll be staying, at least for the time being. It's right down the road. The Schlemmers are a wonderful family, and their bakery has the best bread in town!"

A baggage handler loaded Sally Rose's trunk into the rear of the buggy, and the children scrambled in behind it. While Mr. Powell assisted Mrs. Powell into her seat, Mr. Hernandez offered his hand to Sally Rose and helped her step up into the buggy. Warmth pulsed through her at his gentle touch. Then he slid his hand from hers and gave her a polite nod before walking away.

As Mrs. Powell took the reins and clicked to the horses, Sally Rose collected herself and focused on the town and its buildings.

"I've never seen such white buildings," she said. "What are they made of?"

"We call that *tabby*. It's made from shell. Some call it *coquina*. We have lots of shells around here, so we put them to good use. In fact, you're riding on them as well. They keep the streets from getting so muddy." Mrs. Powell clucked to the horse and shook the reins, encouraging the horse along.

"Shells?"

Sally Rose looked down at the streets paved with broken seashells. She couldn't imagine streets in Cleveland paved this way.

"That's correct. They're mostly oyster shells, since oysters are so plentiful in our waters." She faced Sally Rose. "Do you like oysters?"

"I've never tried them." Sally Rose wasn't sure she was ready to either.

"You'll have the opportunity, since we have them for dinner fairly often. Our cook knows how to smoke them. They're quite tasty."

Perhaps she'd give them a try, just to be polite.

Beyond the main street they traveled, the train tracks extended to the end of the dock on the water. Ships lined alongside, waiting to be loaded or unloaded onto the train. As far as Sally Rose could see, ships and boats large and small dotted the water. Shielding her eyes against the glare with her hand, she spotted another island. Memories of Uncle Joshua taking her along with her brothers and sisters sailing on Lake Erie warmed her heart. Perhaps she'd have an opportunity to go sailing here as well.

"Is that island part of Cedar Key?"

"It's actually another town called Atsenie Otie. The Faber Pencil Mill is over there."

"Truly? They make pencils on that island?"

"The mill actually makes the cedar planks *for* the pencils. There's another pencil company here in town, the Eagle Pencil Company that does the same."

Sally Rose sniffed the air. "I can smell fresh-cut wood."

"We have quite a few sawmills in the area, so I don't even notice the scent anymore." They passed a corner with a sign boasting *Powell and Hobbs Mercantile*.

"That's our store!" Benjamin announced from the rear of the buggy.

Sally Rose quirked an eyebrow and faced Mrs. Powell. "I thought Mr. Powell was a lawyer."

"He is. But he's also a partner in the mercantile. The other partner, Albert Hobbs, runs the store while Mr. Powell handles his law business next door."

And now Bryce Hernandez was Mr. Powell's new law partner. Sally Rose's pulse quickened. Would see him often?

"I suppose the weather is warmer here than in Cleveland." Mrs. Powell drew Sally Rose back from her thoughts about Mr. Hernandez.

"Oh, yes. Quite a bit warmer. We have snow on the ground back home because it's still winter there. And please, call me Sally Rose."

"Of course, and you may call me Ellen. Even though I'm your employer, I hope we can be friends as well."

"All right, Mrs.—that is, Ellen. May I ask you a question?"

"Please do. Ellen glanced at Sally Rose, her expression encouraging. Yes, they would surely forge a friendship. "What do you need?"

"Oh, I don't need anything." Sally Rose smoothed her skirts, brushing away some of the ash from the train and avoiding Ellen's looks as she tried to not sound overly interested. "I was just wondering how long you've know Mr. Hernandez."

"We just met, so I hardly know him at all." Ellen responded to the look of surprise Sally Rose failed to suppress. "Mr. Powell advertised for a law partner in all the major cities, just as he did for a governess. Mr. Hernandez answered the advertisement, and they have been corresponding ever since."

"I see." Sally Rose mulled over the information. "He has a slight accent, and the name Hernandez is of Spanish origin. Is he from Spain or South America?"

"I don't know. He came here from Pittsburgh." Ellen glanced at Sally Rose. "You met on the train?"

"Yes, although we didn't have much conversation." If she'd known Mr. Hernandez was also an employee of the Powells, perhaps she'd been more comfortable conversing with him.

The scenery changed as the wagon left the shops of the town behind. Trees on either side of a slight incline waved their spring-green boughs in the soft sea breeze, as if bidding her welcome. Ellen turned down another street and pulled the carriage up in front of a large house commanding the next corner.

"Here we are."

Ellen tied the reins then climbed down, while the children jumped out the back. Benjamin appeared next to the wagon at her side, offering his hand to assist Sally Rose down.

"What a nice gentleman." Sally Rose beamed at the blushing lad as she gripped his small hand and stepped to the ground.

Ellen came around and patted her son on the back. "We're working on it, aren't we, Benjamin?" The boy nodded and lifted his chin proudly. "Mr. Powell expects his children to be well-mannered."

Sally Rose smiled. "Well, it looks as though they're off to a fine start."

"Joseph will get your trunk." Ellen turned toward an elderly Negro man approaching the wagon.

"I hope it's not too heavy." A pang of guilt bothered Sally Rose as the older man lifted her satchel.

"It's all right, Miss. I been liftin' loads a long time." Joseph eyed her curiously, and she ducked her head. Could he tell?

Ellen touched Sally Rose on the sleeve. "Come on in and let me show you to your room."

"You'll be next to our room." Adele fell in step next to Sally Rose, as if assuming the role of hostess along with her mother.

"Is that so? Well, I can't wait to see." Sally Rose and Adele followed Ellen as the other children trailed behind. The house had two broad porches on the front, one on the second floor and another one on the lower level that wrapped around to the side. Entering the front door, she found herself in a large central hallway with polished wood floors and rooms on either side. A stairway sided by broad-striped rose-covered wallpaper led to the second floor. It was a well-furnished home, though not quite as fine as Mrs. Middleton's house in Cleveland.

"Here's the parlor." Ellen motioned to her right. "This is where you'll conduct your lessons, unless you prefer someplace else."

Sally Rose poked her head in the doorway and glanced around. "This will do just fine."

The room was comfortably large, with two windows facing the side yard and one facing the front of the house, affording plenty of light. A fireplace on one wall boasted a mantel with small family pictures and a gilt-framed mirror hanging above. An ornate, carved fire screen covered the front. Sally Rose envisioned herself sitting in one of the comfortable green velvet chairs with the fringed pillows and antimacassars on the arms, while the children sat on the garnet Oriental rug at her feet studying their lessons. Her heart leaped at the sight of a piano gracing one corner of the room, its bench near the window where she could view the side yard. Yes, this would do just fine for a classroom. She gave Ellen a wide smile, eager to start teaching.

"We can come back down after you get settled in your room." Ellen continued up the stairs.

At the top, the landing opened out to a wide hallway with doors on either side.

The girls rushed past and into the first room on the right, dancing around with excitement.

"This is our room!" they announced in unison.

"What a lovely room you have." Sally Rose scanned the cheerful room, with its colorful pink and white calico quilts that covered three beds and the white lace curtains that graced the windows. A wooden cradle filled with several smiling dolls rested below the window, much like the one Sally Rose and her little sister had played with. On the side of the room with the fireplace, a small table with chairs invited her to tea. Warmth caressed her heart at the miniature tea set, ready to serve more dolls sitting in the chairs. The urge to be a little girl again begged her to relive her childhood in this charming room. There was no doubt that little girls inhabited the space.

Tilly, the little curly-haired blonde, ran over to the cradle and picked up a ragdoll, hugging it to her chest. "This is my doll. Her name's Mary."

Sally Rose touched the threadbare fabric of the well-loved doll, its scant hair evidence of being combed many times, her button eyes barely hanging on. "Nice to meet you, Mary. What a lovely doll. She reminds me of one I had when I was a little girl."

Tilly's bright blue eyes widened. "You did? What was her name?"

"Rebecca. She was very special."

Ellen took Sally Rose by the arm and gently tugged her toward the door. "You can show Miss McFarlane the rest of your toys later." Ellen motioned ahead, opening the next door down the hallway. "This will be your room."

Inside, Sally Rose admired the double four-posted bed covered with a fine crochet topping, a marble-topped night table beside it. Against the opposite wall rested a marble-topped chest of drawers with a mirror, and on it was a wash basin and pitcher. A little gasp escaped her as she spotted two richly upholstered chairs beside a round table near the window.

"Oh, how pretty." She walked over and stroked the red velvet back of one chair as she scanned the room. She'd never had a bedroom so exquisite.

"I didn't expect such fine accommodations. Whose room was it before?"

"It was Grandmother Powell's room," Lucy said from the doorway where she watched with her sisters.

Ellen frowned at Lucy as if admonishing the child for saying something impolite. "Mr. Powell's mother used to stay here when she visited. These furnishings belong to her. She brought them with her from England."

"Oh, I'm sorry. Is she deceased?"

Ellen blanched. "Oh, my, no. She lives in Charleston. We decided it was more practical for you to have the room now, since she doesn't visit often."

"So where will she stay on her next visit?"

"We'll put her up in one of the hotels."

"Won't she be offended?" The last thing Sally Rose wanted was to offend an important family member if the woman expected to stay in her former room.

"She shouldn't be. She was the one who suggested we get a governess." Ellen's face reddened and she glanced away. "I mean, she'll be happy to have the luxury of a hotel staff wait on her." Ellen bit her lip then strode to the window. "You can see the water from here. It's a lovely view, one of the best in the house."

Just outside her window, where the branches of a huge oak tree stretched and yawned, splashes of blue sparkled from the water of the Gulf of Mexico in the distance. She stepped closer to better enjoy the view. "It's delightful. With those branches right outside the window, I feel like I'm in a tree house." Snickers erupted from the children who had followed them into the room. Sally Rose pointed to the gray, hairy-looking masses stringing down from the limbs. "What is that strange matter hanging from the tree?"

Ellen's eyebrows creased then her eyes opened wide. "Oh, that's Spanish moss. You've never seen it before?"

"No, I haven't. It's very interesting, though. Is it part of the tree?"

Again a puzzled look. "I'm not sure. It's very common around here."

A memory of Papa talking about their home in Florida came to mind. So this is what he meant about moss in the trees. Her heart warmed with the connection to her past. She would think of Papa every time she looked at the tree.

"Our room is across the hall." Ellen motioned out the door. "If you need anything, just let us know."

Sally Rose glanced over at Benjamin. "And where is your room, Benjamin?"

The sandy brown-haired boy pointed toward the back of the hall. "It's down there. I got a room all to myself, since I'm the only boy. Do you want to see it?"

"It's not as pretty as ours," Adele said.

Benjamin frowned. "It's not s'posed to be pretty. It's a boy's room."

"I'd love to see your room, Benjamin." Sally Rose stepped into the hallway. "Why don't you show it to me?"

Benjamin skipped ahead and pointed in a doorway. Sally Rose followed and stopped at the door to look in. It was a small room and plain, with a single bed and a table. A little window provided light. In a corner, a small trunk gaped open, revealing a wooden boat, a slingshot, and other toys evident of a boy's domain..

Ellen appeared at Sally Rose's arm. "This room used to be the nursery, but when Tilly got big enough to share a room with her sisters, we gave the room to Benjamin. It's nicer than the attic room he used to sleep in."

"Well, I think it's a perfect room for a boy." Sally Rose gazed at the beaming boy, her heart squeezing.

Poor boy was outnumbered in this household of females. She'd have to make sure he didn't feel left out.

"Let's give Miss McFarlane a chance to relax and freshen up from her long trip." Ellen herded the children away from Sally Rose. "I'm sure you must be starved. We'll have supper as soon as Mr. Powell returns. He shouldn't take long getting Mr. Hernandez checked into his hotel. I made him promise to wait until tomorrow before discussing business with his new partner. Come on down to the dining room when you're ready. It's across the hall from the parlor."

Sally Rose thanked her, then retraced her steps down the hall to her room and closed the door. She removed her hat and placed it on the round table, then poured some water in the basin and splashed it on her face to remove the ashes that clung to her skin from the train ride. The cool water was refreshing after an exhausting day of travel. As she studied her reflection in the cheval mirror, she thought about the mistake the ticket agent had made. What did he see? What did she look like to the Powells? What did Mr. Hernandez see when he looked at her? The image of her own face faded and his face appeared in front of her. Why did he keep coming back into her thoughts?

Maybe because he was mysterious. He didn't smile very much; in fact, he didn't seem to be a very happy man. Why not? There appeared to be pain deep within his eyes, a pain he was trying to hide. What had happened to make him sad? She huffed and grabbed the towel. Why was she thinking about him? He was *not* her concern. Wiping her face, she addressed her own reflection in the mirror.

"You are a governess. That's why you're here. You have an important job to do, and nothing is going to interfere with your doing it."

She changed out of her day suit and put on a fresh white blouse and gray skirt for supper. What a relief to rid herself of the extra layers of clothing. She sighed at the way her traveling suit looked, now coated with a light layer of ash. Hopefully, she could brush that off tomorrow and restore its sheen. However, it might be some time before she wore the suit again in the warm, tropical climate of Florida. Lighter clothing was much cooler and more breathable.

As she made her way down the stairs, she heard male voices coming from the dining room. She stopped in the doorway and stared. Mr. Hernandez stood, his head tilted in Mr. Powell's direction as the two men conversed, but he glanced up and met her gaze. His unwavering eyes denied her the opportunity to look away. What was he doing here? A slight smile tugged at the corner of his lips, and he offered a nod. Her face warmed, and she couldn't help but offer a smile in return.

Mr. Powell's gaze followed that of Mr. Hernandez and fell on her. "Ah, there you are. I trust you've had a chance to relax a bit." Mr. Powell motioned to Mr. Hernandez. "I've asked Mr. Hernandez to join us for dinner as he had no other plans."

Sally Rose wanted to admire the beautifully decorated room, but she couldn't focus on anything other than Mr. Hernandez's presence. Her stomach twisted in strange ways. To not eat during her first meal with the family would appear rude, yet she feared she wouldn't be able to swallow anything. And if those mysterious oysters were on the menu, she'd surely humiliate herself.

Mr. Powell extended his hand toward the dining room, inviting Sally Rose and Mr. Hernandez to enter. Mr. Powell went to one end of the table to pull out a chair for his wife, then held the chair to her right for Sally Rose. The children arrived and sat in their places on each side of the table. Mr. Powell moved to his place at the head of the table, motioning for Mr. Hernandez to sit beside him.

Sally Rose let out a sigh, her stomach untwisting. Thank goodness, the men were at the other end of the table. At least, she could focus her attention on Ellen and the children, instead of battling the jitters that besieged her stomach every time Mr. Hernandez looked at her. Her ears, however, stayed attuned to the men's conversation.

"So when will you be going to Cuba?" Mr. Powell asked.

Sally Rose's heart skipped a beat. He was leaving? Well, good, he wouldn't be in her way. She brushed the thought aside, being none of her concern.

Tilly tugged on her sleeve, and as she bent down to hear the little girl, she missed hearing Mr. Hernandez answer the question.

# Chapter Five

Seated at the Powells' table, Bryce stole glances at Miss McFarlane. When Mr. Powell suggested he join the family for dinner, Bryce had found the idea of sharing a meal in a home with a family sounded inviting, something he'd missed for a long time. Then, there was the lovely Miss McFarlane. His pulse quickened at the thought of seeing her. Not that he was interested in courting her—not at all. However, the idea of her presence at dinner was certainly appealing.

He doubted she had the same interest in seeing him again though. Her reaction to his partnership with Mr. Powell wasn't very welcoming. In fact, she'd seemed shocked. He had to admit he was rather surprised himself that they'd both be working for the same employer. He found the opportunity appealing, but did she disagree?

She was quite relaxed with the children, having quickly settled into her role, as if she'd known them for some time. He envied the children, wishing he was the recipient of one of the smiles that lit up her face. Even though she had changed out of her proper suit and hat, she was still quite striking.

*Bryce, get hold of yourself.*

He tried to concentrate on what Frank Powell was saying—more important things. Mr. Powell had hinted at a matter of concern earlier, and Bryce was interested in finding out what the problem was. But a family meal wasn't the proper place to broach the subject, and dinner passed without discussing anything more serious than the weather.

After supper, the women and children retired to the parlor, and the men went out on the side porch. "Mr. Hernandez, there's something I need to discuss with you."

"Please, call me Bryce." Bryce settled in one of the wooden rocking chairs Frank gestured to, then Frank took the one beside it.

"Yes, of course, and you may call me Frank. You see, your background intrigued me because I need a special kind of assistance."

Bryce raised his eyebrows. "Assistance?"

"Yes. I have a partner, Albert Hobbs, in the mercantile business."

"I recall your telling me that."

"Frankly, I have suspicions that Hobbs is stealing from the business. But I can't prove it and need help finding out. When I saw that not only were you a lawyer but a former Pinkerton detective, I thought you'd be the perfect man to discover any wrongdoing."

"So you hired me to be a detective and not a law partner?" Bryce stroked his chin. Had he made a mistake by coming here? Just when he thought life was calming down...

"Well actually, I need you to be both. However, as far as anyone else knows, you're only my law partner. Not even Mrs. Powell knows of my suspicions."

Bryce ran a hand through his thick hair, staring up at the oak tree near the porch. "I see."

"Is that arrangement acceptable to you?" Uncertainty crept into Frank's voice, and deep furrows creased his brow. "I didn't mean to mislead you. In fact, I only came to this decision since my last letter to you."

"You know I retired from Pinkerton."

"Yes, I know. Was there some problem with the agency that caused you to leave?"

Bryce shook his head. "No, I just got tired of the fighting and tensions involved in handling the unions." He'd traveled hundreds of miles to escape that job, yet it had followed him. "I'm seeking a quieter lifestyle."

"I understand. It's pretty quiet in Cedar Key. I'm sorry. Perhaps I shouldn't have asked."

Bryce studied the pine flooring before raising his head. "It's all right. So you want me to perform my duties as a lawyer for the public but do some detective work secretly?"

"That was my hope."

"Hmm. Let me think about it." The war between coming to the rescue again and putting that life behind him battled inside him. The decision wouldn't be easy. "May I give you an answer later?"

Frank grinned. "Of course. I'll introduce you to Albert tomorrow. We rent some rooms above the store. As soon as we have a vacancy, you can move there. That way, if you decide to investigate him, it'll be easier to keep a close watch on his activities. Our law offices are next door, so it'll be a very convenient location for you."

Bryce gazed out at the nighttime sky, his chest tightening. So Frank had something else in mind when he hired him on as a partner. Was it not possible to leave the life of a private investigator behind him? Yet, his curiosity was piqued, and a new challenge was inviting.

What had he gotten himself into now?

~

Sally Rose helped Ellen clear the dishes and carry them out to the kitchen. She had forgotten most southern homes kept their kitchens away from the main house. As warm as it was already, no doubt the kitchen would heat the house considerably.

Martha, the Powells' cook, was a large Negro woman with a robust grin.

"Nice to meet you, miss. You come all the way down here from Ohio, hmm?"

"Yes, I did. I must say, it was a very long trip."

"No, thank you, I won' be goin' that far. It's far 'nuf to my house."

Where did the woman live? And had she ever been a slave, like Sally Rose's own parents? But she dared not ask these questions, nor could she look Martha in the eyes for very long, lest Martha see her secret.

Ellen patted Sally Rose on the arm. "You must be exhausted. I'll go get the children ready for bed, and you can retire. I'm sure you'll be very busy tomorrow."

After Ellen left, Sally Rose turned to go too, then noticed Martha studying her, looking her up and down and shaking her head. What was she thinking? Did she know?

Sally Rose felt lightheaded. She inched toward the door, desperate for cooler air.

"Don' worry." Martha clucked her tongue. "We'll put some meat on those bones of yours. They must not have good food in Ohio!"

Tension melted from Sally Rose, as only her eating habits were being assessed. "My mother was a very good cook, but I confess I haven't had her cooking lately, since living in Cleveland."

"Your mother did all her own cooking?"

"Yes, well the children helped." Should she tell Martha about her parents? Maybe not just yet. After all, she was in the South now. Even if Negroes were no longer slaves, they were still treated differently than whites, forced to ride in separate railcars and evicted from restaurants. Would the Powells evict her if they learned of Sally Rose's heritage?

"That right? Well, you don't have to worry 'bout doing the cooking here. I does all of that. Mrs. Barnes sometimes helps a little, but if I need mo' help, my daughter will come over."

"I see." Sally Rose suddenly felt very tired. "I'm afraid I must retire now. It's been a long day."

"You go rest up. You gonna need your strength with them children."

Sally Rose smiled and turned back to the house. Just what did Martha mean by that comment?

When Sally Rose returned to her room, she heard male voices through the open window. Was Mr. Hernandez still there? Her pulse quickened, and she strained to listen but couldn't make out the conversation. Earlier during dinner, she could sense him looking at her even without making eye contact. So why was he going to Cuba? Was that part of his duties at the law firm? Perhaps that's where his family was, which would explain his accent. Maybe he had a wife there whom he would bring back to live with him in Cedar Key. Just as well. It wasn't her concern what he did anyway.

Enough thoughts about Mr. Hernandez. She needed to plan tomorrow's lessons for the children. Opening her trunk, she lifted out the books she'd brought—a reading primer, *Aunt Louisa's Alphabet Book*, *Little Women*, *Mother Goose Nursery Rhymes*, *Alice's Adventures in Wonderland* and *Robinson Crusoe*— something for everyone. She ran her fingers over the covers, trembling with anticipation of her first day of teaching. The children would be so excited to read these books—at least, she hoped they would be. If not, she'd find a way to make them more exciting, perhaps with some role playing. What a wonderful idea! She could envision the children dressed up for their parts.

As she settled into bed for the evening, she could hardly rest for thinking about the next day. She had been a good companion to Mrs. Middleton, but she'd be an even better teacher. Sighing, she glanced up at the ceiling and murmured, "I'm here, Papa. And I'm a teacher."

As if in answer, a breeze from the moss-laden tree blew into the room. A tear trickled down her cheek as she closed her eyes.

~

Bryce ate breakfast downstairs in the hotel dining room, then walked across the street towards the Powell law office. Frank had asked him to be there at nine o'clock. Shopkeepers were just opening up as he passed by, noting two other mercantiles, a bank, and a drugstore on the way. A shingle proclaiming *Frank Powell, Attorney at Law* beckoned to him from a wrought-iron bracket above a stately oak door. He lifted the ornate latch, pushed the door open, and stepped inside.

As his eyes adjusted to the dim room, he noted the dark wooden bookcases lining each wall. Thick leather volumes filled the shelves, the more lengthy ones in stacks. On one side of the room, Frank sat behind a massive oak desk. When he saw Bryce, he stood and came around to greet him.

"Good morning, Bryce." He shook Bryce's hand. "Did you sleep well?"

"Most assuredly. I think I could have slept on a log last night, though, after the trip."

Frank laughed. "Well, I hope you're rested up. We have a lot to do. Have you considered my request to investigate Mr. Hobbs?"

"Yes." He'd battled that request in his room last night before conceding to the decision, so he could rest. "And I'll do what I can."

"Splendid!" He shook Bryce's hand again. "I want you to look at some of the store's books before you meet Albert."

Bryce noted the leather-bound books on the desk. "Those?"

"Yes, here you go. That desk over there will be yours." Frank handed the ledgers to Bryce. "Take your time. I'll return them to Albert when you're finished."

"He keeps the records?"

Frank nodded. "That was our arrangement. He had the retail experience, so I let him manage the store. I thought I could trust him, but something isn't right. I think we should be making more money with the shipments we're getting."

"I'll be happy to look at them." Bryce carried the books to the desk across the room. "Will he get suspicious about our looking them over?"

"No, I have a right to look at them whenever I want to since I'm part-owner. I'm not so sure he would want someone else, like you, to look at them, but that'll be our secret. He seldom comes in here, so it shouldn't be a problem. Besides, with his extra duties as postmaster and customs officer, it may be some time before he looks at them again. Look them over this morning, then we'll go next door and I'll introduce you."

For the next few hours, Bryce reviewed the records, scouring them for incongruities. True, the mercantile received a lot of merchandise, but as far as he could tell, it was all accounted for. If Mr. Hobbs was a thief, he was a clever one and knew how to cover his tracks.

Frank had two appointments with clients while Bryce was busy with the books. Shortly before noon, Frank glanced up from his paperwork. "Are you hungry?"

"I could use a bite or two." Bryce pushed back from his desk and stood, reaching for his hat from the hat rack.

"Let's go meet Albert and invite him to lunch with us." Frank reversed the "Open" sign on the door and waited for Bryce to exit.

"I look forward to it." Bryce had developed a mental image of the man who kept the books he'd spent the morning studying and was curious to find out how his image matched the real person. "Wonder if he knows about your suspicions?"

"I don't think so." Frank locked the door and pocketed the large, brass key. "At lunch, you'll have a chance to study him, get a feel for his character. Maybe you'll detect something I haven't noticed."

Bryce nodded as they left the office, then walked alongside Frank on the boardwalk the short distance to the open door of the mercantile on the corner. Boisterous laughter greeted them as they entered.

"Now these are the best cigars you can get anywhere in the world." A portly, red-faced man stood in the center aisle speaking to another man and pointing to something in the glass case between them. "Straight off the boat from Havana; came in yesterday. You must have one." He laughed. "Every man needs a good cigar."

Even though the store temperature was pleasant due to the cool spring morning, sweat dotted the face of the portly man. Reaching into his pocket, he pulled out a handkerchief and wiped his forehead and upper lip. A rusty brown beard ran along the edge of his face from ear to ear, with bushy sideburns jutting out on either side. His thin hair was parted on one side and combed across the top, slicked down with hair wax. As he noticed Frank and Bryce enter, a shadow passed over his face before the wide smile reappeared.

"Well, hello, Frank! To what do I owe this visit, and who is your guest?" He stuck his hand out toward Bryce. "Albert Hobbs. How do you do?"

Bryce extended his hand as Frank made introductions.

"Albert, this is Bryce Hernandez, my new partner."

As the two shook hands, Bryce studied Hobbs. If first impressions were valid, Hobbs's demeanor didn't set well with Bryce. His broad smile and jovial nature were overly effusive. Maybe Bryce's suspicions were due to Frank's, but the man's friendliness seemed extreme, like someone hiding their true feelings.

"Pleased to make your acquaintance, sir." Bryce released the man's sweaty palm.

"Partner, heh? When Frank told me he was searching for a partner, I was surprised to learn he was so busy. Where do you hail from, Mr. Hernandez? Mexico? Spain?"

Bryce suppressed the irritation that rifled his conscience. The man was bereft of manners.

"Most recently, Pittsburgh, although my family lives in Cuba." He was surprised Hobbs noticed his minimal accent.

"Well, I guess you're not a real Yankee then. Ha ha! We finally got rid of them around here. Heh heh."

Frank frowned and cleared his throat. "We were just heading out to lunch and thought you might like to join us, Albert."

Hobbs patted his ample belly. "Ha! I'm not one to pass up an invitation to eat."

"Fine, then. Can you leave now? We're heading to the restaurant in the Bettelini."

"Of course, I can leave." Hobbs turned to the back of the store and shouted, "Lewis! Can you come out here?"

An older, bespectacled gentleman with thin, graying hair and stooped shoulders appeared from a back door. Peering over the top of his glasses, he glanced around at the men. "Yes, Mr. Hobbs?"

"I'll be going to lunch now with these two gentlemen." Hobbs motioned to Bryce and Frank. "I need you to watch the store a while."

Lewis nodded toward the other men. "Yes, sir. I'll do that. Y'all have a nice lunch."

Frank, Bryce, and Hobbs left the store and walked down the sidewalk several blocks to the Bettelini Hotel—or rather, waddled, in Hobbs's case. What an annoying fellow. He talked too loudly and too much for Bryce's liking, and he acted like a politician campaigning for office, when he waved and nodded to several people across the street.

As they entered the restaurant, Hobbs worked his way through the room, laughing and speaking to everyone there, especially flirting with the ladies as he bowed and bobbed between the white cloth-covered tables. The fakery of his behavior repulsed Bryce. Although some of the older women appreciated the attention, Bryce couldn't imagine a lady desiring the man's notice.

When they were seated, Hobbs continued smiling and nodding to the other patrons as he flourished his napkin and tucked it under his chin. The waitress appeared and took their orders, then Hobbs leaned toward Frank with an inquisitive look.

"So, Frank, how's the new governess?"

Bryce's attention piqued at the question. A picture of the lovely Miss McFarlane seated at the table the night before quickened his senses.

"She's very nice, but we haven't had much time to talk yet." Frank sipped the iced tea the waitress brought to the table. "Miss McFarlane arrived at the same time as Mr. Hernandez, so I've been a bit preoccupied. However, she seems pleasant enough. With her outstanding recommendations, I'm sure she'll be fine."

"Don't know why you want some old maid schoolteacher around. First thing you know, she'll be trying to teach you something too!" Hobbs threw his head back and laughed at his own humor.

Frank and Bryce exchanged quick glances.

"You might be surprised when you meet her, Albert."

Hobbs looked at the two of them then shrugged, his attention captured by the food being served to them. "Well, enough talk. Let's eat!"

*She's certainly not what you think, Hobbs.* Bryce cringed, imagining Hobbs meeting Miss McFarlane. No doubt she'd find his flirting objectionable. At least he hoped so.

"Albert, isn't Mr. Dalton leaving today?"

"Checked out this morning. Why do you ask?" Albert lifted the napkin tucked into his collar to wipe the juice running out the corner of his mouth.

"I told Mr. Hernandez he could stay in one of the rooms for a while. There's no reason for him to pay for a room here at the hotel."

Albert choked and grabbed his glass of tea. "Of course. Why, that makes sense. I suppose we could stand to lose the rent." He cut his eyes at Frank, his tone contradicting the words.

Bryce wouldn't let himself be a source of conflict between the business partners, regardless of what he thought of Hobbs. "I will pay the daily fee."

"You'll do no such thing." Frank slapped his hand down on the table. "You're welcome to stay in one of the mercantile rooms until you find something you like better—perhaps one of the houses in town."

"Then I thank you, sirs, for your generosity. I'll bring my things over later today." Bryce focused his words on Albert, who responded with a forced smile. However, the smile didn't reach his eyes, which reflected something Bryce couldn't quite put his finger on, but it certainly wasn't a welcome.

# Chapter Six

"Helloooo!"

Accompanied by persistent knocking, the sing-song voice trilled though the etched glass of the front door, interrupting the children's lessons in the front parlor.

Sally Rose looked up from the primer Lucy was reading to her and searched the room for a volunteer. "Children, would one of you please answer the door?"

"I will." Benjamin dropped his book and strode out of the parlor to the front hallway.

"It's Mrs. Chapman. She's always coming over here." Adele rolled her eyes from her seat at the desk where she worked on her penmanship.

"She's nosy." Lucy flattened her hand on the primer, keeping the book open but losing her place in the lines.

"That's not very kind, girls." Sally Rose raised her eyebrows, attempting to instill a decorum in her young charges, but her nerves tensed at the interruption, as well as the girls' attitudes.

"Hello, Benjamin." A woman's shrill voice came from the foyer. A grating kind of voice that further tightened Sally Rose's nerves. "Where is your mother?"

"She's upstairs at her sewing machine."

"Well, I'll just wait right here while you go fetch her for me." The voice came closer to the parlor.

Sally Rose straightened her spine and shifted the primer fully onto Lucy's lap, curious to meet this Mrs. Chapmen who, if the girls were correct, made a habit of welcoming herself into the Powells' parlor.

Benjamin passed the doorway on his way up the stairs. The floor creaked as someone moved in the foyer. A white feather attached to an oversized hat leaned into the opening, and a gloved hand waved. Soon the whole person was in view. A plump woman in a rose-colored dress stood in the doorway, holding a cloth-covered basket. Smiling, she said, "Oh! You're having your lessons. I didn't mean to interrupt."

Sally Rose stood and smoothed out her dress, then stepped toward the woman. "Hello. I'm Sally Rose McFarlane, the Powells' governess."

Fleshy cheeks puffed out as the woman beamed. "Mary Etta Chapman. I'm the Powell's neighbor." Unnatural black bangs with white roots peeked out below her hat. The woman must use silver nitrate to color her hair. "I live right across the street."

"Mary Etta. I see you've met our governess." Ellen Powell descended the stairs, Benjamin following.

Sally Rose glanced toward Ellen, feeling Mrs. Chapman's gaze roving over her. Sally Rose folded her hands in front of her long navy skirt and held her chin steady, though why Mrs. Chapman's opinion would matter, she didn't know.

Looking back to Ellen, Mary Etta nodded. "Yes, we've met. I didn't expect your governess to be so young." The added emphasis on her last word sounded disdainful.

"Miss McFarlane has excellent credentials. Miss Middleton highly recommended her."

"I see." Mrs. Chapman's examination resumed. Perhaps her opinion *did* matter. At least the woman believed it did. "So you taught at that girls' school for rich folks?"

Sally Rose stiffened, her cheeks growing hot. Taught? She didn't teach there. She stammered, "Yes, I, I mean no, well..."

"Mary Etta, was there a reason for your visit? I'm sorry to be rude, but I have my hands full upstairs, and the children need to get back to their lessons." Ellen clasped her hands in front of her pale green day dress.

"Oh, I'm so sorry to bother you! I just stopped by to welcome Miss McFarlane to town. Here are some cookies I made. I hope you like ginger cookies." She handed the basket to Sally Rose.

"I do! I do!" Benjamin pranced around and trying to peek into the basket.

Sally Rose took the basket and lifted the cloth. "They look delicious. Thank you very much. How nice of you to do this."

"My pleasure. Everyone likes my baking." Mary Etta's nose rose a little, and she brushed a hand over her darkened hair. She glanced back, her steps slowing as Ellen ushered her to the door. "I look forward to seeing you again, Miss McFarlane, perhaps in church Sunday?"

Sally Rose opened her mouth to speak, but Ellen answered first. "Yes, we'll see you on Sunday, Mary Etta. Thank you for coming by."

When she'd closed the door behind her neighbor, Ellen sighed. Her mouth stretched taut as if she sought something polite to tell Sally Rose about the unexpected visitor. "I'm sorry about the interruption. However, I'm not surprised Mary Etta showed up today. She had to quench her curiosity about our new governess. It won't be long before the whole town hears her description of you."

"Well, in that case, I hope I made a favorable impression." Sally Rose kept her voice light, since Ellen didn't appear to place much interest in Mrs. Chapman's opinion. Yet a twist inside her chest reminded her that the truth of her employment at Miss Middleton's School had been confused. Should she attempt to straighten that out? Would she lose her job if she did?

"You never know what Mary Etta will say." Ellen continued providing the benefit of doubt, even though her tone didn't quite agree with her words. "She means well, I believe, but sometimes her tongue gets ahead of her mind."

Sally Rose swallowed hard, stuck on the statement about her teaching credentials. She'd been a companion to Miss Middleton's mother, not one of the teachers. Had the Powells misunderstood? She needed to clarify her experience. "What she said about me and my background…"

"Don't worry your head about that. It doesn't matter that you're young. You have proper qualifications, and I'm confident you'll be a fine teacher." Ellen turned in the directions of the stairs. "If you'll excuse me, I need to finish Adele's dress."

"She always gets the new dresses." Lucy puffed out her lower lip and stared down at her pink and white pinafore, the fabric of which appeared bright and crisp.

Ellen continued up the stairs. "I love the new Singer sewing machine Frank gave me for Christmas, and now that you're here, I have time to make some new clothes for the children. They're growing up so quickly! The younger girls can wear their older sisters' clothes, but Adele has no one ahead of her." She looked down at Lucy. "Maybe I can make you a new dress too, Lucy."

"And me too?" Tilly popped her finger out of her mouth, eyes widening.

"You too, Tilly."

Tilly swished back and forth, holding out her skirt as if imagining a new one.

"Don't make me no new clothes. I don't want none." Benjamin's jaw jutted forward, his eyebrows pulling low over his eyes.

"Don't want *any*, Benjamin." Ellen appealed to Sally Rose, a small half-smile, half-frown twisting her lips. "I hope you can make this boy speak correctly."

"We'll work on it." Sally Rose mentally scanned her resources. Whatever lessons the Powells desired for their children, she could—and would—provide. "I have some grammar techniques I can teach him."

"Thank God you're a teacher." Ellen let out a puff of air, shaking her head as she continued up the stairs. "I just don't have the patience."

Sally Rose ushered the children back into the study. No matter that the Powells mistakenly believed she was a teacher at Miss Middleton's School. She was a teacher for these children now, and that's all that mattered.

~

"Daddy's home!" The children rushed to the front door as Frank Powell entered and placed his hat on the hall tree.

He scooped Tilly up in his arms. "So how were your lessons today? Did you learn something new?"

Sally Rose followed the children to the foyer and stood with her hands clasped together, anticipating their answers. From her perspective, the first day had gone well, but how would the children's report compare?

All four children spoke at once, eager to share the day's events. Surely a good sign.

"I learned some French words—un, deaux, trois ..." Adele enunciated each word with emphasis.

"Excellent!" Mr. Powell peered over the heads of the chattering children at Sally Rose and beamed. "It seems you're off to a grand start!"

"Good afternoon, dear," Ellen called, as she made her way down the stairs. "How was your day?"

Mr. Powell lowered Tilly to the floor and leaned over to kiss his wife on the cheek. "Afternoon, darling. Productive day. Mr. Hernandez will be a fine partner."

Sally Rose's heart fluttered at the reminder of Mr. Powell's new partner. Would she learn more about him at dinner tonight?

"Why, that's nice, dear." Facing her children, Ellen said, "Go wash up for dinner."

As the youngsters scampered away, Sally Rose said, "Please excuse me while I straighten up the classroom."

When Sally Rose returned to the parlor, she heard Ellen. "Mary Etta came by today."

Sally Rose couldn't help but hear the conversation.

"Yes? Well, I'm not surprised," Mr. Powell said. "She had to examine our new governess, I assume."

"You know Mary Etta."

"So you met our neighbor, Miss McFarlane," Mr. Powell said, coming to the doorway of the parlor. "I hope she wasn't rude to you."

Sally Rose turned around. "Oh, no." She didn't want to give the Powells the impression she was concerned about their neighbor. "She was polite, and she also brought some cookies she'd made."

"Of course." Mr. Powell laughed. "Mary Etta wants to make certain her reputation for baking is well-known."

"She acted surprised that Miss McFarlane was so young for a teacher, but I assured Mary Etta our governess was well qualified."

There it was again—her qualification. Sally Rose's chest constricted. But she *was* qualified to teach, even if she didn't have official experience. Hadn't she taught her younger siblings to read and do arithmetic?

"She's probably surprised Miss McFarlane is so pretty as well." Mr. Powell smiled at Sally Rose.

Sally Rose's face warmed, and she lowered her gaze to her clasped, sweaty hands.

Mr. Powell continued speaking, obviously unaware he had embarrassed her. "I'm sure she had to see her rival."

"Rival?" Sally Rose tilted her head as she looked up at him, spreading her hands out to the side. "She needn't worry about that. I don't bake."

He threw his head back and laughed. "Oh, no, it's not baking she's concerned about. She wants to make sure you don't compete with her for the attention of her fellow."

"I assumed she was married, but I can assure you, I have no interest in any gentleman." Except, perhaps, Mr. Powell's new law partner. But no, her purpose was to teach the children, not seek a husband. "Who's the man in question?"

"Albert Hobbs, my partner at the mercantile. She's been vying for his attentions ever since her husband died."

"I see. Well, she has nothing to worry about as far as I'm concerned. Now, if you'll please excuse me, I need freshen up."

"Go ahead, dear. We'll see you at dinner," Ellen said.

Sally Rose walked toward the stairs.

"Oh, I almost forgot!" Mr. Powell reached inside his coat and pulled out a piece of paper. "We got a telegram today. From Mother."

At Ellen's gasp, Sally Rose paused and glanced back. Ellen stared at the telegraph, color drained from her face.

Ellen covered her mouth with one hand. "Oh, dear."

Sally Rose hurried over and placed her hand on Ellen's arm. "Is everything all right?"

Ellen took a deep breath and straightened as she focused on her husband's face. "Yes, of course. Everything is fine." She exhaled. "Mother Powell is coming to visit."

"How nice. I'm looking forward to meeting her." Sally Rose meant her words, curious about the woman whose room she occupied, yet she worried about Ellen's unease.

"She's looking forward to meeting you too," Mr. Powell said.

"When will she be here?"

"She arrives Friday, this Friday." Ellen's hand holding the telegraph dropped to her side.

"So soon? Well, I'll make sure the children can show some new knowledge." A week wasn't much time, but Sally Rose hoped to remove any anxiety Ellen might have about her mother-in-law's expectations. Surely the elder Mrs. Powell wasn't as frightening as Ellen's reactions made her out to be.

Ellen appeared stricken as she replied in a flat tone. "I'm sure she hopes to see some proof of your skills."

Mr. Powell turned to Sally Rose. "Yes, and perhaps you can entertain us with your musical ability. Miss Middleton highly praised your vocal talent."

Sally Rose's pulse quickened. Not only did she have to prove her teaching skills, but she'd have to show her vocal skills as well. "I'll be happy to sing for her if you like. But surely, she's more interested in the children's progress."

"Yes, of course. However, your singing will be a welcome addition to the dinner party."

Sally Rose lifted her eyebrows. "Dinner party?"

"Mother Powell has requested we host a dinner party while she's here." Ellen's voice was tight.

So that explained Ellen's tension, and now Sally Rose shared some as well. Apparently, Mr. Powell's mother did not hesitate to place demands on the family.

Sally Rose's heart went out to Ellen. "I'll be happy to help in any way I can."

"Thank you, dear." Ellen relaxed and offered a meek smile. "Perhaps you can help me make the dinner party more up to the latest social protocols."

Sally Rose patted Ellen's arm. "I might have some ideas from dinner parties we had in Cleveland. I'm sure if we put our heads together, it will be lovely."

"Well, good, then. That's settled." Mr. Powell clapped his hands together, clearly not aware of the work involved in planning a dinner party or the reason for his wife's distress.

"I better get started on the invitations this evening." Ellen wrung her hands, her shoulders sagging as if the preparations already weighed too heavily.

"Let me do those for you." One thing Sally Rose was proud of was her penmanship, having always received compliments for it. This task she could handle confidently and lighten Ellen's burden. "Just tell me whom you would like to invite, and I can take that task off your hands."

"We'll have to ask Albert, of course," Mr. Powell said.

"And Mary Etta," Ellen suggested. "She'll expect an invitation."

"And Mr. Hernandez," Mr. Powell added. "I know Mother will want to meet him as well."

Mr. Hernandez? Sally Rose's stomach flipped.

"Yes, of course. He'll be your escort to the table, Miss McFarlane." Mr. Powell's statement sounded like a mandate. What choice did she have?

"Perhaps Mr. Hernandez should escort Mrs. Powell. I'm sure your mother would like that." Sally Rose made a vain attempt to avoid being paired with Mr. Hernandez, trying to hide any interest in their association.

"Oh, no." Mr. Powell chuckled. "Mother expects Reverend Whitman to be here. She always enjoys engaging him in religious discussions."

Ellen sighed. "So that's eight. Will there be any others?"

Mr. Powell shook his head. "No, eight is quite enough and will allow us all to get to know each other."

Four couples. She hadn't planned on being partnered with anyone. Not that she disliked the man, but she wasn't ready to be matched up with anyone. But what choice did she have? She couldn't be rude, refuse, and spoil the dinner party for the Powells. A shiver of apprehension shook her. She'd been asked to sing as well. Normally, singing would not make her nervous. She had sung in front of many people before. But singing in front of Mr. Hernandez? For some reason, the thought unnerved her. She just wouldn't look at him. He mustn't be a distraction, if that was possible.

# Chapter Seven

After his first day at the law office, Bryce stepped into the small lobby of the hotel attached to the mercantile and strode to the counter. Seeing no one around, he waited, drumming his fingers on the glass top.

Voices came through the doorway leading to the store. Bryce cleared his throat, leaning to peer through the doorway. "Excuse me. Hello?"

The voices stopped, and Hobbs entered from the mercantile, glancing over his shoulder.

"Ah. Mr. Hernandez! I completely forgot you were checking in today." Hobbs walked over to Bryce, his sweaty palm extended.

Forgot? Since lunch? Bryce took the hand offered, wishing to wipe his off soon. "Mr. Hobbs, sorry to interrupt you, but I need the key to my room, so I can get settled."

Hobbs's eyebrows creased together. "I'm afraid I haven't had time to check on the room yet, make it presentable for you. I've been very busy." The man stretched, making himself larger, which Bryce hadn't thought possible. "As you know, I'm also the postmaster and the customs agent here. Perhaps you can come back tomorrow."

"I've already checked out of the hotel, but don't concern yourself about the room. I'm sure it will be fine. If you have fresh linens, I'll change the bed myself."

"Certainly. Well, if you insist." Hobbs reached behind him to a row of nails holding keys. "Hmm. Where is that key now? Oh, here it is." He lifted one, turned back around, and handed it to Bryce. "Up the stairs, all the way at the end of the hall, last door on your right." He stepped over to a cabinet and withdrew some sheets. "There's outside stairs too, so you don't have to come in here to get to your room."

Bryce snapped the key inside his hand and took the linens. "Thank you, Mr. Hobbs." He headed over to the steps leading to the second floor.

"Call me Albert! We'll be seeing quite a bit of each other," Hobbs added with his familiar chuckle.

Bryce looked over his shoulder and gave a brisk nod. "Albert." He didn't reply with "Call me Bryce." He wasn't sure he wanted to be on such familiar terms with the man.

The room wasn't as fancy as the one at the hotel, but it was serviceable. It had a bed, table, washstand, and kerosene lamp— pretty much all he needed. A window opened to the balcony and the street below. As he emptied his valise and arranged his things, he remembered that he needed some lathering soap. How convenient to live above a mercantile.

He headed back down the hall, but when he reached the top of the stairs, he heard Hobbs speaking to someone. How strange that Hobbs spoke in such low tones, when normally he was so loud. As Bryce arrived at the bottom of the stairs, he saw Hobbs with a lanky fellow, engaged in a serious discussion.

Hobbs noticed Bryce and quieted. The other man glanced over, scarcely lifting his head to acknowledge Bryce.

"Yes, sir, Mr. Hernandez, was there something else you needed?" Hobbs's tone was a bit sharper than usual, his customary smile working hard to appear.

Bryce looked at the other man, waiting for an introduction. When none came, he proceeded with his errand. "Excuse me for disturbing you men. Where can I find the lathering soap?"

"No need for apology." Hobbs's usual boisterousness returned, but sounded forced somehow. "This is Ira Gray, the assistant light-keeper over at the lighthouse on Seahorse Key. Mr. Gray has come into town for supplies."

"Bryce Hernandez." He noted Mr. Gray's empty hands.

Where were these supplies? But perhaps the man hadn't had a chance to purchase any yet. No reason to be suspicious. Bryce had yet to find proof of any wrongdoings on Hobbs's part of the business.

Ira Gray had a slumped posture and fidgeted with something in his pocket. He regarded Bryce with one brow lifted. "Mr. Hernandez. Hear you're the new lawyer in town. Didn't know Powell needed help." A smirk crawled across his face.

"Mr. Powell is a busy man. I hope to lighten some of his workload." Bryce put his hands in his pockets when Gray didn't offer a handshake. "You're the lighthouse keeper? I haven't seen a lighthouse. How far is it from here?"

Gray pointed out the door. "Over yonder on that island out there. 'Bout seven miles. But I ain't the main keeper. He's taking a leave right now, so I have to do it all myself."

"And a fine job he's doing too!" Hobbs patted Gray on the back and displayed a toothy grin. "Fine job."

Gray straightened and nodded his thanks to Hobbs for the accolades.

"I'm sure he is. Well, I won't keep you gentlemen from your business any longer. If you can just show me where the soap is, I'll be out of your way." Bryce scanned the room filled with tables and stacks of merchandise looking for the item.

"Here it is." Hobbs strode to a shelf and picked up a bar. As he handed it over, Bryce withdrew some money from his pocket. "No, sir. No charge." Hobbs waved his hand. "You just go ahead and take it."

Bryce gestured with the soap. "Thank you." Turning to Gray, he said, "Mr. Gray, I hope to see your lighthouse someday."

"Sundays, that's the day townspeople can visit the lighthouse. The board doesn't like folks around the rest of the week. Interferes with the work, you know."

"I'll keep that in mind." Bryce gave a nod to the men, then went back out and up to his room. Strange fellow, that Gray. Why did he and Hobbs need to be so quiet with their business dealings? Bryce shook his head. Maybe he was overly suspicious since Frank had asked him to investigate Hobbs's business dealings. However, in the past, Bryce's gut feelings about people had proven he was a pretty good judge of character. Right now, his gut was telling him not to trust either of them.

~

"Miss McFarlane, you really don't need to go to the store for me." Ellen twisted her hands while Sally Rose faced the mirror in the hall tree, adjusting her hat. "I can send Martha or Joseph."

"It's no bother, I assure you." Her hat settled firmly, the blue ribbons hanging off the back and neatly gracing her shoulders, Sally Rose faced Ellen and smiled. "Martha's busy preparing the food, and Joseph's working in the yard getting ready for Mrs. Powell. I just want to see what I can find to accent the room, make it more festive for the party. The children can go with me, and we'll make the trip a learning exercise."

"That's very kind of you, but are you sure you want to take them all? They can be a handful, especially Benjamin." Ellen lowered her voice as she spoke the boy's name, casting uneasy glances up the stairs.

"They'll be fine. There'll be a reward for good behavior." Sally Rose patted Ellen's hand with her gloved one. She leaned in and lowered her voice. "I hope you don't mind if I let them have a sweet treat."

"Of course not. That will be fine, as long as it doesn't spoil their dinner, and they'll enjoy it." The creases beside Ellen's eyes didn't completely fade, but her shoulders relaxed a tad. "All right then, but if you see Mr. Powell, be sure to tell him this was your idea, not mine. He might feel I'm imposing on you."

The children clambered down the steps, Benjamin in the lead and nearly tumbling off the bottom tread in his haste. In contrast, little Tilly gripped the handrail, navigating each step with the same foot first.

"Children!" Ellen clapped to draw their attention to her, and she looked at each one with her brows knitted together. "I expect you to use your best manners with Miss McFarlane. Don't forget, your father will be close by. I don't want him to be disturbed by your noisiness." Ellen turned to Sally Rose. "You'll be taking the buggy?"

"Oh, no. It's a fine day for walking."

"But what if you need to carry something?"

"We can each carry a little, and if we can't carry it all, I'm sure the mercantile will deliver it." As the oldest child on the farm,

Sally Rose had plenty of experience corralling youngsters.

"That's true, they will. Or Joseph can go back with the wagon and get the rest." Ellen studied each child, straightening the ribbons in the girls' hair and brushing off Benjamin's short pants. Hands on her hips, she addressed the children. "You mind Miss McFarlane, understand?"

A chorus answered her. "Yes, Mother. We will. Promise!"

Sally Rose held the front door open while the children filed out. She cast one final look of reassurance to Ellen. "I'm certain you have plenty to do while we're out of your way. Please take advantage of the opportunity."

Ellen sighed and smiled. "You're absolutely correct about that. Thank you so much for understanding."

"Of course." Sally Rose stepped onto the porch behind the children and closed the door. "Tilly, would you like to hold my hand?"

The little girl nodded and slipped her tiny hand inside Sally Rose's. Adele and Lucy joined hands as well, while Benjamin skipped ahead, running his hand along the edges of the picket fences that bordered each yard.

Sally Rose motioned to a large tree with white blossoms. "Who can tell me what kind of tree that is?"

"A magnolia!" Adele was, as usual, first to respond.

"Who cares about some old tree?" Benjamin cocked his head at Sally Rose.

"Have you ever smelled one of the blossoms?" Sally Rose pulled down a low-hanging limb, motioning the children over.

"Ooh. It smells real good!" Tilly stood on tiptoes to poke her little nose into the blossom.

Benjamin hung back, watching the girls, his lips twisted.

"Come on, Benjamin." Sally Rose waved him over. "You smell it too."

"It's nice, Benjamin. You'll like it." Lucy grabbed his arm and pulled him toward the flower.

A distant sniff, then a closer look, and the boy smiled. "It's smells purty, like you, Miss McFarlane."

Sally Rose's face grew warm. "Why, thank you, Benjamin. Now look at the middle of the flower. What do you see?"

The children eagerly pointed out the flower parts while Sally

Rose told them the name for each. "When we get back, we'll draw a picture of the flower and write the parts on it."

Sally Rose inhaled the clean spring air. How refreshing after the coal dust of Cleveland. She enjoyed the slow pace of the town, where only a few wagons were visible up and down the street. Unlike the frantic rush of wagons and noise of the city, Cedar Key was peaceful and quiet, except for the occasional sound of the train whistle, and the sawmill in the opposite direction. So comforting and inviting, like home—her new home and new life. Her heart swelled with satisfaction.

"There it is!" Benjamin pointed down the block to the mercantile on the corner, and began to run.

"Benjamin!" Sally Rose hastened to regain control of her charge. Ellen's admonishment that Mr. Powell's office was close by applied to her actions as well. "Wait, please. Remember, I said there would be a reward for good behavior. I need you to stay with us."

Benjamin halted in the street. "A reward? What is it?"

"It'll be a surprise." Sally Rose gave him a secret little smile, hoping the anticipation would motivate the boy into good behavior.

He tucked his hands in his suspenders and strolled back to the others. "Is it candy?" He peered up at her with head tilted.

"If I tell you now, it won't be a surprise, will it?"

Benjamin shook his head then walked alongside Sally Rose, his gait a little less enthusiastic.

Outside the mercantile, Adele pointed to the sign hanging next door. "That's Papa's office."

Sally Rose paused to study the sign—Frank W. Powell, Attorney at Law. Would there be a new sign soon with Mr. Hernandez's name added? Her heart skipped a beat. Shaking her head to refocus, she entered the open doors of the store.

Smells of leather and coffee, tobacco, kerosene, and lye assaulted her nose. Benjamin dashed to a counter to study the contents of the candy jars sitting on top. The older two girls walked over to the stacks of fabric bolts where they giggled and chattered about the cover of Godey's Ladies Magazine lying on a table. Tilly wandered over to a wicker doll buggy and stared at the delicate doll lying inside. Sally Rose scanned the room, taking in the variety of merchandise in the large mercantile. Not as big as stores in Cleveland, but remarkably large for a small town.

Shelves lined the walls laden with everything from cans of spices to bottles of medicine. One shelf had men's hats and gloves, another pipes and boxes of cigars. Sally Rose noted the stand of umbrellas next to the counter which displayed guns and knives. Barrels of flour, sugar, salt, and cornmeal stood below a hanging scale. Boat oars and fishing nets occupied another corner.

Noting two gentlemen at the rear of the store helping other customers, she joined the girls and peered over their shoulders. "What have you girls found that's so interesting?"

"Oh, Miss McFarlane! Look at this beautiful dress." Adele pointed to the picture of an elaborate evening dress with rows of ruffles.

"Hmm, rather elaborate, isn't it?" Sally Rose studied the details of the dress, a little too ornate for her taste. "There must be ten yards of lace on that dress."

Lucy glanced at Sally Rose and nodded. "It'd be real pretty on you, Miss McFarlane."

Sally Rose's face heated. "Thank you, Lucy, but I don't know where I'd wear such an elegant dress."

Tilly tugged Sally Rose's hand. "Grandmother likes purty dresses."

"I see. Well, I'm afraid there isn't time to make a dress like that before Saturday night." She hadn't expected the dinner party to be quite so extravagant. Surely, she'd be able to make do with one of the dresses she had.

"Ahem! Sonny, keep your hands off that candy!"

Sally Rose jerked to see a portly man charging toward Benjamin whose hand rested atop one of the candy jars.

She hurried to intercept the man. "Benjamin, please wait for me."

The red-faced man with the bushy jowls halted and stared at her. His demeanor changed, and a smile replaced the scowl while his eyes roved over her. "Sorry, ma'am. Didn't realize he was your boy."

"I'm not her boy. I'm Frank Powell's boy. Don't you remember me, Mr. Hobbs?"

Glancing from Sally Rose to Benjamin, his eyes widened with apparent understanding. "Please excuse me, ma'am. My name is

Albert Hobbs, proprietor here. You must be the Powells' new tutor." He attempted to bow by bending in her direction.

"I'm Sally Rose McFarlane, their governess." She nodded her head in return. "I hope the children aren't bothering you. We have a few things to get."

"We're having a party," Tilly announced as she scampered over.

"Ah, yes, Frank dropped off an invitation to me this morning." He reached inside his vest pocket and retrieved a familiar piece of stationery. "I believe the senior Mrs. Powell is coming into town."

"That's correct." So this was the Albert Hobbs that held Mrs. Chapman's interest. Sally Rose Rose fought back a grimace at the realization that this man would be a guest at the party. Thank goodness, Mr. Powell hadn't suggested she be paired up with Mr. Hobbs for the evening.

"Well, now that I know *you'll* be there, I'm even *more* happy to accept the offer."

The man's wide grin made her skin crawl like it was covered with the tiny black bugs that were on the magnolia blossom.

"Albert! Albert! Oh, there you are." A panting Mrs. Chapman huffed into the store and made her way to the group.

"Mary Etta, how are you today?" Mr. Hobbs spoke politely, but his smile wilted at the corners.

The buxom woman fanned herself with the card she was holding while she aimed coy eyes at the man. "I'm just fine, Albert. Just so excited, I couldn't wait to speak to you!"

"I was just speaking to Miss McFarlane here." His hand swept toward Sally Rose, his eyes gleaming.

Mrs. Chapman stared at Sally Rose as if noticing her for the first time. "Oh. Hello, Miss McFarlane. I didn't see you there."

Sally Rose dared her eyebrows to lift. Surely she wasn't invisible. Smiling at the woman, she said, "The children and I had some shopping to do. Mr. Hobbs and I have just met."

A dark cloud passed through Mrs. Chapman's eyes then lifted. "I was going to speak to Albert about the dinner party Saturday night at the Powells'. Will you be joining us, or will you be staying with the children?"

Was the woman taunting her? Then she remembered what Frank Powell had said about Mrs. Chapman having her sights set on Mr. Hobbs. The woman was jealous! Sally Rose stifled an urge to laugh at the absurdity of Mrs. Chapman's concerns. Albert Hobbs held no attraction for Sally Rose whatsoever.

"Mr. Powell's mother has asked me to be at the party, so I must not disappoint her." Sally Rose forced her sweetest smile.

"Of course, dear." Mary Etta reached out and patted Sally Rose on the arm. "I'm sure Mrs. Powell wants to bestow her approval on the governess for her grandchildren."

"I have no doubt about that." Sally Rose glanced around her, looking for a way to distance herself from the two people. "Well, if you two will excuse me, I need to get some things for the dinner party." Nodding to the couple, she turned. "Come along, Benjamin. We'll see about getting you a treat before we leave."

Sally Rose found some thin pink ribbon next to the case of buttons, pins, and other sewing accessories. She took the items to the back counter, where a slight, bespectacled gentleman who introduced himself as Lewis Greene wrote up the sale. While the children studied a display of toys, she asked him to order some items for the classroom. Then he accompanied her back to the candy display, where she let each child choose their favorite candy. Benjamin wanted lemon drops, but the girls chose the white peppermint sticks. Thankfully, Mrs. Chapman had cornered Mr. Hobbs, so Sally Rose could slip out without further conversation.

"Look forward to seeing you again on Saturday!" Mr. Hobbs shouted behind her as she exited. She turned her head to acknowledge him and ran into someone coming inside.

"Oh! I'm sorry." She held her hand against her chest.

A grin hinted on Mr. Hernandez's face as he stepped back and gestured for her to come through.

"Pardon me, Miss McFarlane. I didn't expect to be running into you today."

The twinkle in his eyes rendered her mute. Sally Rose swallowed and commanded her voice to work. "Mr. Hernandez."

His smile broadened. "I look forward to seeing you again on Saturday as well."

Sally Rose, face hot, hurried down the boardwalk, shepherding the children in front of her. Oh my. First Mr. Hobbs, then Mr. Hernandez. One man she enjoyed seeing, but the other…well, hopefully Mrs. Chapman would keep Mr. Hobbs occupied at the party. Or else, how would she ever survive Saturday?

# Chapter Eight

Tilly bounced and pointed toward the tracks. "I see the train!"

"Be still so I can re-tie your sash." Sally Rose raised her voice over the rumbling of the train engine as she looped the white ribbon around on Tilly's Sunday best dress.

Like everything else in the Powell household, the four children had been washed and polished as though they were entertaining royalty, rather than Mrs. Powell, or 'Mother Powell', as Ellen called her. The family poised on the platform as if awaiting inspection. Sally Rose hoped she would pass. Finally, an older, silver-haired lady emerged from the train, fanning herself and searching the crowd.

Mr. Powell rushed forward and caught her as she practically fell into his arms. The rest of the family stayed where they were until he brought her away from the noise of the train. Sally Rose stood back as the children swarmed the woman. Dressed in the latest fashion, a two-toned gray satin walking dress with box pleats at the bottom of the jacket and the dress, the matriarch carried herself in a dignified manner with chin high and back straight as possible. She reminded Sally Rose of the society ladies in Cleveland, yet with a Southern accent.

"Well, look at you children! How much you've grown! Adele, you're almost a young lady now, and Lucille, you must be two inches taller." Tilly let go of Sally Rose's hand and ran to her grandmother, hugging her skirt. "Why, hello little Matilda! You're so much bigger." She patted Tilly on the head while glancing around. "And where is that young man?"

Benjamin emerged from behind his father. "Right here, Grandmother." He doffed his cap and bowed.

"My, my. What a debonair young gentleman." Mother Powell was certainly proud of her grandchildren. Sally Rose hoped the woman would be pleased with the children's new governess as well.

Ellen waited until the children had been appraised, then approached to give the woman a shoulder hug and a kiss on the cheek. "Welcome, Mother Powell. I hope your journey wasn't too unpleasant."

Mother Powell rolled her eyes. "I'm afraid it was quite uncomfortable, what with all that smoke and heat." She glared at the train and fanned herself some more, then drew herself up and huffed. "Thank goodness, I survived. Now I intend to enjoy my family a while before I have to face that monster again."

"Mother, your trunks?" Mr. Powell motioned to a cartload of baggage.

"Yes, dear. I hope that's all of them."

"You must be staying a long time!" Benjamin started counting the trunks and carpetbags. "One, two, three, four . . ."

Frank placed a firm grip on Benjamin's shoulder, silencing him. "I'll have them delivered to your hotel room. Would you like to go straight there or come to the house with us first?"

"I hope you've reserved one of the large suites for me, dear. I couldn't bear a tiny little hotel room." Her eyebrows knit together as she pursed her lips. "And since this is the first time I've stayed in a hotel here. . ." She halted, eyeing Sally Rose standing apart from the group.

Sally Rose held her breath. Did the woman blame her for taking her room at the house? She straightened and attempted a polite smile.

"Frank, is this the new governess? Aren't you going to introduce us?" Mother Powell moved toward Sally Rose with her hand outstretched.

"Of course, Mother. This is Sally Rose McFarlane. Miss McFarlane has been here just over a week now, and we're already quite impressed by her work with the children."

"Hello, dear." She clasped Sally Rose's hand in both of hers. "You're a pretty young thing, I must say. However, your letter of recommendation from Miss Middleton was quite impressive."

"Thank you, Mrs. Powell." Sally Rose curtsied. The woman had seen her letter? Mrs. Powell's influence might stretch further than she'd realized. "The children have something to say to you." She turned to the children and motioned like a conductor with a baton.

"Bonjour, Grand-Maman!" they recited—or at least the sound resembled those words.

"Well, bonjour to you too! How delightful!" The woman's eyes lit up at the children's greeting, then her gaze shifted to Sally Rose. "I can see already that your credentials are bona fide. I look forward to spending more time with you, but I believe I'll go to the hotel first and freshen up. I need to rest before dinner."

~

"I heard the Rockefeller girls attended Miss Middleton's School. What were they like?" Mother Powell continued her interrogation later that evening in the Powells' parlor following a grand welcome dinner. After droning on about Charleston, which sounded like the perfect city where she knew everyone—the mayor, clergy, and anyone of importance—she had targeted Sally Rose with questions about Miss Middletons' School for Young Ladies.

"Elizabeth and Alice attended for a while. They were very nice, well-behaved young women." If the woman was looking for gossip, Sally Rose had no intention of obliging.

"I'm sure they were." Mother Powell probed for more with her sharp blue eyes and insistent tongue. "Were they good students?"

"As far as I know, yes." Sally Rose forced a smile, sealing her lips together to keep a yawn from escaping. She didn't know how much longer she could stay awake and continue to politely answer the woman's questions. The clock on the mantel chimed ten times.

Ellen had excused herself to get the children to bed nearly an hour ago, but Sally Rose had been offered no such relief.

Mr. Powell didn't bother stifling his yawn. "Mother, we need to get you back to the hotel. It's getting late, and we have a big evening tomorrow night. Are you ready to go?"

"Why, yes, as a matter of fact, I am. I had no idea it was so late." She placed her hands on the chair arms and pushed herself up. "I've so enjoyed our conversation and getting to know you, Miss McFarlane."

"Thank you, ma'am. I've enjoyed our discussion as well." That was more a courteous reply instead of the truth. Mother Powell dominated the conversation, but she was a guest, and Sally Rose was an employee, so she didn't have much of a choice.

She bid Mother Powell and Mr. Powell good evening at the door.

When it closed behind them, Sally Rose regained her energy to work on the place cards. She withdrew to the secretary in the parlor where she took the same small note paper she had for the invitations, dipped the pen in the inkwell, and with delicate strokes, wrote out each name in English script, adding flourishes to embellish the lettering. When she finished writing them, she punctured a small hole through the paper with a nail and tied on a piece of the pink ribbon, making a bow at the top.

As she admired her handiwork, the card with "Mr. Bryce Hernandez" drew her like a magnet. Why had he left Pittsburgh to come to Cedar Key? Why wasn't he married? Surely a man as attractive and intelligent as he would have no lack of female admirers. But why did she care?

~

"There! That should do it." Sally Rose placed the last sprig of pink azalea blossoms in the nest of ferns she had arranged for the centerpiece. "We'll put the crystal cake stand right here in the middle with Martha's lemon cake on it, and the candlesticks will go on either side. The plate of bonbons will go here and the tea cakes over there."

"What a lovely arrangement. I never have been artistic enough to make something look so nice." Ellen picked up a fork and studied it before rubbing it on her apron. She'd been around the table at least twice, polishing the silverware. "In fact, I've never had such a lovely table before, but thanks to you, our guests will be impressed."

"Thank you. I enjoy doing things like this, but you're very creative. Why, I've seen the detail you put into the children's clothes."

"Well, I'm not sure I would call that creative. I just enjoy sewing."

"Sometimes when we do something we enjoy, we take it for granted, while another person thinks it's special."

"You know, you have a point." Ellen paused in her silverware polishing, angling her head as she considered Sally Rose's words. "We don't always appreciate our God-given gifts."

Sally Rose pondered Ellen's words. Did she appreciate her God-given gifts? Yes, that was why she'd responded to the Powells' advertisement for a governess. A desire to teach was most certainly a God-given dream.

She stepped back to once again admire the table set with a white damask tablecloth, gleaming dishes, crystal and silver. A salt cellar was placed by every plate next to the attractive place cards she had made.

Her heart had fluttered when she placed Mr. Hernandez's card next to her own as instructed by Ellen. Across from her would be Albert Hobbs and next to him Mary Etta. Thankfully, Ellen would be on the other side of Sally Rose at the end of the table, assuming hostess duties and directing conversation. At the opposite end, Mr. Powell would preside at the head with his mother to his right and Reverend Schilling to his left.

Sally Rose was more than satisfied with their handiwork. "I think that's everything except the food, and Martha has that taken care of."

"I hope so. Let's you and I get dressed. Martha will feed the children their dinner on the back porch and then put them to bed." Ellen untied her apron, giving the table one more glance. "They have strict orders not to come down the front stairs while our company is here."

"Did you say Martha's daughter is going to serve the table?" Sally Rose removed her own apron.

"Yes, Ruth Ann is coming. She's helped us before and does an excellent job."

"What age is she?"

"Oh, I don't know, perhaps early twenties, maybe close to your age. She has two children of her own. Why?"

"No reason, really. When Martha mentioned her daughter, I

thought of a younger, unmarried girl." Did Ellen think she was too curious?

"Oh no. Ruth Ann is married to a German fellow that came to work in the pencil factory."

"I see." Sally Rose decided to ask no more questions, even though this new revelation made her want to know more. As far as she knew, most German men were white. "Well, I better go get dressed."

"Yes, let's get ready for the evening."

Creases still puckered Ellen's forehead as she stepped onto the staircase. Sally Rose touched her arm. "Everything will be fine, I promise."

Upstairs in her room, Sally Rose stood before the mirror and studied the woman wearing a beautiful satin evening dress. The square-necked mauve dress trimmed with lace on the short sleeves and neckline was a perfect color for her. Fitted with tucks down the front, the skirt draped to the back where it poufed in layers behind. She tied a black velvet ribbon around her neck, then caressed the amethyst pendant suspended from it. A gift from Mrs. Middleton. Her eyes misted over. Mrs. Middleton had been like a grandmother and treated her as such while Sally Rose cared for her until her death. Sally Rose never would have been able to purchase such a precious jewel with her own meager earnings.

Exhaling and drawing herself up, she checked to make sure her chestnut hair was securely pinned so the curls cascaded down her back. A tinkle of the bell outside the front door prompted her to grab her ivory fan and go downstairs to greet the guests.

The senior Mrs. Powell already sat in the parlor, having been retrieved by Mr. Powell moments before, and Sally Rose crossed to her side.

"Do you need anything?" Sally Rose bent down to address the woman, and the scent of rosewater tickled her nose.

"No, dear, I'm fine." Mother Powell sat like a queen holding court, her chin level, her back stiff and straight.

Ellen stood at the front door beside her husband as first the reverend, then Albert Hobbs and Mrs. Chapman entered. She immediately pranced across the room to Mother Powell.

"Mrs. Powell, how lovely to see you again."Mrs. Chapman gushed over the elderly woman while sending icy darts in Sally

Rose's direction. "You are looking wonderful. You must tell me all about Charleston."

Mother Powell obliged, and Sally Rose closed her ears to a repeat of the conversation from the first night. She glanced around the room, and every time she scanned past Mr. Hobbs, he seemed to be staring at her. Like the day in the mercantile, his gaze unsettled her in a very unpleasant way, like discovering a snake in the barn back home.

She didn't see Mr. Hernandez's entrance into the room, but she felt it. Jerking her head around, she caught his gaze and subtle smile as he nodded his greeting. Immediately her temperature rose, and she snapped open the fan hanging from her wrist.

"Dinner is served."

Sally Rose joined the others in turning to the voice, which she was surprised to see coming from a formally-attired Joseph. Frank escorted his mother to the dining room, then Mr. Hobbs did the same for Mrs. Chapman.

"Madam?" Sally Rose jolted at the sound of Mr. Hernandez beside her as he offered his arm.

Instinctively, the teacher in her responded. "That's *mademoiselle,* since I'm unmarried."

Her face warmed at the twinkle in his eyes.

"How could I forget?"

She glanced down to hide her embarrassment and focused on his arm. Taking it, a tingle traveled up her own arm. Behind them, the reverend escorted Ellen to her seat. Once seated, the reverend gave the blessing, then the food was served in courses from the sideboard by Ruth Ann on one end of the room and Joseph on the other.

Ruth Ann was tall like her father, yet she resembled Martha. A pretty woman, she wore a long-sleeved black dress with a white apron and cap. Sally Rose didn't hear her utter a word, just offer dishes to each person as she moved around the table. She only nodded her acknowledgement of requests as she served. Sally Rose glanced from Joseph to Ruth Ann and noticed the silent messages exchanged between them. Much like she and her own papa had communicated. Very much the same.

"Miss McFarlane?"

"Yes?" Sally Rose turned toward the other end of the table.

Mother Powell was looking at her expectantly.

"I'm sorry. Did you ask me something?"

"Yes, dear. Mr. Hobbs has suggested an outing for you and the children."

Sally Rose faced the grinning Hobbs across from her.

"I was just saying I could take you over to the lighthouse one Sunday. And the children too, of course."

Sally Rose widened her eyes. Next to her, she sensed Mr. Hernandez stiffen. "Oh, I … well, I wouldn't want to impose on you." She could feel Mrs. Chapman's glare penetrate from across the table. This would not sit well with her.

"Not an imposition at all. I always have a boat ready, since I must go out and inspect the ships anchored in our waters. Got to keep an eye out for smugglers." Mr. Hobbs's booming voice bounced off the dining room walls, and Sally Rose suppressed a wince. "However, since this will not be a business trip, we can relax and even have a picnic if you'd like."

Mrs. Chapman's eyes were shooting sparks. Sally Rose would not have been surprised if her dress caughu fire.

"A boat?" Sally Rose squeaked, her lungs feeling squeezed by an invisible vise. "Where is the lighthouse?"

"Seahorse Key." Hobbs pointed across the room. "About seven miles from here."

"I see. But I'm afraid I don't have the disposition for boating." Maybe that wasn't true, but spending time with Albert Hobbs didn't appeal to her stomach either.

"Didn't you travel by boat to Fernandina?" Hobbs cocked his head, narrowing his eyes.

Mr. Hernandez came to her rescue. "Sometimes larger boats don't have the effect on one's constitution that a small boat does."

"Hmm." Mr. Hobbs narrowed his eyes even more, staring at Mr. Hernandez through thin slits. "Well, I guess you speak from personal experience, Mr. Hernandez."

"Oh, yes, boating has the same effect on me."

Sally Rose stared at her dinner partner. Was he coming to her rescue?

"All right then, if you change your mind, let me know. I'm sure the children would have a grand time."

"It certainly sounds like a splendid opportunity for the

children to learn more about their surroundings." Mother Powell fixed her gaze on her son, her tone commanding.

Sally Rose gulped, her stomach swirling as she pictured the inevitable boat trip with Mr. Hobbs.

"I'm sure it would be." Mr. Powell failed to follow his mother's obvious suggestion and pushed away from the table. "Now, if you'll join me, let's retire to the parlor.

He assisted his mother out of her chair. The couples followed in order and took their places around the room. "Miss McFarlane has offered to entertain us with music." Mr. Powell gestured toward the piano.

A task preferable to further conversation, Sally Rose obliged and took a seat at the bench.

She arranged her sheet music on the piano and began playing Schubert's Serenade. Then she played a few hymns by Fanny Crosby, which drew enthusiastic applause from the reverend. Next, she played another classical piece, receiving more polite applause when she finished.

"Won't you sing something for us too?" Mother Powell glanced at Mr. Powell, then back to Sally Rose. "I've heard you have a lovely voice."

Where would she hear that? It must have been mentioned in the letter of recommendation. Sally Rose nodded and began singing "Dreaming Forever of Thee."

When she finished, she turned to see if Mother Powell approved.

The woman was wiping her eyes with her handkerchief. She waved the cloth at Sally Rose. "That was wonderful, my dear. What else can you sing for us?"

Sally Rose launched into "Beautiful Dreamer," one of her favorites. As she completed the song, she caught Mr. Hernandez staring at her. His gaze was intense, penetrating. Why was he so serious? What was he thinking? Her heart leaped when he nodded and smiled, breaking the tension. She took a deep breath to steady herself. If only she could unlock her gaze from the handsome man across the room long enough to find another song.

# Chapter Nine

"Can you sing something more lively?" Hobbs's sudden suggestion broke the spell between Bryce and the lovely Miss McFarlane.

Bryce sighed. Hobbs was such a boor and obviously had never been trained in manners. The most beautiful woman with a wonderful voice had just sung an enchanting song, and the oaf didn't—no, couldn't—appreciate it. A glance at Miss McFarlane revealed the shock on her face, though she quickly pulled herself together.

"What would you like to hear, Mr. Hobbs?" She responded with an unruffled voice.

"Well, let's see. There's lots of lively songs I heard in New Orleans, but I suppose they might not suit the ladies." Hobbs chuckled and winked at the other men, apparently forgetting the reverend, who cleared his throat. "How about that 'Old Folks at Home' song? Didn't that Foster fellow write that one too?"

The young woman tensed. "I'm afraid I don't know that song, Mr. Hobbs."

Was it his imagination, or did she appear to be angry?

Hobbs guffawed. "I thought everyone knew that song. It's about some old slave who wishes he was still a slave. I think lots of them were better off when they were slaves."

Did she flinch? Bryce had to rescue her from the crude fellow.

"I'm sure Miss McFarlane would like to rest her lovely voice now." Bryce spoke to the group, but kept his eyes on Miss McFarlane. "May I get you something to drink?"

Her shoulders relaxed as her eyes thanked him. "Yes, I'd very much appreciate that, Mr. Hernandez. I'm afraid my throat is quite dry."

He poured a glass of water for her from the serving cart near the fireplace and returned with it.

"Thank you," she whispered, taking the glass from him and sipping it slowly.

The senior Mrs. Powell spoke up. "Thank you, dear, for entertaining us this evening. You are a very talented young lady." She motioned to the piano with her fan. "Are you teaching my grandchildren how to play the piano?"

"Yes, we have music each day. We divide the time between piano and singing." Sally took another sip before handing the glass back to him, her eyes thanking him again. Her poise was captivating, and he couldn't take his eyes off her.

The moment was interrupted by an unwelcome suggestion from Mr. Hobbs. "You know, Miss McFarlane, I've got an idea that could make your trip to the lighthouse more comfortable." He stroked his bushy whiskers while he awaited her response.

The color drained from Miss McFarlane's face as her eyes widened. How could the man be so insistent? It was obvious she didn't want to go with him.

Frank's mother leaned forward. "Do tell, Mr. Hobbs."

"Well, ma'am, we sell peppermint oil at the store. I've heard it gets rid of stomach uneasiness." Hobbs faced Miss McFarlane with a smug grin and continued to cajole. "It would be a shame for you to miss out on an opportunity to educate the children. There's lots to see out there—hundreds of birds. Might even see some dolphins. You know, when that John Muir fellow was here, he was quite interested in the islands. Course, he liked looking at all the flowers and such too."

The man was insufferable. Bryce tried to think of a way to help Miss McFarlane out. After all, the subject had been put to rest at the dinner table. Why must Hobbs insist on resurrecting it?

The elder Mrs. Powell appeared to consider the suggestion. "Miss McFarlane, perhaps you could reconsider. Why, it sounds like a wonderful idea! It could be a nature trip, and I'm sure the children would love it. Have you ever taken peppermint oil? I've also heard that it's good for the stomach."

Bryce was dumbfounded. Surely the woman didn't want Miss McFarlane to accompany this oaf on an outing. But what could he do to stop it? Volunteer to go along too?

"Well, I, no, I haven't . . ."

"She said she got sick, didn't she?" Now Mrs. Chapman, face turning red, jumped into the discussion, an unlikely ally for Bryce.

Hobbs ignored Mrs. Chapman's distress and clapped his hands together. "The weather should be good for a sail tomorrow." Assuming a serious, caring expression, he said, "Of course, we won't go if the water's rough."

The senior Mrs. Powell swept her hands apart. "Well, then, I think we've found a sensible solution. Mr. Hobbs, since tomorrow is Sunday, let's plan on the trip after church services. And you expect the sea to be calm?"

"Yes, I do, Mrs. Powell——just perfect for sailing. But I'm afraid the boat won't be large enough for all of us to go, what with the children and the captain, of course."

"Oh, heavens no, I have no intention of going." Mother Powell waved him off. "I think you and Miss McFarlane and the children should have a lovely time. We can have Martha pack a picnic for you." She beamed a self-approving smile at Miss McFarlane. "How does that sound?"

Bryce saw Frank and his wife exchange glances while their governess wrung her hands. No doubt who was in charge at the moment.

Bryce searched Miss McFarlane's face, noting her obvious discomfort, like a helpless animal caught in a trap. The situation appeared to be out of her hands and his too.

Miss McFarlane swallowed then gave a slight nod. "I suppose I could try the oil. The trip could prove to be educational for the children."

Why did Bryce feel he was the one who should be taking her for a sail? And yet, what she did and with whom was not his business. They weren't courting, and he wasn't planning on it. However, he hadn't expected to meet her either. He so wanted to save her from the experience, but what could he do? Once again, he felt responsible for rescuing someone.

As the guests departed, Bryce waited until the others had left. The reverend paused at the door to thank Frank and his wife before escorting the senior Mrs. Powell back to her hotel.

"We'll be seeing you folks in church tomorrow." He aimed a glance in Bryce's direction. "And will we see you too, Mr. Hernandez?"

Caught off-guard, Bryce hesitated to answer, but tipped his head. The reverend smiled in response, seeming to accept the gesture as affirmation before he turned to leave. Bryce had no intention of discussing his faith at the moment, but truth was, he and God hadn't been on speaking terms for a few years now. Ever since Anna Maria …

Returning his thoughts to the present, he bowed to Mrs. Powell, then turned to Miss McFarlane and bowed to her. She extended her hand, and he took it, holding it perhaps too long while he tried to convey with his eyes his sympathy for her predicament with Hobbs. Her lips tried to turn up at the corners, but didn't quite make it, and the slight nod of her head made him believe she understood. He released her hand, but her touch lingered and pulsated through him. He feared he had failed her, a fear all too familiar.

~

Bryce didn't go to church on Sunday, yet wrestled with guilt. Not that it was unusual for him to miss, as he had long since gotten out of the habit of going. However, this Sunday he was tempted to go only because he wanted to see Miss McFarlane again. But he couldn't be that much of a hypocrite—going to church just to see a woman. Would she expect him to be there? Or would she notice his absence?

After breakfast at the hotel, he strolled around the town, mulling over his spiritual state as families passed him by on their way toward the street where the churches were—the Methodist on one corner and the Episcopal on the other. With all the stores closed, the isolation and loneliness made Sunday Bryce's least favorite day, the day everyone else spent with their families as they enjoyed their day of rest. He didn't feel like resting, so he went back to his hotel room to do some paperwork. After a while, the room got stuffy, so he went outside on the upstairs veranda for some fresh air.

He sat down, propping his feet on the railing, and gazed toward the waterfront. Church must have ended because people were ambling along the street; a few headed toward the boats tied up at the dock. Some ladies carried covered baskets, ready for their afternoon picnics. Soon Miss McFarlane would join Hobbs for their outing. His stomach churned over images of the two of them together. Was there a chance she would cancel? *Could* she?

He had to find out. Leaping to his feet, he strode down the stairs and out the door toward the water. He attempted to look casual as he meandered along the dock, inspecting the various boats and wondering which one they would board. Hearing the sound of children's voices, he turned to see the Powell children scampering along, with Miss McFarlane close behind, holding tightly to the hand of the youngest girl.

"Children, please be careful and don't run." Her voice was as taut as her expression.

"Now, now, children. Right over there." Hobbs laughed out loud as he sauntered behind, pointing out a sloop nearby. "The captain will help you on."

Miss McFarlane was stunning as always, in a pale yellow dress with a matching hat, a perfect contrast for her dark hair and olive skin. One of her gloved hands held a lacy parasol, which she handed to the ship's mate as the captain helped her onboard. She was perfect, except for one thing. There was no evidence of a smile anywhere on her face. Clearly, she was not enjoying the situation. Or was he just hopeful that she wasn't?

As Hobbs clambered into the boat, he noticed Bryce.

"Mr. Hernandez! What brings you out today?" Hobbs scanned the waterfront, grinning as if he'd just won a prize. "Going sailing too?"

Miss McFarlane's head jerked up and her gaze met Bryce's. Her eyes widened, and a smile emerged from her beautiful lips. Was that a hopeful look?

"I'm afraid not. I was just out for a stroll, enjoying the nice weather."

A cloud passed over her face, and the smile vanished.

"Oh yes, I remember you said boating wasn't agreeable to you. That's a shame. I think Miss McFarlane will be fine, though."

Hobbs hooked his thumbs in his suspenders and puffed out his chest. "And we're going to have a grand day, aren't we, children?"

The children all chattered at once, unable to contain their excitement. Bryce clenched his jaw as Hobbs's raucous laughter rang out.

"Well, I hope your trip is pleasurable." Bryce spoke through gritted teeth but tried to mask his ire as he nodded toward Miss McFarlane who barely acknowledged the action. He wasn't sure if he meant what he said or not. On the one hand, he didn't want her to be ill, but he definitely didn't want her to enjoy her time with Hobbs. In his heart, he believed she really wouldn't like spending time with the obnoxious man. He visualized himself with her instead of Hobbs, the two of them having a pleasant outing together.

But would he ever have a chance to find out? Perhaps it was time to recover from his feigned seasickness. Yet he couldn't very well find a boat and run after them. How would that appear? No, he had to quit concerning himself with the matter. The woman could handle herself, of that he was sure. After all, she'd managed to come to Cedar Key unaccompanied and had already distinguished herself with her capabilities. She certainly didn't need his protection. So what was that nagging feeling that made him think she did?

He shook his head as if to clear out the jumbled thoughts. When would he realize he couldn't protect everyone? He hadn't been able to protect Anna Maria, yet would he spend the rest of his life trying to make amends for that? Would he ever realize some things were out of his control? If he were still a praying man, he'd pray about it. But sometimes, it seemed like God wasn't in control either, or He would've saved Anna Maria and the baby.

Right now, Bryce had to concentrate on what he could control. And if Albert Hobbs was guilty of wrongdoing, Bryce would guarantee he didn't get away with it. He watched the boat diminish on the water, then waved it farewell before he strode away. It was time to give those ledgers a closer look.

# Chapter Ten

"How are you feeling, Miss McFarlane?" Mr. Hobbs sat across from her, letting the captain and his deckhand manage the boat. "You see, I promised you a fine day for boating." He waved his arms as if conducting the weather like a maestro.

"Fine. Thank you." Sally Rose nodded, keeping her eyes on the horizon.

"I told you that peppermint oil would do the trick." He sounded pleased with himself and how he had controlled all the circumstances.

Sally Rose inhaled the salt air as the wind brushed her face. In reality, she loved being on the water. Uncle Joshua had taken her and the other children out on Lake Michigan on a friend's schooner when she was younger, and she had never forgotten the thrill of sailing across the waves. Unfortunately, the family farm was not close to the water, so she had only experienced it that one time.

The only other time she'd been on the water was the trip down from New York to Fernandina before taking the train to Cedar Key. However, a steamboat didn't convey the excitement of sailing. She had to be careful not to let Mr. Hobbs know how much she enjoyed the trip, lest, heaven forbid, he wanted to ask her again. Somehow, this would have to be the last voyage she made with him. Poor Mrs. Chapman. Sally Rose would gladly have traded places with the woman, but it hadn't been possible to do so. She must assure her the excursion was purely for the purpose of an educational experience for the children and none other.

With someone else, the trip would be delightful. When she saw Mr. Hernandez on the dock, she thought he might accompany them. But it was not to be. In addition to his apparent propensity for seasickness, he and Mr. Hobbs didn't seem to like each other. Her heart had dropped when she realized he wouldn't be going with them. As they sailed away, he looked so lonely and forlorn standing there, waving with little enthusiasm. Perhaps she was mistaken, but he seemed as disappointed as she. She had sighed as he walked away—for his sake or hers, she wasn't sure.

As they passed the nearest island, Sally Rose's attention was drawn to a large wooden building bearing the sign "Faber Pencil Mill" near the water.

Mr. Hobbs, watching her every move, followed her gaze. "That island's called Atsenie Otie. Everybody who lives over there works at the pencil mill."

Sally Rose shielded her eyes to get a better look beyond the glare off the water. Her light-colored parasol did little to block the sun. "Oh, yes, I recall Ellen talking about it."

"They don't actually make the pencils there. They cut the cedar into planks before they're shipped up north where they're made into pencils." As he talked, Hobbs opened his arms to demonstrate the size of the planks, then drew them together to show the length of the pencils. "The Powell house isn't very far from the pencil mill over in Cedar Key. Lots of cedar around here." Hobbs grinned his customary smile.

"I see." No wonder the town was named Cedar Key.

"It's just a few blocks from our house." Adele turned her head back and forth as she searched the shore behind them, then she pointed. "Over there."

"That's where all the noise comes from," Lucy added, standing next to the bench and trying to maintain her balance by holding onto Sally Rose's shoulders.

Sally Rose had noticed the noise around town and remembered what Ellen said about the sawmills.

"It's fun watching them float the logs in." Benjamin joined the conversation without taking his eyes off the yo-yo moving up and down in his hand. "Sometimes I seen men jump across them on the water."

Sally Rose corrected his English. "I have *seen*."

"You have?" Benjamin looked up, eyes wide as his yo-yo hung limp. "I didn't know you'd been there too."

"I haven't, I was just . . ." She stopped. She'd address his language later. Right now, she'd just let him enjoy the day.

"Mother told us not to go near there. She said it's dangerous." Adele crossed her arms, assuming her big sister rule-enforcer role.

"Look at all the boats!" Benjamin stuck his yo-yo in his pocket and ran to the side of the boat for a better look at the vessels scattered among the islands and beyond. From steamers to schooners, a variety of boats were either anchored or moving off the mainland.

Sally Rose scanned the horizon. "I had no idea Cedar Key was such a busy port."

"Certainly is! With the train coming into town, there's people and goods moving back and forth all the time." Mr. Hobbs spread his arms out toward the water as if displaying his kingdom. "Keeps me very busy."

"Do I understand that you personally inspect every vessel? That must be quite an undertaking."

"Yes, it is. But it's an important job. A lot of people want to avoid paying the customs taxes if they can. Sometimes goods are exchanged before the ship ever comes into port just to evade taxes."

"I see. You must spend a fair amount of time in the water, then."

Hobbs laughter drowned out the cawing of the sea gulls flying overhead. "Like a fish. But I'd prefer to be *on* it rather than *in* it."

Sally Rose's face grew hot at the joke he made of her remark.

Tilly tapped Sally Rose on the arm and pointed ahead of the boat. "Look, Miss Sally."

"Miss Sally?" Mr. Hobbs quirked an eyebrow.

"Yes. Miss McFarlane is difficult for the children. Especially Tilly."

"Of course. And Miss Sally is much more delightful than Miss McFarlane."

Sally Rose stiffened. Oh no. The casual way he used her Christian name was too personal. "But you say Miss McFarlane with much ease, Mr. Hobbs."

He roared with laughter as if she'd made a clever joke. Why did he think everything was so amusing?

Following the direction of Tilly's finger, Sally Rose saw a group of dolphins rolling through the water. "Oh, how wonderful! I wonder how many there are."

The children scrambled to the edge of the boat to glimpse the sea animals, competing to see who could spot them first.

"There's one!"

"There's one over there!"

Sally Rose gasped as they stretched over the side of the boat. "Children, please don't lean too far over the boat."

"There's two more right there!"

Mr. Hobbs laughed loudly. "How do you know you're not counting the same ones twice?"

"Well, I think there's five different ones." Adele shook her head for emphasis. "See?"

"I think there's a baby in the middle of those two." Lucy pointed to a group of three.

"Why, I think you're right, Lucy. How adorable." Sally Rose patted Lucy's hand.

"There's the island up ahead." Mr. Hobbs nodded toward the bow of the boat.

The island grew larger as they drew closer, and Sally Rose was relieved to see other boats at the single long dock. Thank goodness, there wouldn't be alone with Mr. Hobbs. Seagulls cried overhead as they pulled up alongside.

"Looks like there's quite a few families out here today, enjoying the nice weather like we are." Mr. Hobbs motioned to the other boats tied up nearby.

Sally Rose didn't like his use of the word "we." They were certainly not a "family." Grabbing the picnic basket, she lifted it up to the shipmate who had jumped out to tie up the boat. Mr. Hobbs struggled, but managed to get out, grunting as he did. Then the children clambered out and Mr. Hobbs extended his hand to assist Sally Rose.

She accepted the hand just long enough to disembark the boat, then dropped it to pick up the basket. Mr. Hobbs's fleshy hand was like a squishy sponge compared to Mr. Hernandez's firm, but gentle grip.

Sally Rose searched the sandy beach. "Where's the lighthouse?"

"Oh, you can hardly see it from here." Mr. Hobbs waved toward the treetops. "It's up there on top of the hill, but the trees practically hide it until you get up to it."

The children ran ahead and were now scampering along the sandy beach, discovering objects that had washed ashore. A flock of white pelicans came around the bend, skimming low in straight-line formation across the water.

"Children, please wait for us!" Sally Rose lifted her skirt high enough to keep it from getting stuck in the rough boards on the dock and tried to catch up to the youngsters.

"Eeek!" A shrill scream came from Tilly as Benjamin chased her with a piece of driftwood.

Benjamin laughed as he yelled at his sister. "Snake! Snake!"

"Benjamin! Stop that at once!" Sally Rose placed her hands on her hips as Tilly ran to her, crying, and hid behind her.

"It's just some old piece of driftwood." Benjamin stopped running and ambled over, dragging the stick while drawing a line in the sand.

"Please don't scare your sister like that." Sally Rose patted Tilly's head, as she cowered among her teacher's skirts.

Mr. Hobbs arrived then, panting and out of breath as he waddled up to them. "There's plenty of real snakes around here." He swiped his forehead with his handkerchief.

Sally Rose arched her eyebrows. "I hope we're not in danger of meeting one."

"Ha. Well, you better stay close to the path and close to me, if you want to be safe."

The man grinned broadly as he tucked his thumbs in his waistband.

Was that a wink? Her stomach lurched, and it wasn't from seasickness.

"Children, stay close to me on the path." Sally Rose reached toward the youngsters and beckoned for them to come.

"I'm hungry!" Benjamin reached for the basket on her arm. "Can't we eat now?"

Sally Rose gently pushed back his hand. "Benjamin, we need to wait until everyone is ready to eat."

"As a matter of fact, I am too, son." Mr. Hobbs indicated a small sand dune not too far away. "We can spread out the quilt over there."

While they were having their lunch, some seagulls arrived, squawking as they hovered over them, eyeing the food. Benjamin threw a piece of biscuit up in the air; suddenly, more seagulls materialized, begging for morsels.

"Oh my!" Sally Rose lifted her hands over her head to protect herself from unwanted falling debris.

"We'll take care of these pests." Mr. Hobbs pulled a pistol out from under his jacket and aimed it at the birds.

"No!" Sally Rose flailed her arms, trying to stop him before he murdered a poor, innocent bird. And in front of the children too.

"Hahaha!" Mr. Hobbs bellowed at her reaction and returned the pistol to its hiding place. "Don't worry. You don't think I'd really shoot one, do you?"

Sally Rose placed a hand over her heart to still it, glaring at him before she glanced over at the children, who watched wide-eyed. "I certainly hope not." Although she wasn't sure what he would have done if she hadn't stopped him.

Several flocks of large, black birds flew past, providing grateful distraction. "There are certainly a lot of birds here." Sally Rose watched them land out in the water. "I haven't seen all these varieties before." Hopefully, he'd keep the gun tucked away.

"Those are cormorants. You watch them; they'll dive under and come up quite a ways off."

"Look! That one just went under!" Lucy pointed to her left. "Wonder where it'll come up."

"There it is!" Adele's finger indicated an area some twenty feet away from where bird dove.

"Yep, the snakes like all these birds," Mr. Hobbs announced. "They hide out under the trees and wait for a baby bird or an egg to fall out of a nest, then 'gulp!'"

Sally Rose shuddered. She couldn't think of anything she disliked more than snakes.

Mr. Hobbs continued matter-of-factly. "Mr. Gray told me if it weren't for the rats, the place would be crawling with snakes!"

Rat or snakes. Which would be worse? She covered her mouth with her hand. Stifling a scream and fighting repulsion, Sally Rose tried to hide her disgust. She took a deep breath before replying.

"Mr. Gray?"

"The assistant keeper here. You'll meet him when we go up there to the lighthouse. He's in charge now while the main keeper's on leave." Mr. Hobbs directed them up the hill. "We've known each other a long time." He paused, his brows furrowed as though in deep thought.

"Can we go to the lighthouse now?" Benjamin jumped to his feet, ready to run.

"*May* we?" Sally Rose corrected.

"'Course we can!" Mr. Hobbs answered, oblivious to the response. "It's a bit of a hike up there, but stay on the path and it's a little easier."

Since Sally Rose had long since lost her appetite, she began to gather up the napkins and plates they'd used for the picnic, and the girls helped put them back in the basket.

"You can leave that here until we get back." Mr. Hobbs struggled to stand up then reached for her hand.

She accepted his hand long enough to get to her feet, then let go of his to take Tilly's, brushing off sand from both herself and the child. "Girls, brush your skirts off." Adele and Lucy followed suit.

Benjamin had disappeared from view as he followed the path up the hill through the thick tangle of twisted windswept trunks and palmetto. Sally Rose hurried the girls along to catch up, with Mr. Hobbs tottering behind.

Sally Rose caught sight of the boy's knickers up ahead. "Benjamin, please slow down and wait for us."

He obeyed, stepping to the edge of the trail, and when they reached him, he was staring at a couple of headstones lying a ways off the path.

"A graveyard?" Sally Rose lifted her eyebrows and turned to address the panting and red-faced Mr. Hobbs as he joined them.

"Couple of soldiers killed in the War."

"I heard there's ghosts here." Benjamin headed toward the markers.

"Better not do that, son." Mr. Hobbs grabbed the boy by the shoulder, jerking him back. "Snakes, you know."

"Johnny Thomas said there's a headless horseman." Benjamin picked up a stick and galloped in circles, mimicking riding a horse. "It rides when the moon is full."

Sally Rose felt a chill. "Benjamin, you shouldn't believe in those stories."

"They say it's true." Mr. Hobbs's voice took on a gravelly, sinister tone. "Seems the story is about one of Jean Lafitte's pirates he left here to guard some treasure. Some men—fishermen, I think—stopped on the island and started drinking with the pirate. Next thing you know, the fishermen are gone, the treasure's gone, and so is the pirate's head. Some have seen his horse riding on the island with his headless body." Mr. Hobbs laughed when he saw the expression on Sally Rose's face. He lowered his voice. "Only comes out at night, though, so you better not be here after dark." He threw his head back and hooted with laughter.

Sally Rose shook her head in disgust. "Mr. Hobbs, I really don't believe in such nonsense. And I don't think the children need to hear such tales, either." Little did he know her grandfather had been one of Lafitte's pirates, but no one here knew her true heritage anyway, a secret she would keep.

"Let's go to the lighthouse. Last one there's a rotten egg!" Benjamin took off up the hill again. Adele and Lucy took up the challenge and raced to catch him.

"Children!" Sally Rose's voice was lost amidst the sound of the children calling out to each other.

"Miss Sally, I'm scared." Tilly tugged on Sally Rose's hand, peering up at her with wide, fearful eyes.

Sally Rose glared at Mr. Hobbs. "I'll thank you, sir, to keep your conversation on more pleasant things."

Mr. Hobbs lowered his gaze and pretended remorse. "Yes, my lady. I will behave myself."

Sally Rose huffed and marched up the hill with Tilly in tow. As the path opened out to a clearing, a white frame house appeared, perched on the crest. She was surprised at the modest home, which boasted the lighthouse tower in the center. Unlike the tall lighthouses she was familiar with along the coast of Lake Michigan, this lighthouse was scarcely two stories high.

People milled around the building, some sitting on the front porch, while children raced about the grounds. Up on the light tower, some people stood on the catwalk that surrounded the light. Benjamin was standing by the building, displaying his yo-yo skills with another boy, while Adele and Lucy waited for the rest of their party to catch up.

"There you are." Sally Rose huffed her displeasure, putting her hands on her hips as she faced her young male charge.

"Well, we waited for you before we climbed to the top of the tower." Adele frowned at her brother as she copied Sally Rose's stance.

"Thank you, Adele. Please hold Lucy's hand, so you won't get separated. Benjamin, please come over here." Turning to Mr. Hobbs, Sally Rose said, "Is it safe to climb up there, Mr. Hobbs?"

"Oh, yes, just a short flight of steps and you're in the light room. Have to take turns, though, because there's not much space up there." He walked alongside her to the front porch steps then stopped. "You folks go on up there. I'll wait here for you."

Sally Rose tilted her head at him. "You're not coming too?" She silently breathed a sigh of relief. Finally, she was free of the man for the time being. "Very well, then. We'll be back down shortly. Come, children."

"Oh, you take your time. Enjoy the view." Mr. Hobbs swept his arms out wide. "You can see for miles up there."

When Sally Rose entered the central hallway and saw the narrow spiral stairs, she understood why Mr. Hobbs didn't want to join them. He most likely wouldn't fit, or if he did, it would be very difficult for him. When they reached the top, an opening in the floor allowed just enough room for a normal-sized person to squeeze through. Sally Rose pushed the children up before she pulled herself into the opening. Once upright in the small lantern room, they went through a short door to the outside where several others were already gathered by the railing.

"Children, please be careful. Girls, hold hands."

Sally Rose moved cautiously around the gallery, holding the railing with one hand and Tilly's hand with the other. The panorama spread out above the treetops, giving a view of water encircling the island and several smaller islands in the distance. A refreshing breeze carrying the scent of the sea swept through Sally Rose's hair, lifting her spirit.

Lucy scanned the view. "I can see our house."

"No, you can't; it's too far away." Adele crossed her arms and shook her head. "Besides, it's the other direction."

"I can't see anything." Tilly stood on tiptoe, stretching her little nose toward the top of the railing.

"Let's just enjoy this beautiful view, girls. When we get home, we'll get a map and find all the islands on it." Sally Rose watched a white bird with an orange, curved beak light in a nearby tree. "I don't believe I've ever seen such a variety of birds." She'd have to check her bird book to see what it was called.

Benjamin still held onto his yo-yo, until the boy next to him asked if he could play with it, and Benjamin complied.

"Hey, look!" The boy dangled the yo-yo over the railing.

"Don't drop it!" Benjamin lunged for the toy, but it slipped out of the boy's hand, falling to the ground below.

"I'll get it!" The boy ducked in the door.

"No, you won't! It's mine!" Before Sally Rose could stop him, Benjamin had run in after the other boy.

*Dear Lord, what now?* Should she run after Benjamin and leave the girls? What if he tumbled down those tricky stairs? Or had a fight with the other boy? But leave the girls up here, where they could fall off the edge? Sally Rose inhaled a deep, calming breath.

"Adele, you hold on tightly to Tilly's hand and help her and Lucy get back downstairs. I'll go get Benjamin." Sally Rose ducked through the small door and carefully climbed back down the stairs. As she reached the bottom, she looked to her right and left to catch a glimpse of the boy. At either end of the wide hallway a door led out of the house, one to the back and the other out the front. Which way did he go?

She took a few steps toward the back door and heard voices. Two men were talking, but what caught her attention was the fact that they were speaking in French. How odd. She didn't mean to eavesdrop, but occasionally, the voices were loud enough to hear clearly. She peered through the open window. Outside on the porch, Mr. Hobbs spoke to a lanky fellow in a uniform. That must be Mr. Gray, the assistant keeper.

Bits and pieces of the conversation entered her mind, but she made no sense of it. Instinctively, she heard "hiding place," "ship signal," "watch out for," "crates." She pushed it back in her mind to concentrate on finding Benjamin. She needn't concern herself with others' conversations. Afraid to interrupt the men and preferring to avoid Mr. Hobbs, she decided to go out the front door. As she stepped toward it, however, the back door opened and she turned to face Mr. Hobbs, the other man behind him.

Mr. Hobbs's usual jovial countenance contorted into a menacing glare, his face reddened and eyes narrowed upon finding her there.

"Miss McFarlane, what are *you* doing here? I thought you were with your charges on the tower." He raised his eyebrows awaiting her answer.

A chill raced down her spine. Why did she feel like he was accusing her of something? Being negligent of her duties to care for the children? Or was there something more important that concerned him?

# Chapter Eleven

"Miss McFarlane, are you lost?" Mr. Hobbs scanned the area.

"Benjamin . . . Have you seen him?" She avoided his eyes, hoping he didn't think she'd been listening to their conversation. "He dropped his yo-yo off the top and ran out to find it."

Mr. Hobbs emitted one of his noisy laughs, sounding a bit contrived. "You know boys. Always getting into mischief. We'll see if we can find him." Noting her glance at the uniformed man beside him, he waved him forward. "Ah, I don't believe you two have met. My apologies. Miss McFarlane, this is Ira Gray, the assistant keeper."

"How do you do?' Sally Rose gave a slight bow with her head. The man reminded her of one of the cranes she'd seen on the beach, lanky and stealthy, with beady eyes.

"How do you do, ma'am? You like our lighthouse? Did you go up top and look out?"

He glanced from side to side, looking like a child with his hand caught in the cookie jar. The man's demeanor made her skin crawl, and she searched behind him for a glimpse of Benjamin as an excuse to leave the conversation.

"Yes, we did, and I enjoyed the view very much. But if you'll excuse me, I need to find Benjamin."

Children's voices were heard coming down the stairs then, and soon the girls emerged.

"We saw Benjamin. He waved to us from over there by the water tower." Adele gripped Tilly's hand and kept an eye on each step the child took until she reached the bottom. "I told him he better come back before he got in trouble."

"Well, let's go out and find that young man." She looked over her shoulder at Mr. Hobbs as she approached the door. "We should leave as soon as I locate him. I believe we need to get the children back home."

"I'll be right there." Mr. Hobbs nodded in her direction then turned to the keeper, patting him on the back. "Mr. Gray, it was very nice to see you again, sir. You're doing a fine job." More laughter followed his remarks.

Sally Rose ushered the children outside and found a disheveled Benjamin standing by the back porch, playing with his yo-yo.

"Benjamin! Look at you! What happened to your clothes?" She rushed over to him and began to straighten his clothing and brush off the sandy dirt. His shirt hung crooked outside of his pants, which were soiled all over. One of his stockings was down around his ankles, the other displayed a large hole, and his hair was tousled as if it had seen no comb that morning. She couldn't let his parents, much less anyone else, see him in this state. What would they think of her chaperoning ability?

The boy shrugged and glanced down at himself to see what all the fuss was about. "Toby tried to take my yo-yo, but I got it back!" He held his toy up and waved it around, as if showing off a trophy while he grinned with pride.

"Mother's going to be angry with you for ruining your clothes." Adele crossed her arms and accused her brother.

"Did you give him a black eye?" Lucy leaned forward, eyes rounded.

Sally Rose gasped and covered her mouth with her hand. "Oh my, Benjamin. You didn't hurt him, did you?"

"Will you give me a black eye too, Benjamin?" Tilly reached her open palm out to her brother.

"Tilly, it's not a marble!" Adele leaned over and instructed her little sister. "It means—"

Sally Rose hurried to take Tilly's hand as the child's face radiated confusion. "Come, children. It's time to go home." She grabbed Benjamin and steered him around the lighthouse, just as Mr. Hobbs was coming down the steps.

"Boy had a little tussle, I see." Mr. Hobbs chortled.

Sally Rose glared at him. She found nothing humorous about the situation. "I hope he'll be presentable when his parents see him. Is there a pump where I can clean him off?"

"Right over there."

The group went around to the other end of the house where the water pump was, and Sally Rose washed Benjamin's hands and face and finger-combed his hair. Better than before, but what would be Ellen's reaction to seeing him this way? When finished, they returned to the dock and boarded the waiting boat for the trip home.

Once the children were safely situated in the boat, with the three oldest seated on the deck, Sally Rose sank down on one of the benches. She pulled Tilly onto the bench, and the child promptly leaned against her. Sally Rose closed her eyes and tried to catch her breath. It was one thing to take care of one's own siblings, but quite another to be responsible for someone else's children. The gentle rocking of waves against the boat threatened to put her to sleep. Her eyes popped open; no time for sleep now. She still needed to deliver the children to their home.

She gazed ahead at the water, thinking about the day's events. A sense of being watched pulled her glance toward Mr. Hobbs, sitting on the side of the boat. Despite the ocean breeze, heat flooded her face when she met his stare. Why was he looking at her that way, as if studying her? A forced smile made its way across his fatty cheeks.

"Busy day for you, Miss McFarlane?"

"Yes, quite." She attempted a smile back.

"I do hope you enjoyed your visit. Perhaps next time, you can come without bringing the young ones along." He nodded toward the children.

Sally Rose tried to hide the shock of his offer as her stomach turned over and a bitter taste rose in her throat. Next time? Alone with him? Did he not understand the reason she agreed to the trip was for the children, not for his company? She must avoid that situation at all costs. In addition to her dislike for the man, she now sensed something even worse. Danger? As he emitted his annoying chortle, a chill trickled down her back.

~

Bryce paced back and forth on the hotel veranda, stealing glances out toward the wharf. Shouldn't they be back by now?

The sun had begun its descent to the water as other families arrived in boats and strolled down the dock back to town. Bryce scanned each face, watching for the one he wanted to see. But so far, hers wasn't among them.

Studying ledgers all afternoon had diverted his attention somewhat, yet his inner clock kept ticking, waiting for Miss McFarlane and Hobbs to return. No amount of self-talk would still the clock. What was she doing? Was she enjoying herself? Visions of her smiling face appeared unsummoned in his mind while he tried to concentrate on the numbers in front of him. What a poor way to spend a Sunday afternoon. Work had proved a worthy escape from his lonely life before, but today, he yearned for more. Another's company, perhaps?

However, when he did manage to focus on his task, he noticed a few peculiarities. It appeared that quite a few times numbers had been erased. Often the quantity of items ordered were not matched by the number received, and many times the adjusted number was written over an erased number. Perhaps altering the quantities would not be unusual except for the frequency of these changes. He would ask Hobbs's clerk about it first thing tomorrow. Perhaps the clerk could shed some light on the messy bookkeeping.

Bryce pulled the watch chain out of his vest pocket and checked the time. Almost five. His stomach rumbled, giving him a reason to leave the building. He'd grab dinner at one of the hotel restaurants then take a stroll through town to stretch his legs. Taking his hat and coat off the peg on the wall, he went out the door, donning them as he descended the stairs. In the lobby, the closed doors of the mercantile reminded him again that it was Sunday, when most people worshipped and did not work. It had been a long time since he was one of them.

He stopped and peered through the glass doors into the store. There was certainly a variety of goods as well as ample space for them. Where did they keep their back stock? He'd ask Frank about that. Whoever placed the orders recorded in the ledgers certainly purchased a large quantity of merchandise. If they had received all of it, they would need a large place for storage. It was almost as if they'd ordered a surplus not expecting to receive what they ordered. That struck him as odd. Was this typical of other merchants in the area?

As he stepped outside, he had the urge to walk along the dock before going to dinner. But what if Miss McFarlane arrived and saw him there again? She'd surely think he had nothing else to do but hang around the dock all day. He grimaced. That wasn't far from the truth. While many unmarried men would spend their leisure time drinking with other men, Bryce had never developed the habit. He'd seen too many brawls that were the result of overindulgence.

A raucous laugh drew his attention in the direction of the docks. He knew that laugh and, unfortunately, knew its owner. Hobbs. So they had returned.

A tremor of excitement raced through him in anticipation of seeing Miss McFarlane again. Had she enjoyed herself? He walked a comfortable distance away from the juncture of the dock and the sidewalk where he could still see the group yet not appear so obvious. Standing in the shade of the bank, he leaned against one of its columns and watched.

The children walked in front, showing less enthusiasm than they had when departing, all except the little boy who darted along the dock from boat to boat, investigating each one. An amused smile crept over Bryce's lips when he noticed the boy's clothes. What an impossible task to keep such an active youngster neat and clean all day. When he saw Miss McFarlane, he read the fatigue on her face. Had the boy been too difficult to handle?

Hobbs was the only one smiling, putting on his show for all to observe as he paraded behind the group. He acted like this was his family and proud of them too. Bryce's collar tightened, and he clenched his jaw. The man savored his self-importance, strutting along as he did. He said something to Miss McFarlane, which made her frown. When they reached the sidewalk and turned in the direction of the Powell house, she glanced back over her shoulder.

He didn't think she saw him before she looked away. But the expression on her face bothered him. Was she tired, angry, or something else? An uneasy feeling told him it was fear.

# Chapter Twelve

"I do wish you could join us." Ellen paused at the front door as she and Mother Powell were leaving. "I'm sure you would enjoy having tea with the ladies in the guild."

"Come, Ellen. I like to be early." Mother Powell appeared to be top-heavy with her elaborate hat piled high with bows and feathers. Were it not for the generous bustle of her beige satin dress, she'd be unbalanced. She turned to look back at her daughter-in-law as she stepped out on the porch. "Miss McFarlane needs to be with the children. After all, that *is* what a governess does, my dear." Glancing over at Sally Rose, she gave a patronizing smile.

"Mother Powell is right." Sally Rose stood in the foyer, hands clasped in front of her as she watched the ladies leave. "I have some exciting lessons planned for the children." She was certain Ellen only asked her to be polite, but Sally Rose had no interest in joining the guild ladies. She truly preferred the company of the children, where she was warmly accepted.

Ellen, dressed in a gray suit trimmed in black, adjusted the small black hat on her head and gave Sally Rose an apologetic, timid smile before she followed the older lady out the door.

"You'll have a lovely time, I'm sure," Sally Rose called to Ellen.

Once they were gone, Sally Rose exhaled a sigh of relief. Mother Powell meant well, of course, but she was constantly interfering with the lessons and interjecting her own opinion of how the children should be taught. *Thank you, Ellen.* Sally Rose was confident Ellen had invited her mother-in-law to the guild meeting to get her out of Sally Rose's way, even though Ellen hated social gatherings of that nature, where the town's ladies met to impress each other and discuss everyone else's business.

She settled in the parlor and opened one of her most-prized possessions, the Royal Octavo version of Audubon's *Birds of America.* Her eyes misted over as she ran her fingers across the page featuring one of Audubon's prints. Her former employer, recognizing Sally Rose's admiration for the book, had given it to her, refusing Sally Rose's offer to pay for it. Of course, it would've taken Sally Rose a long time to save the money for the expensive book, one of only 1200 printed. But since the school already owned one of the original, larger volumes, Miss Middleton was willing to part with it.

A thrill of excitement quickened her pulse as she carefully turned the pages, looking for the birds she'd seen on their island excursion.

"Children, come here and let's find the birds we saw when we went to see the lighthouse." The children scampered over to gather around her chair, their eyes wide with curiosity.

"We saw that one!" Lucy was the first to point out the brown pelican.

"Look at that one! We saw the white kind too!" Adele laid her hand on the picture of the white pelican.

"Careful, children. This is a very special book given to me by a very special lady, so let's take care of it, shall we?" It warmed her heart to see the children enjoy the book as much as she did, even though she needed to protect the book.

"What's that black bird?" Benjamin, on his knees, pointed as Sally Rose turned the page. "I saw lots of them too."

"Those are called cormorants." Sally Rose smiled at the children's enthusiasm. "Can you say 'cor-mor-ant'?"

"Cor-mor-ant!"

"Miss Sally, I saw that big bird." Tilly tugged on Sally Rose's sleeve, indicating the picture of a large bird with blue-gray feathers.

"Great Blue Heron." Adele peered over Sally Rose's shoulder and read the name. "It didn't look blue to me. I'd say it was gray."

Lucy waved at the opposite page. "There's a white one too! I saw that one."

"Yes, it may also be called an egret." Sally Rose showed them the words at the bottom of the picture.

She continued to flip gently through the pages as more birds were recognized. The children laughed at the illustration of the anhinga, with its wings spread wide to dry.

"There it is!" Sally Rose stopped at the page showing a white bird with an orange, curved bill. "White ibis. So that's what it was."

She turned her attention away from the book. "All right, children. What I'd like you to do is choose one of the birds we saw and draw your own picture of it."

The children quickly got to work with their pencils and tablets, while Sally Rose watched their progress. Her heart swelled with satisfaction as she witnessed their enthusiasm. It was so fulfilling to see them enjoy learning new things.

A knock on the door startled her. Who would be coming by at this time? She opened the door to find Mary Etta Chapman standing with crossed arms.

"Mary Etta? I'm afraid Ellen's not here. She's at the guild meeting."

"That's Mrs. Chapman to you, dear. You need to remember your place." The scowl on the woman's face contorted her fleshy features, reminding Sally Rose of a gargoyle.

Sally Rose's face flamed at her slip, as well as, the woman's reaction. "I'm sorry, Mrs. Chapman." She straightened and said, " Can I help you?"

Mrs. Chapman glanced from side to side. "Can you help me? What you can do is stay away from my fiancé."

"Your fiancé? Who . . . ?"

"Albert Hobbs, that's who. Who do you think you are, waltzing into town and attracting all the decent men?"

"Why, I never! Mrs. Chapman, I have no interest in Mr. Hobbs, I assure you. I didn't realize you were betrothed, but . . ."

Mrs. Chapman stepped forward and aimed an accusing finger at Sally Rose's face.

"Well, you mark my word, young lady! You'd better watch your step. I've got some old acquaintances in Chicago, and I plan to find out about you—what you're hiding, and what you're doing here."

A heavy weight dropped down inside Sally Rose's chest. She gasped and stepped back then took a deep breath and drew herself up to regain her composure. "Mrs. Chapman, I came here as a governess. That is my job and all I am interested in here. I have no notions nor interests in any man, especially Mr. Hobbs." She squared her shoulders. "Now if you'll excuse me, I have lessons to teach."

She closed the door as a red-faced Mrs. Chapman opened her mouth. Through the open window, Sally Rose heard, "You'd better keep your distance. I've got my eye on you."

Sally Rose fell back against the door, her pulse racing. What if the woman found out she hadn't really been a teacher at Miss Middleton's school? What if she discovered Sally Rose had Negro blood? Would she still be allowed to teach white children? Her head began to spin as she saw the new life she had begun now crumbling around her.

~

"I'm sorry, Mr. Hernandez. Mr. Hobbs isn't here today. Had to go out to check the boats." Mr. Greene shook his head. "'Fraid I'm the only one mindin' the store. Not that I mind, of course, what with Mr. Hobbs havin' to leave so much."

"I see. Well, perhaps *you* can help me then." Bryce had watched from the balcony, making sure Hobbs was gone before going downstairs to talk with Mr. Greene. Perhaps the employee could reveal information to support Frank's suspicions without his boss around.

"Yes, sir. I'll try." Mr. Greene's spectacles slid to the end of his narrow nose, where he pushed them back up.

"I noticed you carry quite the variety of goods here. Do you order them yourself, or does Mr. Hobbs?"

"Mostly it's Mr. Hobbs that does the ordering. I keep a list of what we need then he writes up the orders."

Bryce swept his arms out to encompass the entire room. "With this big a store, it must be difficult to keep up with all the items."

Mr. Greene lifted his chin. "Yes, sir, it is. We'd have aplenty if we got all we ordered though. Wouldn't be running out of things all the time."

Bryce raised his eyebrows. "Is that right? So you have a problem getting your orders filled?"

"Constantly. It's enough to make a man lose his hair, worryin' about it." Greene winked and pointed to his shining scalp.

"Ha. Well, that's a shame. One would think with the train coming in every day and so many ships delivering here, you'd have more than enough inventory."

"I agree, Mr. Hernandez. But we're always havin' to adjust the books. They're plum messy."

Bryce rubbed his chin. His sentiments exactly.

Mr. Greene bent over the counter and glanced sideways before lowering his voice. "I've got my own suspicions about what happens to the goods."

Bryce leaned toward him. "What might that be?"

"Smugglers. They're thick as ants out there."

Bryce straightened, the news surprising. He hadn't realized there was so much smuggling going on. "That so? Are they really so numerous?"

Greene bobbed his head. "That's the truth. I hear 'em all the time, talkin' about the goin's on out there." He stood upright and pulled down on his vest. "Mind you, I don't associate with those ruffians, but I sometimes take a bit of refreshment at one of the taverns they frequent on my way home."

"Wouldn't Mr. Hobbs be aware of this, since he's the customs agent?"

"Of course he knows. Poor man can't catch them all though. There's so many places a little boat can hide out there along the shore and on the islands." Greene shrugged and waved his hand towards the water in a helpless gesture, as if the problem was unpreventable. "All they have to do is take some freight off one of the big ships out there before Mr. Hobbs gets a chance to see it."

"It must be very frustrating for him."

"It certainly is. You wouldn't want to be around him when he gets angry." Greene shook his head.

"So I assume all the stores in town have the same problem?"

"Yes and no." Greene shook his head. "My friend, Mr. Clayton, is a clerk down at the Lutterloh store. They have some problems getting their merchandise too, but they don't seem to have as much trouble as we do." Greene pushed his glasses up again. "Or maybe he just doesn't want me to know if they do."

"Are there certain items that are harder to get than others?"

Greene pointed down at the glass countertop. "See them ceegars? They're real hard to get."

"You have ships from Cuba, don't you?"

"That's right. But for some reason, we never get enough. Taxes on 'em are sky-high too."

"Anything else a problem to get?"

"Liquor, especially rum from Cuba and South America. I know for a fact the smugglers love to get their hands on it. Like liquid gold. Can make a pretty penny selling it if they don't have to pay the taxes on it. Hmm. Lutterloh don't sell liquor—he don't believe in strong spirits, so he don't sell it in his store."

"No wonder." Bryce pulled his watch out of the pocket on his vest and opened it, revealing a clock face and the faded photo of a man and woman. After reading the time, he raised his head and returned the watch to the vest. Straightening his coat, he donned his bowler and turned to leave. "Well, I won't take up any more of your time, and I must get to work myself."

"Enjoyed talkin' to you." Greene shook Bryce's hand. "Say, why are you so interested in how we get our merchandise?"

"My parents run a store in Cuba." That much was partially true. "They've been having some problems obtaining some goods as well." That part wasn't. "I was just wondering if you shared the same dilemma."

# Chapter Thirteen

"Well, I've done my civic duty for the day, if not the month." Ellen removed her hatpins as soon as she came in the door, then took off the hat. She frowned at her reflection in the hall-tree mirror then turned to Sally Rose, who had come into the foyer to greet Ellen when she arrived. "I left Mother Powell at her hotel. She wanted to rest before dinner."

"I trust you had a nice meeting."

"It was bearable and somewhat informative. I heard who's courting whom, whose daughter is with child, and complaints about the deplorable taverns on the other side of town where all the undesirables gather, fight, and so on."

"I see." Sally Rose clasped her hands together in front of her skirt.

"Oh, yes, and let's see what else. We discussed bustles and whether or not we liked them. Of course, Mother Powell said all the society ladies in Charleston wear them now—the bigger, the better. I do wish that fashion would go away. It's so impractical."

"I agree that it can be, especially if too large."

"I almost forgot. Eliza Hearn wants to start a school."

Sally Rose's chest tightened. Would she be unnecessary if that happened?

Ellen grabbed Sally Rose by the arm. "Dear me, I've alarmed you. Rest assured, whatever Eliza does won't affect us. We're quite pleased with the way you're instructing the children. They appear to be flourishing as well as enjoying your tutelage."

Sally Rose exhaled slowly. "Thank you. I very much enjoy teaching them. They're quite amenable to learning."

As the women entered the parlor, Lucy jumped up from her chair and ran over to her mother with a drawing. "Mother, look what I drew!"

"Look at mine!" Tilly scampered to Ellen as well, her paper held aloft.

"Mine too!" Benjamin dashed over with his sketch. "They're pictures of birds we saw over at the island. It's a anhinga!" He posed with arms outstretched like the black bird in the picture.

"How lovely! You're quite the artists." Ellen glanced over at Adele standing with her arms crossed. "Adele, did you draw one too?"

"Yes, ma'am. It's on the mantle so it won't get messed up." Adele nodded toward the fireplace where her sketch rested against the wall.

Ellen strode over to view the artwork. "Very nice, Adele."

As she turned from the fireplace, she scanned the children's faces. "What is it? Did something happen that I should know about?" She put her hands on her hips and cocked her head.

"Miss Mary Etta came over," Lucy volunteered.

Sally Rose shot her a glance, trying to quiet her. She had told the children the visit was not important enough to share with their mother.

"She was mean to Miss Sally!" Tilly crossed her arms and gave an emphatic nod.

"Mean? But how . . . ? Why?" Ellen's eyes widened and she turned to Sally Rose for an answer.

"She told her to stay away from Mr. Hobbs!" Benjamin stomped his foot on the wood floor, rattling the prisms that hung from the lamp.

Ellen gaped. "She did? Oh, my. What nerve! I knew she was unhappy about your going to the island with him, but I never thought she'd act this way. What else did she say?"

"That was all, really. I tried to assure her I had no intentions toward him, but I don't think she believed me." Sally Rose lifted her hands to the side. Hopefully, the children hadn't heard everything Mrs. Chapman said to her. They parroted so much of what they heard, and she didn't want Ellen to learn of the woman's threats and create questions within her employers' minds.

"Dear me. I am *so* sorry. Mary Etta Chapman has no hold on Albert, whether she likes it or not." Ellen's forehead creased as she turned her head in the direction of Mrs. Chapman's house.

"She told me he was her fiancé."

"Fiancé? I doubt if Albert would concur with that. If it were true, there would have been a formal announcement, and there hasn't been. I'm afraid her expectations are getting ahead of her."

"Well, it really doesn't matter to me. I'm not interested in Mr. Hobbs—or any other man, for that matter. I came here to be a governess, not to court."

"And we're so happy to have you." Ellen placed her hand on Sally Rose's arm. "We'll speak to Mary Etta about this."

Ellen's caring touch was comforting, yet what if she knew the truth about her? She hadn't intended to mislead them, but until she figured out how to tell them, she was afraid she'd lose her position.

"No! I mean, please don't. I'd just as soon let it pass. I don't intend to put myself between her and Mr. Hobbs again, so there's no need."

"Are you certain? I don't want her to think she can take such liberties whenever she pleases."

"Yes, I'm certain. She's just a jealous woman and must be very concerned about her relationship with Mr. Hobbs."

"Apparently more concerned than I realized. But I'll not mention the incident if you'd prefer."

"Thank you." Sally Rose walked to the secretary and lifted an envelope. She caressed the edges of the textured ivory paper as she carried it to Ellen. "I do have a favor to ask of you, however."

"Yes, of course. Do you need to post something?"

"I do. I need to send a letter to Cleveland. Do you think there's still time today?" She desperately wanted to get a letter off to Miss Middleton and tell her about her new position, hoping to defray any negative information Mrs. Chapman might find out. However, Sally Rose wasn't sure Miss Middleton had returned from her trip to Europe yet. If only she could talk to her former employer and determine what she had told the Powells regarding her credentials.

Ellen glanced at the mantel clock. "Three o'clock. Yes, you have time. I'd send Joseph, but he's gone on another errand."

"I can do it myself. Where's the post office?"

"It's in our store, at the back of the mercantile."

Sally Rose's stomach turned over. The last person she wanted to see was Mr. Hobbs.

As if reading her mind, Ellen added, "Mr. Hobbs is usually not there on Mondays. He's out inspecting the ships. I don't think you have to worry about running into him today."

"That's a relief." Sally Rose blew out a breath and her stomach settled. "I suppose I can't avoid him all the time, but I'd prefer not giving Mrs. Chapman anymore anxiety."

"And what if you run into her? Does that concern you?"

"No. I don't think she'd create a scene in public." At least, she hoped not. "I'd better be going. I'll be back soon." She turned to Adele. "Adele, I believe it's your turn to practice on the piano. If you'd like to, you can help Lucy with her chords. Benjamin, will you please help Tilly with her alphabet?"

"And I'll be here to help them carry out your instructions." Ellen eyed her children, her love for them evident her voice. She turned back to Sally Rose and smiled. "Go on now. I'll make sure the children comply with your instructions."

~

Bryce entered the lobby of the mercantile building and headed to the stairs. As he passed the open doors of the store, he glanced inside. Miss McFarlane walked to the back of the room, her rose-colored dress flattering her olive skin. He halted. What was it he needed from the store today? There must be something. Perhaps if he wandered in and looked around, he'd find something.

He strolled in and pretended to examine the merchandise, watching her out of the corner of his eye. She went to the counter with the "Post Office" sign hanging above. Mr. Greene scurried over from his place behind the grocery counter to help her, putting on the official postmaster visor in the process. Bryce eavesdropped on the conversation.

"Can I help you, miss?" A grin covered his face as the eager clerk took on his other job as assistant postmaster.

"Yes. I'd like to send this letter, please." She handed the envelope over.

"Cleveland, eh? That where you're from?" Greene peered over the top of his glasses.

"Yes … well, no, actually, I was last employed there." Miss McFarlane appeared to be nervous, glancing to the side as she answered. "Can you tell me how long it will take to get there?"

"Well, depends. First, it goes on the train to Fernandina, then it goes on the boat to New York, then it goes on the train again to Cleveland. Might take a week or two."

"I see. I suppose it takes as long to get there as it took me to get here."

"Heh heh. You're right! Same train route, same ship. You could almost get there as fast as your letter!" Greene chuckled at his joke, but Miss McFarlane didn't appear to be amused.

"Thank you, then." She reached for the drawstring of her reticule. "What do I owe you?"

"Say, you're the lady that ordered those slate boards, aren't you?"

"Yes, I am. Have they arrived yet?"

"They sure have. Got 'em in the storeroom. Just came in today. I'll go get 'em for you." Greene turned to leave the counter then remembered to take off his visor and put it down first.

Bryce watched her sigh, then fidget with her reticule. She looked over her shoulder and saw him staring at her. Her cheeks flushed then she lifted her eyebrows. He'd been caught.

"Mr. Hernandez? I didn't hear you come in."

Bryce cleared his throat. "Er, yes. I needed to do some shopping."

Her gaze shifted to what he was holding. A slight smile crept across her face. "You're buying fabric? Are you planning to do some sewing?"

Bryce glanced down to see that he was fingering some material on the fabric table. Heat rushed to his face. "Buttons. I need buttons. And thread." He pointed to his shirt. "Need to sew some buttons on. Keep falling off for some reason."

Her hand covered her mouth, and she laughed. "Do tell, Mr. Hernandez. I didn't take you for a seamstress. Apparently, lawyers are talented in many ways." Her eyes sparkled, dazzling him.

"Here they are." Greene walked out carrying a crate. "They're kind of expensive, you know, so I hope the children don't break them." He held up one of the slate boards trimmed in wood. "Where's your buggy? I'll carry them out for you."

"I don't have a buggy. I walked."

"I'll carry them for her." How did those words come out so fast? Bryce stepped to the counter and reached for the box.

"Mr. Hernandez. Didn't know you were back. Say, I've got a letter for you. Came from Cuba."

His mother, no doubt, responding to his letter giving her his new address. "Thank you. I'll take it now." After he took the payment from Sally Rose for her supplies, Mr. Greene put his visor back on before stepping over to the post office window. Bryce stuffed the envelope in his jacket pocket as Miss McFarlane eyed him with curiosity.

Returning to the grocery counter, Greene addressed Miss McFarlane. "Is there anything else I can help you with, young lady? You need some chalk too?"

"Yes, of course. And something else. Let's see … " She scanned the store then her face brightened. "Do you have a map of the area?"

"Cedar Key?"

"Yes, and the islands around it too."

"Yes'm. We have a nautical chart over here." Greene moved to a shelf and took down a large, rolled-up paper, then stretched it out on the glass counter top.

"That will be perfect." She practically glowed with excitement as her eyes roved over the chart.

"Going sailing again?" Bryce couldn't help himself as thoughts of her on Hobbs's boat ran through his mind.

A cloud passed over her face. "No, Mr. Hernandez. I'm teaching geography."

Why did he have to remind her of her sailing trip with Hobbs? Her excitement had lifted his own spirits, energizing him after sitting in the law office all day, but his question had abruptly changed her mood.

"Of course. I should have known." Did that sound like an apology? Because he meant it to.

"Well, my purchases are completed. How about yours?"

"Mine?" Then he remembered his ruse and smiled. "Oh, the buttons can wait. That's one of the benefits in living above the store."

She raised an eyebrow as if considering his statement, then picked up the parcel containing the map.

"I put your chalk in the box with the slate boards." Greene gave her his biggest smile. "Let me know if you need anything else!"

She nodded then turned to Bryce, who held her box. "It isn't necessary for you to carry that for me. I can send Joseph tomorrow."

"I don't mind. Need to stretch my legs anyway, since I've been cooped up in the office all day." Whatever it took to spend more time with her. She intrigued him, drawing him like a magnet. Walking the short distance to the Powells' house would allow the opportunity for conversation and perhaps, to get to know her better.

They exited the store and headed down the street, walking in silence. The call of seagulls fighting over the latest catch by the waterfront faded into the background as they strolled up the hill away from town. As if on cue, they both started speaking at once. The embarrassing moment caught them off-guard, and they laughed. It was so refreshing to see her laugh again.

"So Miss McFarlane, slate and chalk? You couldn't find enough pencils around here?"

"That's definitely not a problem." The tinkling sound of her laugh was pleasant to hear. "But it's so messy when we have to erase. Slate boards are easier to use and reuse. I think the children will be very happy to get them."

"I'm sure they will."

"I wish I could find something to add color to their paper drawings, but paint is just too difficult for them to use."

"I saw some wax crayons in Europe. Perhaps you could get some of those."

"That would be wonderful, but I'm not sure how to acquire them." As she spoke, she gave him the most delightful smile.

"I'll see if I can find out for you." It would be well worth the effort to see that smile again.

"That would be very nice of you." She paused, as if considering her next statement. "May I ask you a question?"

"Anything." And he meant it. He was willing to share himself and his story with this woman.

"I understand you're from Cuba. Do you have family there?"

"My parents. That is, my mother and stepfather, plus two stepsisters."

"I see. Do you visit them often?"

"No. But one of the reasons I took the position here is its proximity to Cuba and the steamships that run back and forth. My mother has been begging me to come back home and help my stepfather run his sugar plantation." He shifted the weight of the box in his arms.

"Do you think you'll do that someday?"

"I don't want to, at least not now. I had planned to, but then . . . things changed." He didn't care to talk about Anna Maria.

"Oh?" She turned to him with a raised eyebrow. "You came to the states to go to college and didn't want to return home?"

"Something like that." Exhaling deeply, he decided to go ahead and be forthright with her about his life. "I did come to the states to study law at Harvard." He paused and glanced at her as she waited for him to continue. He turned back and looked straight ahead, while his throat constricted. Taking a deep breath, he continued, trying not to show any emotion. "Then I returned to Cuba, married, and went to work with my stepfather." Swallowing hard, he continued. "My wife died giving birth to our child. He died too."

"Oh! I'm so sorry." She reached out a hand and touched him on the arm, sending a gentle surge of warmth throughout his body. He blinked away the moisture in his eyes.

"So I left Cuba and came back to the States. Worked with the Pinkerton Agency a few years before coming here."

"You were a detective?"

"Yes, but please don't discuss that with anyone." He lowered his voice. Seeing the confusion on her face, he hurried to explain. "Mr. Powell has asked me to investigate something for him, and it's best no one knows."

"So are you a detective or a lawyer?"

"I guess you could say 'both.' But I came here to be a lawyer. It was after I arrived that Frank, Mr. Powell, asked me about the other. That's really all I can tell you now."

She smiled and nodded. "I appreciate your honesty, Mr. Hernandez. You can trust me with this confidence."

Bryce smiled back, feeling a burden had been lifted from him. Confiding in her felt good. But she hadn't told him anything about herself. He had been doing all the talking, yet, his intention was trying to know her better. And now they were almost at the Powell house.

"So now you know all about me. It's your turn to tell me about yourself—your family, home, education, everything."

"Well, we're already here." She hurried the last few steps to the front door of the house. "I can take those now. Thank you so much for carrying them for me."

"My pleasure." He hurried up the steps after her. "Perhaps we can continue our conversation another time?"

"Perhaps. Good day, Mr. Hernandez."

He stared at the door as it closed. What unfortunate timing. Just when they were getting to know each other. And yet, something told him she didn't want him to know her. Why not?

# Chapter Fourteen

Sally Rose stood in the foyer holding the box, her heart racing as perspiration beaded her hairline. He had carried the box all the way to the house for her, and she didn't even invite him in and offer him refreshment. She had run from him like a wild animal avoiding a trap, instead of being polite. What must he think of her?

She hadn't meant to be rude. In fact, she had enjoyed their conversation. He wasn't nearly as cool and distant as she had originally thought. Far from it. He had been engaging, as well as honest with her. Her heart twisted at the pain she saw in his eyes when he mentioned the death of his wife and child. How she'd wanted to wrap her arms around him and console him. Of course, that wasn't possible. She must try to keep her distance.

What should she tell him about her past? The truth? She regretted her sudden departure, but she certainly didn't want to lie. But how could she be honest with him without revealing her dishonesty to everyone else? She sighed. Until she could clear everything up, she simply must avoid him, even though part of her yearned to spend time with him again.

"Miss McFarlane? Are you all right?" Ellen stood in front of her, tilting her head and giving her an odd look. "I thought I heard you come in. Have you carried that box all the way from the mercantile?"

Sally Rose glanced down at the box and remembered what it was. "Actually, Mr. Hernandez carried it for me."

Ellen looked around and behind Sally Rose. "Did he leave already?"

"Yes, he needed to go." That wasn't entirely a lie. It didn't stop her face from growing hot, though.

"Oh, that's unfortunate. He could have come in and rested awhile. I haven't seen him since our dinner party, but he seems like a gentleman. We should have him over for dinner again."

Oh, no. How would she avoid him then?

Ellen smiled and reached for the box in Sally Rose's arms. "Let me help you with that." She peered into the crate. "What did you buy?"

Grateful to move the subject away from Mr. Hernandez, Sally Rose peeked into the empty parlor. "Where are the children?"

"I sent them outside to play awhile. They were losing interest in here, I'm afraid. I don't have your gift for holding their attention."

"I'm sure they needed some fresh air. Children need to move around too, especially Benjamin." Sally Rose pushed aside the lace curtains and peered through window. The children darted around the side yard, apparently in a game of tag.

Ellen chuckled. "Oh, my dear, that boy has such a hard time sitting still, a fact I'm sure you've noticed."

Sally Rose let the curtain fall back and faced Ellen. "He's just a boy, that's all. I had two younger brothers and quite a few boy cousins, so I'm very familiar with their behavior."

"I'm sorry he has all these girls to play with. I wish he had a brother, but I'm afraid that won't be possible." Ellen placed the box on the floor in the parlor, then stood and stared out the window.

"Well, let me show you what I purchased." Sally Rose bent down and picked up the package wrapped in parchment and tied with string. "I think the children will enjoy these."

Ellen's eyes widened when she saw the box's contents. "Slate boards! What a wonderful idea." Ellen picked one up and examined the gray, clean surface.

"I thought we'd use less paper and make less mess with slate boards."

"Absolutely. Oh, they'll love them!"

"I hope so. I'll wrap them back up and show them to the children tomorrow." Sally Rose placed the boards back in the box. "I believe lessons are over for today."

"Oh, were you able to send your mail?"

"Yes. Mr. Greene indicated it would leave on the morning train." If only she knew how long she'd have to wait for news from Ohio. Avoiding Mr. Hernandez was going to be difficult to bear.

~

Bryce took his time going back to his room, deciding to take another route in the opposite direction from town. Around the corner from the Powell house and down at the end of the street was the pencil factory. The clamor of men shouting and a sawmill running temporarily distracted him from his thoughts.

He stood near the water's edge and watched men rolling logs toward the mill. Thousands of logs tied together in rafts floated along as men jumped on top and maneuvered them with long poles. Occasionally, one of the men would fall in the water, then climb out and go back to the logs. In a nearby building, a saw whined as it reduced the logs to planks. Bryce inhaled the scent of fresh-cut wood. However, despite all the activity going on around him, he couldn't erase the image of Sally Rose from his mind.

One minute they were strolling along, enjoying each other's company, and the next she was shooing him away. Perhaps he had misread her actions. Maybe she was only being polite because he was carrying her purchases for her. He picked up a stone and threw it in the water. *Bryce, you needn't be thinking about this woman so much. Why are you so concerned? She's just doing her job, and you need to do yours.* He shook his head, but he couldn't shake the disappointment he felt about the abrupt end to their time together.

He reached into his pocket for his handkerchief to wipe the sand from the rock off his fingers, and the edges of the envelope he had tucked in there earlier stabbed under his fingernail. The letter from home. He had forgotten about it. He pulled it out then slit it open with his pocket knife. Recognizing Mother's handwriting in her native Spanish, he read the latest news from home—about his sisters and his nieces and nephews, this year's crop, and how the business was performing. As usual, she appealed to him to come for a visit and expressed concern over his stepfather's health. Mother loved to make him feel guilty about staying in the States.

He refolded the letter and put it back in the envelope. Perhaps he should go for a short visit and appease her for a while. Yet now might not be the most advantageous time to leave. He hadn't been in Cedar Key long, and Frank wanted him to find out about Hobbs. He needed to make more progress on the investigation before he went back to Cuba. As he turned to walk back to town, he slapped the envelope a couple of times in his hand then stuffed it back in his pocket.

Something out of the corner of his eye caught his attention. Benjamin Powell attempted to stand on a log near the shore in the shallow water. He slipped off a couple of times onto the sand and got back on. The next time he lost his balance and fell backwards with a splash.

"Help!" Benjamin called, apparently not aware that the water wasn't over his head.

Bryce covered the distance to the boy in no time, lifting him out. He was unhurt, but soaked and dripping sandy, dirty water.

"Benjamin, what are you doing here? Do your parents know where you are?"

Benjamin lowered his head. "No, sir." He lifted his arm and gestured at the floating logs. "I was just trying to stand on a log, like those men. But I was trying to stay on the sand."

"Next time, make sure the log is completely on shore." Bryce ruffled the boy's wet hair. "Come on, I'll walk you home."

"No!" Benjamin pulled back. "I'll get a paddling for sure!"

"You might at that, but where else will you go? Your family will certainly be looking for you and getting pretty worried when they don't find you."

"Couldn't you tell them I fell in a puddle or something?" The boy's big blue eyes pleaded for help.

"I don't see any puddles around here. In fact, I haven't seen any rain. Besides, that would be telling a lie, now wouldn't it? You know lying is wrong, don't you?"

Benjamin's shoulders drooped. "Yes, sir. It's one of the Ten Commandments."

"It is, isn't it?" Bryce had forgotten that rules about lying were based on the Bible.

"So will you go with me all the way to the house? Maybe they won't whip me if you're there."

Bryce chuckled. "I can't promise you they won't punish you, but I'll go all the way home with you." Just to make sure the boy did, in fact, go straight home.

The prospect of seeing Miss McFarlane again brightened his mood. He wondered how she'd react. Would she be pleased to see him again, or would it be an inconvenience? After the way she'd hurried away before, he wasn't certain.

As he and Benjamin walked back up to the house, he saw Mary Etta Chapman on the front porch of her house across the street. She appeared to be watering her flowers, yet she held the same position an inordinate amount of time. He nodded to her and she gave a little wave then scurried inside. A few moments later, the curtains shook. Was she peeking through her window, watching him?

He and Benjamin mounted the steps to the Powell home, then Bryce knocked on the front door.

"I could have gone in the back way and they wouldn't have seen me," Benjamin muttered with his head down.

Bryce heard voices inside.

"Can you get the door, Miss McFarlane?" The question seemed to come from upstairs.

"Yes, ma'am." Her voice.

The door opened and she stood there, eyes widening as she looked from Bryce to Benjamin. Her mouth fell open and her hand flew to her chest.

"What …? Benjamin! Look at you! You're soaked!" She glanced at Bryce for an answer.

"Miss McFarlane, seems the boy wanted to try his hand at rolling logs."

"Benjamin!" Ellen hurried down the stairs, her dark skirt billowing behind her. "Did you go down to the mill?"

The boy kept his head lowered as he peered up through his lashes, his lips puffing out.

Ellen leaned down and grabbed hold of Benjamin's shoulders, her face close to his. "You were supposed to be in the yard. What if you'd drowned?"

"I wouldn't get no whippin' if I'd drowned."

Bryce raised his hand to his mouth and feigned a cough to keep from laughing.

Ellen turned to him. "Mr. Hernandez, thank you for bringing him home. How did you find him?"

"I was observing the activities of the mill when I saw him. He was on a log along the water's edge by the shore. Apparently, he fell off the wrong way."

"Young man, your father will deal with you when he gets home, which should be any minute now." Ellen gripped Benjamin and turned him around. "You march yourself out around back and get those clothes off, and then wash up before dinner." Ellen pushed the boy in front of her out the door and around the porch to the back. "Please excuse us, Mr. Hernandez. But do come in. Miss McFarlane, please get Mr. Hernandez some refreshment."

Ellen and Benjamin disappeared around the corner, leaving Bryce and Miss McFarlane facing each other in the doorway. She blushed, and then stepped aside, sweeping her arm to welcome him in.

"I'm afraid I was rude earlier by not offering you refreshment. Perhaps you'll allow me to make up for my poor manners and get you something now." She closed the door and escorted him to the parlor.

"There's no apology necessary. I know you were in a hurry to show the children their new slates."

She posed a finger in front of her lips. "They don't know yet. They were outside in the yard when I came back, so I decided to wait until tomorrow and surprise them."

"Oh." He put his hand over his mouth. "I can keep a secret."

Her eyes widened and her cheeks pinked. Was she thinking about the secret he asked her to keep? She wiped her hands on her skirt and walked to a small table where a silver tray held a pitcher of yellow liquid and punch cups.

"Would you like some lemonade? Martha just made it."

"Lemonade would be wonderful, thank you."

She poured the drink and gave it to him, her hand shaking slightly. "Won't you have some too?"

She looked back at the pitcher then nodded. "I think I will."

When she came back with her cup, he lifted his and said, "To your health."

She cocked her head, but accepted the toast and raised hers too. As she did, the smile returned to her eyes, and a tremor of excitement pulsed through him.

"Miss McFarlane, I enjoyed our walk this afternoon. Would you be interested in joining me for another tomorrow—after work?"

She paused with the cup at her lips, eyes fixed on him. "Perhaps." But this time, she answered with a sparkle in her eyes that looked like "yes."

# Chapter Fifteen

"So Mother Powell is leaving us?" Sally Rose placed the silverware on the table beside the china plate as she waited for Ellen's response. She hadn't expected the older woman to leave only a month after her arrival, but wasn't disappointed. Mother Powell had frequently visited the Powells since she'd been in town, often observing Sally Rose's teaching and sometimes interjecting suggestions.

"Yes. She says it's getting too temperate here for her." On the opposite side of the table, Ellen folded a linen napkin and laid it down next to another plate.

"Is Charleston that much cooler?" She'd always thought Charleston was in the south too. Apparently, Cedar Key was much warmer than the elder Mrs. Powell's hometown.

"She's not going back to Charleston yet. She has a sister in Boston and plans to visit her awhile." Ellen looked up, smiling at Sally Rose. "I'm sure she'll have plenty to share with her sister."

Sally Rose laughed. "I suppose you're right." With Mother Powell's affinity for gossip, she'd be eager to tell all about her visit to the family in Cedar Key.

"Frank should be here with her soon. What time did you tell Mr. Hernandez to come?"

"Six. I wanted to give Mr. Powell time to collect his mother after work." Sally Rose felt a rush of excitement as she placed a glass on the table at his place.

"That's perfect. I'm so glad you agreed to invite him." Ellen arranged another napkin. "I like that young man. And I believe you do too." She glanced up at Sally Rose with raised eyebrows.

It was getting very warm in the room. "He's a gentleman." In the last two weeks, Sally Rose had become accustomed to their after-dinner walks, enjoying the setting sun of the lengthening days. In fact, she looked forward to that time of day when they could talk alone. He was becoming a good friend—too good to lose by sharing information that could only hurt their friendship.

"He certainly likes you." Ellen straightened and faced Sally Rose with teasing eyes and a sparkling tone. "His face brightens every time he sees you."

"Please, Ellen. He's just a friend, nothing more." She needed to remind herself of that too, as she begged her heart to slow down.

"If you insist." Ellen walked over and placed her hand on Sally Rose's arm. "But a woman knows when she sees that special light in someone's eyes, and I see it in his. And maybe in yours too."

The front door opened, and Sally Rose sighed a breath of relief as Mother Powell entered the foyer accompanied by her son. Ellen rushed to greet them, taking Mother Powell's hands in hers and kissing her on the cheek. Her enthusiasm toward her mother-in-law had increased with the prospect of the visit's end. Then she turned to Mr. Powell and stood on tiptoe as he leaned down to kiss her.

"Good afternoon, darling." Mr. Powell removed his hat and put it on the hall tree, as Ellen took Mother Powell's hat, gloves, and shawl from her.

"Would you like some cold tea? I'll bring it into the parlor."

"Yes, indeed. Thank goodness you have an icebox to keep things cool." Mother Powell entered the parlor and fell into the red brocade chair by the window. "It's quite unbearably warm here." She studied the open window beside her as if willing a breeze to blow through.

Sally Rose greeted them as well, glancing out the door behind Mr. Powell to see if Mr. Hernandez was in sight.

"Bryce will be along shortly. He said he had a matter to handle first."

Her face flushed, afraid Mr. Powell had read her mind. A twinge of disappointment twisted her chest. "I do hope he won't be late."

"You needn't worry about that. One thing I know about that young man is that he's reliable as the sunrise."

Mother Powell opened her ivory fan, creating her own breeze, and nodded. "He's a handsome young man too. Would make some young woman a fine husband."

Perspiration moistened Sally Rose's forehead. Was Mother Powell suggesting Bryce would be a good husband for her? She handed a glass to the older woman as Ellen handed one to Frank.

Mother Powell continued. "I wonder why we've never seen him in church. Do you think he attends the Baptist Church?"

"No, Mother. I've invited him." Mr. Powell sat back in the armchair and crossed his legs. "He doesn't want to discuss it, but I think he's not comfortable in church right now. Although he said he used to be very committed."

"Perhaps he'd come if Sally Rose invited him." Ellen's voice lifted as she fixed her gaze on Sally Rose.

"I believe one's faith is very personal," she answered quickly, "and I wouldn't want to impose on his convictions." Much as she wanted him to go to church, she wouldn't dare goad him into attendance. But what was his reluctance? She made a mental note to ask him later.

The sound of the door knocker made her jump.

"Miss McFarlane, would you please let Mr. Hernandez in?"

Sally Rose nodded to Mr. Powell and hurried to the door. She opened it to find Mr. Hernandez standing there grinning with his hands behind his back.

"Good afternoon." She raised an eyebrow and placed her hands on her hips. "Sir, you have a devilish smirk on your face. What, pray tell, have you done?"

"Might I come in?"

She stepped aside and swept her arm to invite him in. "Of course." Eyeing the position of his hands, she crossed her arms. "Whatever are you hiding?"

"A surprise for the teacher."

She couldn't help but smile back at him. "Oh? Are you trying to bribe the teacher?"

He nodded. "Guilty. Do you want to see it?"

The suspense was interminable. "Yes, please!" She clasped her hands in anticipation.

He moved a parcel from behind his back to his front and handed it to her. "I hope you like them."

Her fingers trembled as she unwrapped the parcel, eyes widening when she saw its contents. "Wax crayons!"

"Yes, ma'am. All the way from France."

She clapped her hands with the package in between. "Oh, thank you, thank you! These are wonderful. The children will love them."

"Anything to see the teacher so happy." He grinned and bowed slightly. "It is well worth the effort to see her smile."

She couldn't take her eyes from him, even though she wanted to look away. Her heart swelled with happiness as warmth spread down to her toes.

"How can I repay you?" Oh, dear. Why had she said that? What would he answer?

"I'll have to think about it. Perhaps we can discuss it on our walk this evening."

"Perhaps." Her smile wouldn't stop. She took a deep breath then motioned to the parlor. "Won't you join us for some tea?"

He moved into the parlor and greeted each Mrs. Powell, offering his hand. Then he nodded to Mr. Powell before going over to stand beside the mantel. Sally Rose handed him a glass of tea, then poured one for herself.

"What was all the excitement about?" Mr. Powell glanced from Sally Rose to Mr. Hernandez, his eyebrows raised.

"Mr. Hernandez brought some wax crayons for the children to use." She displayed the open parcel to the others in the room. "They will be so happy to add color to their drawings."

"Wax crayons? How nice. I've not seen them before." Mr. Powell leaned in for a closer look, then reached out to touch them.

"I saw them in Europe when I was there last year." Mr. Hernandez motioned to the crayons. "Miss McFarlane had mentioned a desire for the children to have some color other than paint."

"How thoughtful of you." Ellen beamed as she glanced from Sally Rose to Mr. Hernandez.

"Seems like one of our companies in the States would produce something like that," Mr. Powell said.

"No doubt one of them will someday." Mr. Hernandez gave an affirming nod. "Perhaps even the Faber Company could make them."

"Ha! I can't imagine that, unless they make them with wood." Mr. Powell slapped his knee.

Dinner was enjoyable and peaceful, without the activity of the children, who had been fed earlier and were upstairs in their rooms. Sally Rose felt comfortable at the table, sitting next to Mr. Hernandez and feeling like part of the family. Despite the space between them, it seemed they were touching as a sense of closeness embraced her. She inhaled the scent of him, mixed with the lavender soap he had obviously just washed with. When their hands touched to pass the butter, a ripple tingled up her arm.

"Mrs. Powell, I understand you'll be leaving us soon." Mr. Hernandez directed his attention to the woman across the table from him.

"Yes, I am. I'll be taking the train on Saturday to go visit my sister in Boston. I hope it will be cooler there."

"Boston should be nice this time of year. When I lived there, it was comfortable."

"I recall Frank said you lived in Boston. Were you an attorney there? My sister may have heard of you."

Mr. Hernandez shook his head. "Not the entire time. After college, I practiced law in Boston for a while, but then I did some other work," He shifted in his chair. "However, I wanted to return to the law practice, and Frank's offer came at the right time." He smiled and glanced at Sally Rose, and she blushed.

"And I'm quite happy he did!" Mr. Powell placed his hands on either side of his plate for emphasis. "He has certainly helped me with my work load."

Mother Powell continued. "Mr. Hernandez, I understand you're from Cuba."

"Actually, I was born in Florida, but when I was two years old, my father died of yellow fever and my mother moved us back to her birthplace in Cuba. She married my stepfather there, and that's where I was raised."

"So you were born in Florida. How interesting." The spoon clinked against her glass as Mother Powell stirred her tea thoughtfully. "Do you know where in Florida you were born?"

"Yes. Apalachicola. I don't remember much about the place of course."

Sally Rose stiffened. Apalachicola. That's where she was born too. But her family moved when she was an infant. Was it possible his mother knew her family? Granny Sally lived there a long time before she moved to Ohio. She hadn't shared that information with him, and now she definitely wouldn't. If he found out her parents had once been slaves, she'd surely lose her job with the Powells. And she mustn't let that happen.

"Will you be going back to Cuba?"

"To visit, yes. My mother sent me a letter recently, imploring me to come, so I must find the time to do so."

"Do you think you'll ever live there again?" Mother Powell could be so insistent.

"I prefer it here now." He gave a sideways glance to Sally Rose, and for just a moment, she wondered if she was the reason.

~

Mrs. Powell boarded the train while the rest of the family waved goodbye. Bryce had accompanied them as an excuse to see Sally Rose again, and she had finally agreed to let him call her by her given name, and she his.

Every day he had more trouble concentrating on his work as he watched the clock, looking forward to their evening walks. How fortunate the days were long enough to allow for that time after dinner. Their talks had become quite comfortable as they discussed the affairs of the day, the antics of the children, or just the latest events in town. Certain topics seemed forbidden though, and a wall seemed to separate them when these topics arose. Someday, she would be more open, he told himself. Just give her time.

"May I walk you back to your house?" Behind her, he leaned forward to ask as she watched the train depart.

She twirled, with a twinkle in her eye. "Yes, you may, but I'd like to stop at the mercantile on the way back, if you don't mind."

"Can we go too?" Benjamin, standing nearby, had overheard them.

The girls turned around as well. "Go where?"

"Mr. Hernandez and I are going to stop at the mercantile on the way home."

"I want to go!" Tilly jumped up and down, clapping her hands.

Sally Rose turned to Ellen. "Do you mind if they all go with us?"

"Of course not, if Mr. Hernandez doesn't mind." Ellen beamed at Bryce like she was quite pleased with him.

"It would be my pleasure." Bryce bowed slightly. "You and Frank go on and leave the children with us." *Us.* He liked the sound of that. Of course, he'd rather be alone with her, but he was willing to be with her any time he had the opportunity.

"All right then. We'll see you back at the house." Frank waved as he helped Ellen into the buggy.

Ellen turned back. "You'll join us for supper, Mr. Hernandez?"

He glanced at Sally Rose who gave an affirming smile.

"Thank you, I'd enjoy that."

He and Sally Rose began walking from the depot toward the mercantile, shepherding the children as they stopped to look into the windows of storefronts along the way. As they passed the Bettelini Hotel, Mary Etta Chapman came out the door, accompanied by Albert Hobbs. Her eyebrows lifted and her lips pursed when she saw Sally Rose.

"Good afternoon!" Hobbs nodded to them, eyeing Sally Rose curiously. "Why, you look like a happy family!" He chortled loudly.

Sally Rose flinched then reddened before looking away.

"Good afternoon to you too, Albert, Mrs. Chapman." Bryce nodded to them both, unfazed by Hobbs's attempt to embarrass them.

Mary Etta lifted her nose in the air, barely acknowledging the greeting. As they turned to go the opposite direction, She flashed a warning glance at Sally Rose. What was going on here?

"Mrs. Chapman wasn't very friendly." Bryce took Sally Rose's hand and placed it in his elbow. She looked straight ahead but sighed.

"No, she hasn't been very friendly to me ever since I went to the island with Mr. Hobbs."

Bryce threw his head back and laughed. "Jealous, huh?"

Sally Rose glared at him. "I don't find that humorous. She had no reason to be."

"My dear, it's humorous that you would have any interest in Mr. Hobbs." He patted her hand. "Don't you agree?"

Another sigh then a slight smile. "I suppose so. My feelings toward Mr. Hobbs are quite the opposite of attraction."

"I'm happy to hear that." Bryce grinned at her. "I'd hate to have to fight him for your attention."

"Humph! Don't be ridiculous."

"Here we are." Bryce stopped and waited for her to enter the open doorway, the children going ahead of them.

Mr. Greene waved from the rear of the store. "How're you folks today? Be with you when I can." The store was busy with customers, as it was the weekend and the sawmills were closed.

"I've never seen so many people in here," Sally Rose mused aloud as she turned to Bryce.

"It must have been payday yesterday."

They meandered through the store while the children looked at the latest toys. Benjamin was especially enthralled with some tin soldiers painted with bright red and blue uniforms. The girls had discovered some new dolls with delicate china heads and hands, dressed in lacy gowns.

"What was it you wanted here?" Bryce cocked his head as she fidgeted and eyed someone at the back of the store.

Before she could answer, Hobbs came in, sans Mrs. Chapman. Sally Rose stiffened and averted her gaze. At that moment Bryce noticed Ira Gray lurking near the back counter. Hobbs appeared agitated as he hurried over to the man.

"Miss Sally!" Adele pointed to a hat on a shelf nearby. "*Chapeau.*"

Not to be outdone by her older sister, Lucy held up a doll. "*Poupee.*"

Sally Rose smiled and nodded. "Very good, girls."

She turned to Benjamin, still engrossed with the toy soldiers. "Benjamin, how many soldiers are you holding? Can you tell me in French?"

"*Un, deaux.* . . I can't remember what comes next!" The boy stomped his foot.

"*Trois!*" Adele and Lucy answered together.

Someone cleared their throat nearby. Sally Rose drew back as Hobbs approached, then stood with his arms crossed and eyebrows raised, while Mr. Gray loitered behind him.

"Sounds like the children are learning to speak French." Hobbs nodded to the youngsters.

"Yes, they are." Sally Rose smiled at her prodigies.

"Well, well, I didn't know you were fluent in French, Miss McFarlane." He looked her over as if inspecting cargo on a ship. She shuddered.

A shrill scream pierced the air, pulling them all back to the children. Sally Rose rushed to the area near the back side of the store where Tilly stood staring wide-eyed at an enormous alligator hide. Sally Rose picked up the child and held her close while the girl trembled and pointed at the animal. Bryce sprinted to her side as she tried to console the frightened child.

Hobbs sauntered up behind and bellowed his annoying laugh. He walked over to the hide, lifting the head which was still attached and then dropping it. "It can't hurt you, little girl. It's dead."

Sally Rose spun around to face him. "Where did you get that … that monstrosity?"

"Why, Miss McFarlane, this is a prize hide. Came in this morning."

Benjamin ran over to it and examined the reptile, pointing to the head. "Look at those teeth! Wonder what happened to it?"

"Must've been where it didn't belong." Hobbs cast a serious glare at Sally Rose before the familiar laugh returned.

Sally Rose jerked then turned to Bryce, her eyes pleading. "I believe we need to get the children home." She headed toward the door holding Tilly. "I don't really need anything here."

Bryce put his hand on her back and guided her away as they gathered the children and left the store. He looked over his shoulder and saw Gray leaning toward Hobbs and saying something while the two men watched them leave.

Hobbs frightened Sally Rose, that was certain, but why? And why did it seem the man was threatening her?

# Chapter Sixteen

Sally Rose hustled the children down the sidewalk toward their house, the sound of her heartbeat pounding in her ears.

"Hey, slow down." Bryce grabbed her arm gently. "No one's chasing you. Except me." He flashed an endearing smile.

She glanced down at his arm and started to pull hers away from his grasp then reconsidered. As she looked at his inquisitive expression, she sighed. "I'm sorry."

"What's troubling you, Sally Rose? It's Mr. Hobbs, isn't it?"

Sally Rose nodded her head toward the children and lowered her voice. "I'd rather not discuss this right now."

Bryce followed her gaze to the children. "I understand. But can we talk about it later, after dinner?"

She didn't answer him, but continued to look ahead. What could she tell him? That the man frightened her? That she sensed evil around Mr. Hobbs? And Mr. Gray? Yet there was something in the way Mr. Hobbs spoke to her today that sent a chill down her spine. It felt like a warning, but why? What would he be warning her about?

*Lord, why do I have enemies when I haven't intended to create any?*

After dinner, Sally Rose and Bryce excused themselves for their customary walk.

"It's so nice and quiet now." She relaxed as she allowed Bryce to tuck her hand in his arm.

"Isn't it, though? No sawmills, no train whistles or boat horns." Bryce scanned the scene around them. "Everyone gets a day of rest on Saturday."

"And Sunday as well. That's when even the stores are closed." She studied him. "When most people go to church."

He didn't answer, so she decided to press him further. "Bryce, do you attend a church here? I've not seen you at the Methodist church. Do you attend the Episcopal church?"

He glanced her way. "No, I'm afraid I've not had time to attend the services."

"No? Do you work on Sunday? Mr. Powell doesn't work on Sundays, so I'd hardly expect you to."

"Oh, no, he doesn't require me to work Sundays. I just prefer to stay ahead in my job."

"I see. But what about 'Remember the Sabbath, to keep it holy,' one of the Ten Commandments?" She cocked her head as she waited for his answer, not satisfied that work was the reason he stayed away from church.

"Yes, well, I'm sure the Lord knows I'm busy and doesn't mind my absence. Plus there's that other matter I mentioned before."

She raised her eyebrows and tried to remember what matter he meant. "Oh, the investigation. Can you only do that on Sundays?"

"Not entirely. However, on Sundays it doesn't interfere with the law practice."

How could he be so busy that he had no time for church? She heard his reasons, but didn't agree with them. Work shouldn't be more important than worship.

"Bryce, do you think you could possibly free yourself from work long enough to accompany me to church sometime?"

He stopped walking and faced her, searching her eyes. "Would you like that, Sally Rose?"

She smiled up at him. "Yes, I would like that very much. However, I hope you would attend because you want to be in the House of the Lord, not just because I asked. Didn't you attend church in Pittsburgh?"

He shook his head. "No."

"I suppose you were too busy there as well?"

Bryce shrugged and appeared agitated. Perhaps she had overstepped herself.

"I'm sorry. I shouldn't be interfering with your business. Your reasons are private, between you and God. You have no obligation to explain anything to me." Sally Rose put her other hand atop his forearm and patted it.

He inhaled deeply and then blew out a breath. "No, I do need to explain. When my wife died, I thought God had forsaken me. After all, I prayed for her to live, and she didn't. I assumed God didn't care enough about me or her to answer my prayers, so I decided I wouldn't bother Him anymore. I haven't set foot in a church since her funeral." He wiped his eyes with the back of his hand.

As her heart went out to him, her eyes filled with tears. What could she say to ease his pain? She honestly didn't know why God didn't answer his prayer.

"Sometimes it seems He doesn't hear us, especially when we don't get the answer we want," she said, praying she was saying what God wanted Bryce to hear. "And I don't know why He answers some prayers and doesn't answer others, but I do know He cares. In fact, I believe He cared enough about me to answer my prayer to be a teacher by allowing me to have the position with the Powells. It's been such a blessing, more than I could ever have imagined."

His face brightened as he turned to her. "Well, that's one prayer I'm glad He answered, or we wouldn't have met."

Heat rushed to her face. "I'm glad too."

"So how about tomorrow?"

"Tomorrow? What . . . ?" Her pulse quickened.

"Tomorrow's Sunday, I believe. May I have the honor of accompanying you to church?"

~

As Sally Rose stood in front of her mirror that night and unpinned her hair, she pondered the events of the day. A myriad of feelings had assaulted her as they had gone from one extreme to the other. First, saying goodbye to Mother Powell had been somewhat of a relief. At least she and the family would not be under her watchful eye for a while. Not that she was unpleasant;

she was actually a nice lady, but her presence did connote that of a taskmaster.

Then running into Mr. Hobbs and Mary Etta Chapman. She shuddered as she recalled Mrs. Chapman's nasty glance. Had the woman heard from her friends in Cleveland? If she had, what did they tell her about Sally Rose?

And Mr. Hobbs—his demeanor toward her had certainly changed. From being pleasant if not flirtatious previously, he had become somewhat antagonistic. Was it because of something Mrs. Chapman told him?

Sally Rose brushed her hair and put on her nightgown. She climbed into bed and leaned against the headboard.

Why did it feel like Mr. Hobbs was threatening her at the mercantile? She shivered at the memory of the huge alligator and knew how poor little Tilly must have felt. It had frightened her, just like Mr. Hobbs frightened Sally Rose. Thank God Bryce had been there. His presence was protective and welcome.

And he was accompanying her to church in the morning! A broad smile crossed her face. It would be wonderful to have him alongside her at worship. She turned out the lamp and lay down, closing her eyes.

But her heart raced with expectation about tomorrow. How could she sleep? Granny Sally used to say, "When you can't sleep, count sheep." Visualizing sheep, she began to count, "*Un, deaux, trois. . .*" She sat up in bed.

French! That's why Mr. Hobbs threatened her. He knew she spoke French. The memory of the day at the lighthouse came to her when she had come down the stairs looking for Benjamin. She had heard two men speaking French on the back porch. When Mr. Hobbs and Mr. Gray saw her, they acted as if she'd been eavesdropping on their conversation. But why would she? And why would they speak in French anyway, unless they didn't want anyone else to know what they were saying? And now they thought she knew, even though she couldn't remember what she'd heard ... or could she?

~

Bryce sat rigidly in the pew and scanned the room, noting the small crowd of approximately thirty people. It was a modest church, unlike the cathedral in Pittsburgh, but of course, Cedar Key wasn't the size of Pittsburgh.

Laughter in the back announced the arrival of Albert Hobbs. Bryce gave a quick glance toward the noise. Mary Etta Chapman, whose ample form was besot with rows of yellow ruffles tightly bound across her dress as they strained to meet the exaggerated bustle in the rear. The woman reminded Bryce of a frilly duck as she waddled along. He covered his mouth with his gloved hand to hide his amusement.

Sally Rose, seated on his left, followed his gaze, and then pursed her lips, refusing to respond to the sight.

As the piano began to play the chords of a hymn, everyone rose while the minister made his way to the lectern. Bryce loved to hear the sweet melodic voice of the woman next to him who sang along with the music. Though he didn't join her, he couldn't help but warm inside at the radiance on her face as she sang. She obviously truly believed the words of praise in the hymn.

If only he could feel the same way.

As the minister began to speak from Luke 6:42, Bryce shifted in his seat. "Thou hypocrite!" the pastor boomed.

Sally Rose jumped in her place beside him. Bryce turned to see her eyes widen and cheeks flush. He ran his finger around the inside of his tightening collar. It was getting uncomfortably warm in the room. He had the urge to burst outside for fresh air, but he fought it, closing his eyes, afraid to look at the preacher who seemed to be talking to him. Was it his imagination or was Sally Rose just as uncomfortable?

When the sermon ended, Bryce released a breath. He kept thinking the minister would point his finger at him and ask him why he was in church if he doubted God. Why, indeed? Perhaps he *was* a hypocrite. Just like Albert Hobbs who pretended to be an honorable person while Bryce was sure he wasn't. Somehow, Bryce would have to decline any further requests to attend church. Apparently, he and God were still not on speaking terms.

He followed Sally Rose outside with the rest of the family where they had stopped to visit with other church members. She regarded Hobbs with even more trepidation today than yesterday. Obviously, the encounter in the store still upset her. Pulling her aside, he leaned over and whispered.

"Do you think Frank and Ellen would mind if I steal you away for lunch?"

Her eyes widened as her eyebrows arched. "Steal me away?"

"With your consent, of course. I was hoping you would join me at the hotel restaurant."

She glanced over at the Powells, then at Hobbs and Mary Etta, who were walking away from the church. From the way she shied away from them, he could tell she didn't want to be in the company of the latter.

"How about this? If we see a certain couple go in there ahead of us, we'll change our plans and go somewhere else. Does that sound agreeable?"

She smiled and her shoulders relaxed. "Yes, that sounds like a good idea. I'll tell Ellen not to expect us."

After speaking with the Powells, Bryce and Sally Rose strolled toward the hotel. The sunlight danced through her white lace parasol, casting a glow on her lovely face. She moved with such grace, like a feather floating along on the breeze. His heart raced as he watched her.

"Sally Rose is such a lovely name." *Like its owner*, he thought but refused to let himself say it. "Are you named for someone?"

"Yes, for two people. My Granny Sally and my Aunt Katherine, whose nickname is Rose."

"Well, it's a unique name for a unique lady." Bryce noted the color in her cheeks deepen.

"Thank you for coming to church today." She glanced up and studied his face. "Did you find it to your liking?"

Not particularly, to tell the truth. Bryce cleared his throat. She didn't want to hear that he preferred spending Sundays alone and working instead of sitting in a pew being accused by the pastor. But what could he tell her that wouldn't spoil their time together?

"I'm still not comfortable, I'm sorry to say. Maybe I've been away so long I've forgotten what it feels like to be in church." He turned to her, remembering her response to the minister. "And did you enjoy the sermon?"

"Enjoy?" Her face flushed, and she fanned herself rapidly. "Is one supposed to *enjoy* a sermon?"

"Perhaps *enjoy* is not the proper word. Let me put it this way. What did you think of the sermon?"

She walked on in silence, apparently pondering her answer. "It made me think. And examine myself."

"As any good sermon should, I assume. I examined myself too, and found myself wanting, as the Scriptures say." They stopped and he looked down at her. "I'm afraid I *am* a hypocrite, Sally Rose. And I think God knows I wasn't there for Him, but for you."

Tiny beads of perspiration sparkled at her hairline. She glanced away, then back. "Perhaps we're all hypocrites, Bryce, when we're not being honest."

"I can't imagine you being dishonest in any way." He put her hand in his elbow and patted it as they continued walking. Maybe this would be a good time to find out about her fear of Hobbs. "May I ask you something?"

Her eyes widened as something like fear flitted through them. She nodded slowly.

"I'll just come right out and say it. Am I mistaken or does Albert Hobbs frighten you? I've noticed how uncomfortable you are around him, especially since yesterday at the store."

She shuddered, then relaxed. "Truthfully, yes. The man *does* frighten me. I don't understand his actions. He appears friendly, but he doesn't seem sincere."

"Is this because of yesterday, or did something else happen to disturb you?"

She hesitated before speaking again. "Bryce, do you carry a gun?"

"A gun? No, not here. I used to when I worked for the Pinkerton agency, but I haven't needed one since. Why? Does Mr. Hobbs carry a gun?"

"Unfortunately, yes. And he frightened the children and myself when he drew it to shoot a seagull."

"He shot a seagull?"

"No, but I believe he would have if I hadn't pleaded with him to stop."

"Well, as a customs agent, he may need to carry a weapon to enforce his job, but not to shoot seagulls." No wonder she was scared of the man. He'd frightened the children in her care. "So that's why you're afraid of him."

She paused then glanced around as if making sure no one else could hear her. "No, that's not all. I just realized last night why he may be threatening me. He thinks I overheard something he didn't want me to hear."

Bryce's eyebrows lifted. "Why do you say that? What did you hear?"

She told him about the incident at the lighthouse and how she overheard a conversation in French, then discovered the people talking were Hobbs and Gray. She went on to say that the way the two men reacted in the store to her familiarity with the French language supported her fears.

Bryce ran his fingers through his hair. He had already suspected something unethical about the relationship between Hobbs and Gray. Was it possible the two were working together to steal from the business?

He faced Sally Rose and placed his hands on her shoulders. "Sally Rose, you must try to remember what you heard. It could be very important to the case I'm working on."

Fear filled her wide eyes as the possibility registered. "Oh, my. Do you think Mr. Hobbs and Mr. Gray have something to do with smuggling?"

He nodded. "They might. And if you have information about it, you're a threat to them."

"Me? A threat?" She shuddered again.

"I'm afraid so." But he didn't tell her they were a very real threat to her too.

# Chapter Seventeen

"Miss Sally, did you see what Benjamin did?" Adele stood beside Sally Rose's chair, tapping her on the shoulder.

"Hmm?" Sally Rose snapped out of her trance at the voice beside her. "Adele, did you say something? I'm sorry, my mind was elsewhere."

"Where'd it go?" Lucy asked as she came to stand on the other side of her teacher.

"Oh, it's not important." Only a matter of life and death. Trying to remember what she heard at the lighthouse was consuming her thoughts. "So how are you doing with your assignments?" Sally Rose pressed her hands against her skirt, pushing out the wrinkles.

"We're finished!" Adele displayed her slate showing rows of addition, while Lucy ran to get hers and bring it over.

"Tilly, let me see yours too." The little girl hurried over and held up her slate. Sally Rose smiled her approval. "Very good, Tilly. You're doing quite well writing your numbers. Benjamin, show me what you've done."

Benjamin stopped playing with his yo-yo long enough to pick up his slate off the floor. He approached, holding it down by his side, and then reluctantly handed it to her.

"Why, Benjamin, what's this?" Sally Rose pointed to some drawings on his board. "It doesn't look like arithmetic to me."

"I did my 'rithmetic, but I finished, so I drew something."

"I see a few numbers, but it looks like you rubbed the rest off. What exactly is this picture about?"

"That there's the big alligator, and that's Mr. Hobbs there with a gun. He shot the alligator." Benjamin pretended to shoot at the floor, puffing out his chest like Mr. Hobbs.

Her stomach tensed, Sally Rose pointed to other forms on the slate. "I see. And so tell me what are these?"

"Those are all the dead seagulls he shot. And that's you back there, running away."

"Running away?" The knots in her stomach tightened.

"Yes, ma'am. You're scared Mr. Hobbs is going to shoot you too."

Was she? The slate shook in her hands. Had she somehow conveyed that fear to the children?

"Benjamin, you have a very active imagination, which is a trait useful to artists." Sally Rose took a deep breath and clapped her hands. "All right, children. Time to clean up. Wipe off your slate boards and let's put our things away."

"Do I have to erase my picture?" Benjamin gave her a pouty look.

"Yes, dear. We'll need to use that board again tomorrow. Perhaps next time you can use the crayons and draw a picture on paper."

The sooner he erased that picture, the better, as far as she was concerned. If it were only as easy to wipe the image from her mind. She had been reliving the trip to the lighthouse all day, trying to recall what she heard. Every time she thought she remembered something, she shook her head, not sure if she was actually remembering or simply reconstructing. The more she thought about the conversation, the less certain she was. Had she imagined the entire scene? Yet the reaction of the two men was not her imagination. Even Bryce had noticed.

She rubbed her forehead as the children put away their school supplies. Her head pounded; she was tired of thinking about the men's conversation and trying to focus on the children's lessons at the same time. She stood and brushed off her skirt.

"Children, you may go play outside in the yard. But stay where we can see you." She aimed the last statement at Benjamin.

As the children ran out the door, Sally Rose went to find Ellen and tell her the children were finished for the day. Then she went to her room to lie down and rest. Sleep had eluded her the night before, and she was tired. Tired of trying to remember, tired of being afraid, tired of hiding the truth about herself. How could she ever rest again?

~

Bryce entered the law office early that morning, hoping Frank was already there, which he was.

"Bryce. Good Morning. You're early today."

Bryce pulled up a chair close to Frank's desk. "I needed to ask you about Albert Hobbs and wanted to do so before we were interrupted by clients."

"Have you found out anything yet?"

"I believe I've found a connection, but I need more information." Bryce put his hand on the desk and leaned forward. "How long have you known Hobbs?"

"Oh, let me see. Well, he's been my partner about two years now. Moved here shortly before that to take the job as customs agent." Frank stroked his beard, gazing at the ceiling. "I must admit, I didn't know him at all before we became partners. The building next door was for sale, and Albert approached me with the idea of opening a mercantile in it and renting out the rooms upstairs. He's a mighty convincing fellow. Told me he'd run the store and all I had to do was invest half the money, so I took him up on it."

"I see." How convenient for Hobbs to have a silent partner. "And where did he live before?"

"New Orleans. Was in the shipping business over there, he said. That's how he got the customs agent position."

"Do you know if he knew Ira Gray before he moved here?"

"I believe he mentioned they had been acquaintances at some time before, maybe in New Orleans." Frank sat up straight, his eyes lighting up as if a sudden realization popped into his mind. "Come to think of it, Hobbs recommended Gray for the assistant light-keeper position."

"Is that a fact? And the current keeper took his recommendation?"

"Yes. Poor Mr. Wilson was rather desperate. His mother had served as his assistant for some time until she passed away, leaving him with no help. He wanted to take her body back up north where she could be buried in the family cemetery. Albert told him Mr. Gray had been an assistant keeper in Louisiana."

So Hobbs put his friend in a strategic position to carry out their smuggling scenes. Bryce could see how easily the plan had fallen into place for the two.

Frank leaned forward, lowering his voice. "Do you think they are working together?"

"If I'm right, it's a definite possibility." He wouldn't tell him Sally Rose's story just yet. He didn't think she wanted that information to be shared with anyone else, at least not now. She was worried enough about Hobbs; he certainly didn't want her worried about her employer's reaction as well. He tensed, remembering the fear in her eyes. How dare that man threaten her!

"Bryce? You look angry. Can you tell me more?" Frank's brow creased as he studied his partner.

"I'd rather wait until I can prove my suspicions, if you don't mind." He stood and pushed back the chair. "Please excuse me. I need to go to the mercantile while Hobbs is away this morning and see what else I can find out."

Bryce strode into the store and spotted Mr. Greene arranging bottles of medicine on a shelf. He glanced toward the place where the alligator hide had been the day before and saw that it was gone.

"I see you sold the hide." He walked up behind Mr. Greene, startling the man.

"Oh, I didn't hear you come in, Mr. Hernandez." Greene turned to face Bryce, then nodded toward the back corner. "Yep. Mr. Hobbs took it with him today. Said he had a buyer for it."

At least Sally Rose and the children wouldn't have to see it again.

"Business must be pretty good. Seems like even more boats have been at the docks."

"Yes, it has been, but it could be better." Greene leaned toward him and lowered his voice. "Remember that problem I told you about?"

Bryce's eyebrows lifted, but he feigned ignorance. "Problem? What was that?"

"You know, about us never getting all we ordered." Greene gestured to the empty shelves beside him. "Well, it's gotten really bad lately. That's the only bottle of rum in the store." He nodded toward a bottle of Bacardi rum on the top shelf and shook his head. "I just don't understand."

So the shortages had increased. What was the cause? Taking a chance, Bryce decided to press the man for more information. "I've been meaning to ask you something."

"Yes, sir, what's that?"

"Mr. Gray, the assistant keeper at the lighthouse … I wonder if he might be related to a friend of mine in New Orleans named Gray, Ernest Gray."

"Don't rightly know. Could be, I suppose, since he's from New Orleans."

"Maybe I'll have a chance to ask him next time he's in town. Do you know when that might be?"

"I don't expect him to be around here anytime soon." Greene shook his head as he went back behind the counter to get another crate of bottles.

"That so? Why is that?"

"You know he ain't the main keeper; he's just the assistant. He got a telegram the other day from Mr. Wilson, the main keeper, saying he'll be back at the end of the month. Guess Mr. Gray will be working extra hard cleaning and shining, so the lighthouse will look good when Wilson gets back."

"I see." Perhaps there was some other unfinished business to take care of before the keeper got back as well. "Then I suppose my question can wait." Bryce turned to leave. "Thank you for your time."

"Sorry I couldn't be more help." Greene lifted his arm to wave goodbye then stopped. "Say, are you going to be seeing Miss McFarlane today? I have a letter here for her."

Bryce returned to the counter. "As a matter of fact, I am. I'll see that she gets it."

Mr. Greene positioned his visor to hand Bryce the letter.

He took the envelope from the clerk, noting the return address before he put it in his pocket. Cleveland. So she must be getting news from home. He'd make sure she received it. As he walked back to the law office, he recounted to himself what Sally Rose told him about hearing something at the lighthouse. Had she remembered any of the conversation yet? He needed to find a way to catch Hobbs and Gray in the act. But he also needed to know when they carried on their illicit activities. He was pretty sure he knew where——the lighthouse and the island.

# Chapter Eighteen

"Sally Rose?" A soft knock on the door accompanied Ellen's voice. "Are you coming down for dinner?"

Sally Rose lifted her head and looked at the fading light outside the window. She must've dozed off. What time was it? Still groggy, she sat up and answered.

"Yes, Ellen. I'll be right down. I was napping."

She walked over to the mirror, hoping she didn't look as tired as she felt. Unfortunately, she did. She poured some water from the pitcher into the basin and splashed her face, then grabbed the towel beside it and patted dry. Maybe that would help. Straightening her blouse and skirt, she tucked in a few strands of hair and went downstairs.

"I'm sorry to make you wait." She entered the dining room where everyone else was already seated. Mr. Powell stood to assist her in her chair.

"Are you feeling all right?" Ellen's look of concern warmed Sally Rose's heart. "I do hope you're not getting ill."

"No, I'm fine. Just a little tired and I needed to rest." She smiled at her employer who was feeling more like a friend these days.

Lucy quickly volunteered her reason for Sally Rose's problem. "Her mind went away today."

Mr. Powell frowned at his daughter. "What are you saying, Lucy?"

"Please," Sally Rose interjected. "I'm afraid she didn't understand what I said today when I told her I was preoccupied with something."

"You do seem to be troubled." Ellen turned to Sally Rose, worry lines creasing her own brow. "Is there anything we can do to help? Is everything all right with your family?"

"Thank you, but there's no need for you to worry. I'll be fine." She hoped so, but would she ever really be safe again?

After dinner, Bryce came by for their customary walk. His eyebrows knit together when he saw her.

"You look tired." He took her by the arm and led her down the steps.

"Apparently I look terrible, since everyone has commented on my appearance today."

"You could never look terrible." His smile comforted her. As she gazed into the depth of his eyes, she saw his concern—and something else. Something familiar. But what?

"Bryce, I've been trying so hard to remember what I heard, but I'm just not certain."

"Quit trying then. It'll come to you eventually." He patted her arm. "I found out some information today that might prove helpful."

"You did? What did you learn?"

"Seems the principal keeper of the lighthouse is returning soon."

"Oh, I forgot that Mr. Gray isn't the keeper himself but the assistant. How does this news affect the situation?"

"I suspect the smuggling activity has increased recently because the smugglers want to take care of their business before the keeper returns and notices the illegal activity."

"Which implicates Mr. Gray." She stopped walking and faced him.

"That's my belief. If only I can find out how to catch the two together."

"And maybe what I heard would enable you to do that. I'm so sorry, Bryce. I wish I could help."

Bryce lifted her chin with his forefinger and looked into her eyes. "You *are* helping me. Just being able to discuss it with you has provided me with greater understanding of the situation."

She nodded. "Could we go back now? The sun is about to set, and I need to return to the house."

As they passed Mary Etta's home, Sally Rose cut her eyes in that direction. The window curtains moved as a shadow shifted behind them.

"She's still watching you, I assume."

"Apparently so. I can feel it every time I go out the door."

"Still thinks you're out to get her man, does she?" Bryce chuckled and gave her a wink.

"Lord only knows what she thinks. All I know is she's developed a great dislike for me, despite my efforts to be polite to her."

"Well, I'm sure the woman's harmless. She only wishes she were as lovely as you."

Heat rushed to Sally Rose's face, and she glanced away.

He walked her back to the house and said goodbye at the door. Just as he was turning to leave, he stopped. "Almost forgot to give you this." He pulled out an envelope from his coat pocket.

Sally Rose saw the return address, and her heart raced. With shaking hands, she took the letter then glanced up at Bryce with questioning eyes. Did he have an idea how important this letter was to her?

He smiled down at her, reassuring her heart. "Mr. Greene asked me to deliver it to you. I hope you don't mind that I took the liberty."

"No, of course not." She shook her head. "Thank you."

"Then I'll bid you good night and let you get some rest."

"Good night, Bryce."

He smiled and turned to go as she was closing the door. Across the street, Mrs. Chapman was leaving her house on the arm of Albert Hobbs. He tipped his hat her direction, but his companion jerked her head away, avoiding eye contact with Sally Rose.

What on earth was wrong with that woman? She couldn't answer that question, so she closed the door and hurried upstairs to the privacy of her room. She tore the letter open, recognizing the signature at the bottom—Alice Wilson. Alice had been the head cook at Miss Middleton's School and her closest friend she had when she worked there.

According to the letter, Miss Middleton had not yet returned from her trip abroad and wasn't expected back for almost a year. Apparently, the death of her mother had deeply affected her, and she needed time away before she could return home. The school would remain closed until then.

Sally Rose plopped on the bed and sighed. So there was no one at the school for Mrs. Chapman to contact. The weight on her shoulders lightened. She'd be safe from Mrs. Chapman's threats for a while at least.

"Miss Sally?" A child's voice came through the door, followed by a timid knock.

Sally Rose went to the door and opened it to find Tilly standing outside, shifting from one foot to the other.

"What is it, Tilly?"

"I need to go to the privy, and Adele and Lucy are already undressed. Will you please take me? Mama's in the back, washing Benjamin."

Sally Rose glanced outside and saw the flaming fire of the sun settling behind the trees as it ended the day. It would be dark soon.

"Of course. Let's hurry while it's still light."

Sally Rose followed Tilly to the privy that stood in the back corner of the property. Tilly was always afraid of the place, surrounded on three sides by shrubs, and refused to go alone.

"You promise you'll stay right outside?" Tilly's wide eyes appealed as she slipped behind the wooden door.

"Yes, dear. I'll be right here."

Sally Rose stood near the side, pulling her shawl around her to ward off the mosquitos buzzing about. An uncomfortable sensation sent a chill down her spine. Was she being watched? A rustle disturbed the bushes nearby, and she jumped.

"Are you all right, Tilly?"

"Yes, ma'am."

She pulled the shawl even tighter, rubbing her arms and slapping at insects. The bushes moved again. What was that? An animal? A rabbit hopped out from under the shrubs and she breathed a sigh of relief. Why was she so fearful? She had to be exaggerating Mr. Hobbs's intentions. *Lord, please take this fear away from me.*

Tilly came out of the privy and took her hand. "It's getting dark out here. I'm scared."

Sally Rose trembled but tried to keep her voice from shaking. "Let's hurry to the house then." She escorted Tilly back to the girls' room and spoke a "good night" to Adele and Lucy before returning to the safety of her own room.

At last back in her room, Sally Rose calmed down. Did Mr. Hobbs really threaten her or did she imagine it? She sank onto the bed as tears trickled down her face. This had seemed to be such a wonderful place, but she had unintentionally made enemies. Mr. Hobbs, just because she understood French, and Mrs. Chapman, because Mr. Hobbs had taken Sally Rose to the island.

She still didn't remember what she heard, and she really didn't want to anymore. What if she remembered and told Bryce, then Hobbs and Gray found out? Then Bryce would be in danger.

No, she wouldn't risk that. Even if she remembered, she wouldn't tell him. Maybe she should just avoid him altogether, so they wouldn't think she had told him. The tears increased and her heart ached at the thought. One of the things she loved about her new life was seeing Bryce every day after work. They had become such good friends—maybe even more than friends. But how could she evade him, especially when he came to the house to see her?

She set her jaw and made her decision. She had to keep her distance from Bryce. It would be better for everyone if she did— even if it hurt her to do so.

# Chapter Nineteen

Bryce sealed the envelope, then laid down the letter to his mother and withdrew his pocket watch. He opened it and studied the small picture inside the lid. The couple that looked back at him were strangers, yet they weren't. As he gazed intently at the man's face, he saw some of his own features. The black, wavy hair, the deep dark eyes, the square jaw—he and his father looked so much alike. Did they have anything else in common? What would life have been if his father hadn't died, and he had grown up in the States instead of Cuba? Bryce barely recognized the younger version of his mother, much thinner and without the gray hair she now had.

What a coincidence that his birth surname had been McFarlane, same as Sally Rose's. He wished he knew more about his American ancestors, but only his mother could tell him. Perhaps he'd ask her about them on his next visit to Cuba.

There was another letter he needed to write—one to his cousin back home, but he couldn't risk Greene or Hobbs seeing it. If they were indeed running a liquor smuggling business, they'd recognize his cousin's name as a rum producer in Cuba. A trip back home might be necessary after all.

Bryce ran his fingers through his thick hair and blew out a breath. He needed to catch Hobbs and Gray soon, before the lighthouse keeper returned. He doubted their activity would continue afterwards or they'd be more difficult to catch red-handed. But how could he catch them red-handed? If only Sally Rose could remember what she heard. And if his suspicions were right, he'd be able to use information from his contacts in Cuba to establish his case, but he'd have to go there to get it. Yet if he went to Cuba, his mother would surely beg him to extend his stay. Truth was, he didn't want to leave Sally Rose. She might be in danger, but even if she weren't, the thought of not seeing her for any length of time made him uneasy. Why couldn't he think straight? How had he let his feelings interfere with his job?

Still, he needed to let her know his plans. Hopefully, he would be able to make his trip back home a short one. Would Sally Rose even care if he left? He wanted to believe she would. Although they had become more familiar with each other, there was still an air of mystery about her, something she wouldn't, or couldn't, explain. He'd tell her his plans tomorrow when they went for their walk. He stood and stretched his tense muscles. The sooner he told her, the better.

~

The men moved quietly on the dock, the full moon lengthening their shadows while they unloaded crates from the boat. A larger ship was anchored farther out, the source of the crates.

"This will be the biggest haul we've made." The thin man towered over his portly accomplice who puffed on a cigar.

"Better be, since it'll be the last for a while," the other man said.

"What about the woman? What if she gives us away?" Ira Gray asked.

"Ha! She won't be a problem. We'll feed Miss McFarlane to the gators," the voice of Albert Hobbs answered, followed by raucous laughter.

Sally Rose tried to scream but couldn't make a sound. Her eyes popped open. Her heart raced. Where was she? She blinked a few times until the dark shapes around her came into focus. The washstand, the dresser—her room. Gripping the covers, she realized she was in her bed. Sweat beaded her face, yet she shivered. It had been a dream. A nightmare. But it had seemed so real. She could still see them, Albert Hobbs and Ira Gray, standing there talking about her. Would they not leave her alone, even in her sleep? Was this a premonition? Mama used to say dreams could tell the future. Or was that only in the Bible?

She closed her eyes and murmured, "Lord, please don't let this dream come true."

The sky outside was changing to light gray as dawn approached. She might as well get up and get dressed now, since there was no chance of going back to sleep, even if she wanted to—which she didn't for fear of the dream returning. She dressed quickly, then tiptoed downstairs in the still silent home. Smells from the outside kitchen told her Martha was already there, preparing breakfast for the family. Surely the coffee was ready. Sally Rose headed to the small building behind the house to get a cup.

As she approached the kitchen, the aroma of bacon frying wafted out the door. But when she entered, she stopped short, seeing Ruth Ann instead of Martha. The tall, slender Negro woman stirred a pot on the stove and glanced up at Sally Rose.

Sally Rose blinked in surprise. "Oh! Good morning, Ruth Ann. I didn't expect to see you here."

"Mornin', Miss McFarlane." She let go of the wooden spoon and wiped her hands on her apron. "Mama's not feelin' well today, so I'm working for her. Breakfast isn't finished yet. I got started a little later than Mama usually does. Did you need somethin'?"

"I don't mean to bother you. I was just hoping to get a cup of coffee."

"It's ready." Ruth Ann picked up the coffee pot off the back burner and looked at Sally Rose's empty hands. "I'll go to the house and get you a cup."

"Oh, no. Don't bother." Sally Rose pointed to some plain china ones on the shelf above the stove. "May I use one of those?"

"Those are the ones Mama and Daddy use out here. They're not good dishes like y'all use in the house."

"I don't care how nice they are, if they're clean." Sally Rose's words blurted out of her mouth before she could think, reacting to being one of "y'all." She and Ruth Ann had more in common than the woman knew. Seeing her eyebrows lift, Sally Rose hoped she hadn't misspoken. "Of course, I don't mean to use yours. I can go get one from the dining room myself."

"They're clean. You can use one if you want to." Ruth Ann reached for one of the least chipped cups, poured coffee into it, then handed it to Sally Rose. "You want cream or sugar? There's some sugar over there in that bin. Cream's in the icebox on the porch. You want me to get it for you?"

"No, no. I can get it myself." She found the bin and added some sugar to her coffee but decided to forego the cream. She wanted to know more about this well-spoken yet quiet woman, so much like herself yet so different.

"Is there something else?" Ruth Ann glanced around the room.

"No, you go ahead with what you're doing." Sally Rose moved behind the rough wooden table in the center of the room to get out of Ruth Ann's way. "Ruth Ann, how old are your children?"

Ruth Ann cocked her head at Sally Rose then smiled. "My little girl Mary's three, and my boy Jacob's five."

"So they're about the same age as Tilly and Benjamin."

"Yes, ma'am." Ruth Ann returned to her stirring.

"Where are they when you're at work?"

"Home with Mama right now. Hope they don't worry her none so she can rest."

"I'm sorry to hear Martha's sick."

Ruth Ann walked over to a bowl of eggs on the table and started cracking them into another bowl. "Mama's not sick, just threw her back out again. Most the time I'm home with my kids. I take in laundry, so I don't have to leave them."

"I heard your husband works at the Eagle Mill. Have you been married long?"

Ruth Ann shot her a glance, a shadow passing over her face. "About six years."

What was that expression? Much as she hated to pry, perhaps the woman needed a friend, despite her reticence. Or maybe, she herself was the one who needed the friend.

"You and I are about the same age, I suppose. And yet, you're married with children. Makes me feel like an old maid."

"I'm twenty-three. Mama and Daddy didn't want Karl and me to get married, but we did anyway."

"So your parents thought you were too young?"

Ruth Ann stopped and sighed. "Guess you don't know. My husband's a white man. Mama and Daddy were afraid we'd have trouble if we got married."

Hot coffee sloshed onto Sally Rose's hand, making her flinch. "Trouble?"

"Yes, ma'am. Some folks don't like whites marrying coloreds and try to make life miserable for people like us. Then that law passed."

"Dear me! What law?" Sally Rose gripped the hot cup with both hands to steady it.

Ruth Ann let her gaze drop and resumed her egg-cracking. "Sorry, miss. I don't mean to bother you with such things."

"Please, I want to know. I'm not familiar with your local laws."

"Well, if you really want to know ... After the War ended, the Federals, they stayed here awhile and kept things peaceful. Made sure the freed slaves got treated right. Some of them were even on the town council. That's when my husband and I started courting. He's German. Came to town to work at the pencil factory. About the time the Federals left, we decided to get married. But at the same time, things changed. The state started passin' laws to separate the coloreds and the whites again."

"I wasn't aware of that." So that's when the signs appeared that said "Whites Only."

"Um hmm. But we got married anyway and put up with some mean-spirited people, but then they passed a law two years ago that says whites can't marry anyone with any Negro blood, even a little bit."

Sally Rose leaned against the heavy table for support. "Wha...what would happen if they did marry?"

"They have to pay a big fine and go to jail."

"Oh, my. But did that affect your marriage? You were already married and had children, didn't you?"

Ruth Ann bent over and pulled a pan of biscuits out of the oven. "They threatened us with it, but Mr. Powell put a stop to it, thank the Lord."

"He did? What did he do?" Sally Rose squeezed her cup tighter, feeling its heat penetrating her hands.

"Paid the fine for us. Told them the debt was settled, and that's that. Leave us alone or he'd bring charges against them for something." She carried the bowl to the skillet. "The Powells, they're good folks."

"So they are. And how nice of Mr. Powell to do that for you. Obviously, Mr. and Mrs. Powell value you and your family." Sally Rose let her shoulders fall. Would they value her if they knew she was a liar? At least Ruth Ann and her husband were honest about who they were. "I suppose I should get back to the house. Everyone else will be getting up now." She placed her cup on the table. "Thank you for the coffee." *And the company.* "I hope I didn't interfere with your work. The food smells wonderful, and I'm sure it will be delicious as usual."

Ruth Ann straightened and smiled at her. "I could do this in my sleep, I think. Been cooking since I was a little girl. Used to come here and help Mama when I was a child." She folded her arms across her chest and studied Sally Rose. "You don't need to worry about being an old maid, Miss McFarlane. As pretty and smart as you are, I'm surprised some man hasn't claimed you already. Mama told me that Mr. Hernandez has been spending time with you. Maybe he's the one?"

Sally Rose opened her mouth to reply then closed it. What could she say? She smiled as she hurried out the door, heat flooding her face. Bryce—the one? That was impossible, especially now.

# Chapter Twenty

Bryce strolled down Main Street after dinner, his heart growing lighter with each step. Noticing a patch of wildflowers growing between two buildings, he ambled over and, on a whim, picked a bouquet of the yellow blossoms with black centers. Hopefully, Sally Rose would appreciate the gesture, if not the flowers. At least, he'd get one of those stunning smiles that turned his insides to butter. A warm breeze blew from the harbor, drying the beads of perspiration on his face. His pulse quickened as he got closer to the Powell house. Something had certainly come over him. It had been a long time since he was so eager to see a woman.

As he turned the corner and the house came into view, he strained his eyes to see if she was outside on the veranda. A few times, she had been there resting in a wicker chair, reading a book. He wanted to believe she was waiting for him. But she wasn't there this time.

He trotted up the steps and knocked on the door. Time dragged by with no response, so he knocked harder. With the bouquet behind his back, Bryce rocked back and forth on his heels.

When the door finally opened, it was Ellen Powell's face that greeted him and not Sally Rose's. He mustered a polite smile despite his disappointment. "Good evening, Mrs. Powell."

"Good evening, Mr. Hernandez." She returned his smile but looked apologetic.

Bryce glanced behind her for a sign of Sally Rose. "Is Sally Rose available for a walk?"

"I'm sorry, Mr. Hernandez, but she isn't feeling well. She asked me to tell you she would not be able to join you this evening."

His heart plummeted. "She's ill? I hope it's not serious."

Mrs. Powell shook her head. "No, I don't think it is. But she's been having some terrible headaches and has to lie down."

"Well, please send her my regards. Oh, and give her these. They're just wildflowers, but I thought she'd like them."

"Black-eyed Susans! How lovely. I'm sure these will help her feel better."

Bryce fidgeted with the edge of his sleeve. Should he tell Ellen his plans so she could tell Sally Rose?

"Was there something else, Mr. Hernandez?"

"No. No, just tell her I hope she feels better soon. I'll come by to check on her tomorrow."

He'd delay his trip a few more days so he could see Sally Rose before he left. He couldn't imagine leaving without seeing her. As he left the house, he looked up to see if she might be at the window upstairs. He had no idea which side of the house her bedroom was on, but maybe he could catch a glimpse of her. Turning away abruptly, he chided himself. Why would she be standing at the window if she was sick? He kicked at the shells in the coquina-laid street and plodded away.

~

Sally Rose leaned against the door frame of her room where she'd been standing, door slightly ajar, as she listened to the conversation downstairs. Her heart twisted in her chest, knowing she had lost the opportunity to be with him again. On an impulse, she raced across the hallway to the Powells' bedroom on the other side of the house to look out their window. She longed to see his face, if only for an instant, yet when he looked up, she jerked away from the glass so she wouldn't be seen. She waited a few minutes, then leaned back to look again.

He was walking away.

Sally Rose watched until he rounded the corner, then trudged back to her room. She fought the tears filling her eyes. How long could she avoid him? Would he continue to come to the house? Of course he would. He didn't know why she couldn't see him again or allow the bond between them to strengthen. But how could she tell him? What would he do if he knew she had Negro blood coursing through her veins just like Ruth Ann? He'd surely lose interest in her, especially knowing the law as he did.

She walked to the window in her room and gazed beyond the large oak tree to glimpse the waters of the Gulf of Mexico beyond. Exhaling a heavy sigh, she leaned against the sill. Why had she even entertained the thought of a future with him? When did she lose her priorities? She had come to be a governess, a teacher to these precious children, and to give them an education worthy of their inquisitive minds. A smile crept across her face as a tear slid down her cheek.

She loved these children. Adele, the oldest, enjoyed her role as the oldest, perhaps too much. She could see Adele becoming a teacher someday. Lucy was the outspoken one who had a mind of her own, but she also had musical talent and had already surpassed the others with her skill on the piano. And little Tilly, the baby girl, got far more attention than she needed. But, oh, what a precious, precocious child she was! Yet she seemed to have keen ability to draw, even at such a young age.

Benjamin … well that one was all boy. Bless Benjamin's heart, he was no doubt the liveliest one in the nest. He struggled to sit still for any length of time, as if his muscles were resisting the urge to jump and run. She hadn't decided where his strength lay, but perhaps it was in his curiosity. Goodness knows, he was fascinated with bugs as well as other creatures, great and small.

She couldn't help but compare these children with her own siblings and cousins back home. They were so fortunate to have so much space to roam on the farm. And they were fortunate too, blessed even, to be part of one big family. Color didn't matter where she grew up. She had sisters and brothers both lighter and darker than she, but they'd grown up with the McFarlane children like they were blood-related. In fact, she wasn't even sure if they all knew they weren't really. Aunt Kate and Uncle Joshua, who weren't really their aunt and uncle, treated them as kin anyway. And Granny Sally and Granny Mac had treated them the same way as well.

She sighed again. What kind of future would they face? Would there be laws that separated them? Heaven forbid.

As she glanced down into the side yard, she saw Ruth Ann leaving through the gate. It was unfair that she had to face such a hostile environment. Wasn't it equally unfair that Sally Rose didn't? How she wanted to tell Ruth Ann the truth, to let her know there was no social barrier between them. Yet there was. Sally Rose lived the privileged life, and Ruth Ann didn't.

Sally Rose lifted her eyes to heaven. *Lord, what should I do? I know you hate lying, but here I am, living a lie. How can I tell the truth without losing my chance to make something of myself? Without losing everyone I've come to care about here?*

The dream came back that night. She watched them, Albert Hobbs and Ira Gray, as they supervised other men unloading crates from a sloop onto the dock.

"We'll hide these in the oil house until the other ship arrives from New Orleans. Telegram said it'd be the thirtieth." Hobbs spoke to Gray out of the hearing of the others.

"Just in time to get rid of them before my boss comes back." Gray chortled after his remark. "Just in time to get rid of that nosy woman too."

Their rowdy laughter awakened her again. Heart pounding against her rib cage, she gasped, kicking the covers to get free. She threw them back and leaped out of bed, and then ran to the basin to splash water on her sweating face. Placing both hands on top of the washstand, she leaned forward to catch her breath. How could she make these dreams stop? Were they a foreboding?

~

Three days later, Sally Rose continued her new habit of escaping to her room as soon as the children's lessons ended. After the children went outside to play, Sally Rose grabbed the banister and began to climb the stairs, then turned and faced her employer. "I'm not feeling well, Ellen. I believe I'll lie down and rest.

"Oh dear. Again?" Ellen's forehead puckered. "Should we fetch the doctor?"

Each time Bryce came to the door, Ellen told him Sally Rose was either tired or not feeling well. Finally, Ellen confronted her.

"Sally Rose, wait," Ellen said, stopping her before she could escape to her room again. "I don't mean to be inconsiderate, but I wonder why you seem well enough to teach the children during the day, but when Mr. Hernandez arrives, you're ill."

"I don't know why, but I seem to tire by the end of the day." Sally Rose paused, glancing down at Ellen standing at the bottom of the stairs. Bryce might arrive any minute, and she had to avoid him.

"He looks so sad when I tell him you can't come down. I wish you could greet him yourself."

Sally Rose's eyes widened. "Oh, no, I couldn't. I mean to say, I just need to lie down. Thank you for giving him my apologies."

"Sally Rose?" Ellen placed her hands on her hips. "Are you sure there's no other reason you don't want to see him? Has he offended you in some way?"

"No, no, he hasn't done anything inappropriate."

"I'm beginning to wonder *when* you'll see him again."

Sally Rose studied Ellen's caring face, trying to find an answer. "I wonder that too, Ellen. I really do."

"Well, maybe you'll feel well enough to attend church Sunday. And if he comes, you'll see him then."

Sunday? Would he even go to church Sunday? As her face grew warm, she nodded then continued up the stairs and into her room, closing the door and the outside world behind her. Truly she was tired, but not because she was ill. She was tired of the lying, the pretending, the hiding. What indeed would she do about church?

She couldn't miss church to avoid him. Why, how much more could she compound her sin to lie and miss church? *Lord, what should I do?*

All she could do was prepare her lessons for tomorrow. She'd taken the volume on French upstairs earlier in the day so she'd remember to work on the children's language study. Sitting at the round table in the corner, she flipped open the book and began perusing the pages. If she could only concentrate. She leaned on her elbow, resting her chin in her hand, and stared out the window. The moon rose above the treetop, glowing like a giant pearl.

"*La lune,* the moon," she whispered to herself. "*La pleine lune.* The full moon." But it wasn't. Not yet. She jerked upright. Why did that come to her? She had heard someone say it. She squinted and tried to remember whose voice spoke the words and when.

The scene in her dream came to mind. It had been a full moon. But they were speaking in English. Or were they? Maybe she had automatically translated. No, that wasn't it. But it was the same voices. Mr. Hobbs and Mr. Gray! Suddenly the phrases she'd heard at the lighthouse came rushing back to her.

"... *le plus grand chargement au dock pendant la pleine lune, avant que le guardian du phare revienne. Notre client à Nouvelle-Orléans va payer au prix fort.* The biggest shipment will arrive at the dock during the full moon, before Hobday gets back. Our customer in New Orleans is going to pay top dollar for it."

She remembered. They had been talking about getting a large shipment. And it would happen during the full moon, before the keeper returned. She knew their plans, and they knew she did. No wonder she'd been threatened. A chill shivered down her spine.

Bryce needed to know this information. But how could she get it to him without talking to him? And what would happen if they knew she'd told him? A memory from her dream came back. Something about getting rid of the woman. They had to be talking about her. But how would they get rid of her? Did they say "feed her to the gators" in the other dream?

She buried her face in her hands. If only she could talk to Papa about it. He'd know the right thing to do. He always did. But he was gone. She began sobbing, her shoulders shaking. She was all alone in this, and no one could help her.

*Oh, God, what do I do?*

# Chapter Twenty-One

Another sleepless night forced Sally Rose to give up all hope of rest and get up early again. The dark night was fading to light gray while she dressed then tiptoed downstairs. She went out to the side porch just in time to see Ruth Ann arrive at the back gate and let herself in. As the woman turned toward the kitchen, she glanced over at the house, spotting Sally Rose standing there. Sally Rose gave a little wave in greeting. Ruth Ann cocked her head and smiled, then motioned her to come back to the kitchen.

Sally Rose breathed a sigh of relief at the prospect of company. It would be nice to share her burden with someone. Yet, could she reveal everything? Propelled by her desire for a friend, Sally Rose followed Ruth Ann. Although she considered Ellen a friend, she was also her employer and Sally Rose didn't know what her reaction might be. Ruth Ann was getting the fire going in the stove as Sally Rose entered the room.

"Good morning, Ruth Ann."

"Mornin', Miss McFarlane. You're up mighty early today. I'll have some coffee on in a minute." Ruth Ann went to the coffee grinder, poured some coffee beans in, and turned the crank.

"Is Martha's back still bothering her?"

"Yes, ma'am. She wanted to come this morning, but I told her to stay home another day and rest some more." Ruth Ann put the ground coffee into the basket of the drip pot, poured some water in the top section, then placed it on the stove. I expect she'll be back next week, though."

"I see." Sally Rose stared at the coffee pot while Ruth Ann moved around the kitchen, getting ingredients assembled to make breakfast. She grabbed a large bowl, sifted some flour into it, then dropped in a hunk of lard and started mixing it with her hands. Sally Rose broke her gaze from the stove to watch Ruth Ann make the biscuit dough. "Can I help?"

Ruth Ann tilted her head and eyed Sally Rose. "I don't think Mrs. Powell would like it if the governess helped cook."

"Oh, I don't think Ellen … Mrs. Powell … would mind. Doesn't she help cook sometimes?"

"Sometimes." Ruth Ann nodded then smiled. "If Mama lets her in the kitchen. Mama don't like to share her kitchen with nobody else."

Sally Rose smiled. "Why don't you let me roll out the biscuits? I can do that."

"You really want to?"

"Please. I need to stay busy. I used to help my mother make biscuits. Besides, I hate to stand here, just watching you."

"Well, I suppose that'll be all right. Rollin' pin's right over there. Get that apron so you won't mess your nice dress." Ruth Ann pointed to a hook on the wall of the kitchen where an extra apron hung.

Sally Rose put the apron on, grabbed the rolling pin, and spread a cup of flour out on the table. Then she took the bowl of dough from Ruth Ann's hands. She dropped the ball of dough onto the table and flattened it out with her hands, then started to roll it with the pin.

"You havin' trouble sleepin'?"

Sally Rose jerked her head up. "What?"

"You havin' trouble sleepin,' ain't you? You look kind of tired around the eyes."

She nodded and exhaled a deep breath. "Yes, I must admit I have been."

"Somethin' on your mind?" Ruth Ann cracked eggs into a bowl.

The rolling pin pressed against the dough until it spread out across the table top. Sally Rose shoved the pin, creating a thin layer. It felt good to exert her muscles.

"I think that's thin enough." Ruth Ann nodded at the dough.

Sally Rose stopped to see what she'd done. "Oh. I guess I got carried away."

"Uh huh, somethin's on your mind, all right."

Sally Rose found the biscuit cutter and started making circles in the dough. "Ruth Ann, what if you knew something somebody else needed to know, but you couldn't tell them?"

Ruth Ann placed a hand on her hip. "Why can't you tell them?"

"Perhaps telling them would get them, or you, in trouble."

"Trouble? Like get somebody mad, or somethin' worse?

"Worse."

"Hmm. But if they didn't find out, what would happen? Somethin' else bad?"

Sally Rose held the cutter aloft, searching the dough for a circle-less space, and looked up at Ruth Ann. "Yes, something else bad."

"Sounds pretty confusin.' So this is what's keepin' you awake at night?"

Sally Rose lifted the edge of her apron to dab the tears filling her eyes.

Ruth Ann poured a cup of coffee and handed it to her. "Here. I'll pan up the biscuits and get them in the oven. Why don't you go sit over there on that bench?"

Sally Rose took the hot cup over to a bench against the wall, sighing as she sank down. "I don't know what to do." She bit her lip to stop it from trembling.

"Well, I don't know what it's all about, and I don't know how to tell you what to do. But I'm thinkin' about somethin' Papa said in his sermon last week."

"Joseph's a preacher?" Sally Rose sat upright and leaned forward.

"Yes, ma'am. He preaches at our church."

Our church. Obviously, she meant the Negro church in town. She hadn't seen any Negroes in the church she'd attended with the Powells. "I didn't know that."

"Yes, ma'am. Well, Papa preached about telling the truth, and he said there was a verse in the Bible that says if you know the right thing to do and don't do it, then that's a sin."

The words cut through Sally Rose like the biscuit cutter through the dough.

"So I suppose in this here problem you got, you gotta make up your mind what's the right thing to do."

"The right thing to do," Sally Rose repeated. What was the right thing to do? "I'll have to think about that."

"You do that, but you better do somethin' else too." Ruth Ann pointed at her with her wooden spoon.

"Something else? What is that?"

"Pray, Miss McFarlane. You gotta pray. God will tell you what's right."

"Thank you, Ruth Ann ... for everything. I'll try to take your advice."

When Sally Rose went back inside, the children were scrambling downstairs for breakfast. Ellen and Mr. Powell sat in the dining room.

"Sally Rose, good morning! Are you feeling better today?" Mr. Powell stood as she entered then pulled out a chair for her to sit.

"A little, I believe."

The children clambered into their chairs just as Ruth Ann entered the room with a pot of coffee and a bowl of scrambled eggs. Joseph followed with a dish of biscuits.

Ellen glanced up at Joseph and Ruth Ann. "So Martha's still not feeling better?"

Joseph shook his head. "No, ma'am. Well, she's some better, but Ruth Ann thought she needed another day to rest." He held the plate of biscuits while she chose one, then set them down beside Mr. Powell.

"Ruth Ann, you're very considerate of your mother to take over her duties for her."

"Yes, ma'am, but it's no bother. Mama needed some rest."

"Well, please tell her we miss her and not to come back before she's completely ready." Mr. Powell picked up a biscuit and spread some butter on it.

"Yes, sir. I'll do that."

When Ruth Ann and Joseph left the room, Sally Rose leaned toward Ellen. "I didn't know Joseph was a preacher. Ruth Ann told me he was."

"Well, he preaches at the Negro church. But I don't know how trained he is—I mean, if you could call him a 'preacher.'"

Mr. Powell sipped his coffee then put the cup down beside his plate. "Well, Ellen, if he preaches, I suppose that makes him a preacher. I'll tell you one thing, though." He slapped the table. "I bet he knows as much of the Bible as any white preacher in town."

"Frank, do you really think so?" Ellen studied her husband's face.

"Yes, I do. You ask him where any verse is, and I guarantee he'll know where to find it."

No wonder Joseph reminded her of her father. Both men knew the Word. And lived it.

Ellen turned to Sally Rose. "I need to go into town today to run some errands. Joseph is taking me in the buggy, so is there anything I can get for you?"

"No, thank you. I don't believe there's anything I need." Nothing Ellen could provide, at any rate.

"All right, then. I'll be leaving shortly after breakfast."

"Enjoy your day." Sally Rose gave Ellen a smile.

Mr. Powell left for work right after breakfast and Ellen left soon after. Sally Rose settled into the parlor with the children. Geography would be today's lesson. She unrolled the map of the surrounding area and spread it out on the floor as the children gathered around.

"See that island?" Sally Rose pointed to the largest of the islands on the chart. "That's where we are—Cedar Key."

Adele pointed to the island nearest Cedar Key. "That's Atsenie Otie."

"Look at all these others," Benjamin said, running his finger over the map. "That one's Snake Key. I wonder if it's covered with snakes slithering all over it."

"Ooh! I don't want to go there!" Tilly covered her eyes.

"Dog Island. Does that one have dogs on it?" Lucy tapped a spot on the map. "Wonder why it's not called Dog Key?"

"Deadman's Key! If you go there, do you get killed?"

"Benjamin, please." If she let Benjamin continue with his overactive imagination, the girls wouldn't sleep either. "Who knows why these were named what they were?"

"Well, we're named Cedar Key because of all the cedar." Adele crossed her arms.

"That's right! See?" Benjamin jumped up.

"Benjamin, settle down. So how many islands can you see?"

"One, two, three, four . . . ten?" Lucy jabbed each one as she counted.

"No, there's more than that. I can count fifteen!" Adele was better with her arithmetic.

"There are quite a few, aren't there? But many are very small. Can you tell me where the lighthouse is?"

"Here it is. Seahorse Key." Adele proudly motioned to one of the larger islands.

"Why isn't it called Lighthouse Key?" Tilly asked.

"Because the lighthouse wasn't there when the island was named." Sally Rose patted the little girl on top of her flaxen hair. "I suppose the shape could be a seahorse, do you?"

"Sure. There's the tail and there's the nose!" Benjamin traced the island with his finger.

Sally Rose scanned the map, noting all the islands. Lots of places for people to hide ... and lots of places to hide people. A chill raced down her spine as a frightening scene from one of her dreams crossed her mind.

After they made a list of the names of the islands, Sally Rose rolled the map back up and proceeded with the French lesson. As the children counted in French, then pointed out colors of various items in the room in French, her mind kept hearing the conversation between Mr. Hobbs and Mr. Gray. *Do the right thing,* Ruth Ann had said. But what was the right thing?

After Ruth Ann brought their lunch, Sally Rose assigned reading to each of them. Tilly sat by Lucy and listened to her read a primer out loud. While they were reading, Sally Rose went to the piano and played, something that usually relaxed her. Her shoulders stayed tense this time, however, and the music didn't soothe. After reading, she sent the children outside to play in the yard, while she took a book out on the veranda to read.

An uneasy feeling alerted her that someone was watching. She jerked her head right and left, searching for who it was. Down the street, men were busy at the mill, but no one loitered on the road. As she scanned the houses along the street, movement in the window of Mrs. Chapman's house caught her eye. Mary Etta Chapman was still spying on her. The woman was a nuisance, but not the threat she worried about before—before she had discovered a more serious danger.

However, while she watched Mrs. Chapman's house, the door opened, and the woman came strutting out and marched straight toward her, holding a handkerchief over her nose. What now? Sally Rose searched for a quick escape, but too late. The woman was at the edge of the yard before Sally Rose could get off the porch. She stood and smoothed her skirt then faced the woman.

"Mrs. Chapman? If you're looking for Ellen, she's not here."

Mrs. Chapman huffed. "You're the one I'm looking for, young lady! That is, if you *are* a lady." A big sneeze followed the comment.

"Excuse me? What do you mean?"

A menacing grin contorted the woman's red-nosed face. "So you taught at Miss Middleton's School for Young Ladies, eh? Well I happen to know you didn't. You just took care of the old lady. You're not a teacher at all. You're a fake. A fraud. And even worse, a liar!"

Sally Rose's insides seemed to crumble and fall to the ground. She was found out. She searched for words but couldn't find any. She wanted to run, but her feet were fixed to the spot.

Mrs. Chapman sniffed, then came closer and jabbed a finger at Sally Rose's face. "You'd better pack your bags and leave before I tell the Powells. How do you think they'll feel when they find out you lied to them? Do you think you'll be able to keep your position here? Ha! Of course not! Why would they want a liar teaching their children?"

Putting her hands on her hips, Mrs. Chapman chortled. "I told you I'd find out about you. Looks like your stay in Cedar Key is over." She spun around and marched down the steps, then stopped to turn and face Sally Rose again. "Goodbye, *Miss* McFarlane," the woman said before strutting back toward her house.

Sally Rose leaned against the porch railing, hoping it would keep her from collapsing. Her heart thumped against the walls of her chest and she gasped for breath.

Ruth Ann came out into the yard carrying a basket of laundry to hang on the clothesline, but stopped short when she saw Sally Rose. The maid glanced at her, then at the back of Mrs. Chapman.

"Miss McFarlane, are you all right?"

Sally Rose could only stare at her, another person she'd lied to. She grabbed hold of one of the porch columns for more support.

Ruth Ann dropped the laundry basket and rushed over, put her arms around her and led her to a chair. "What happened? What did that woman say to you?"

"Ruth Ann, I've done something terrible."

"No, you ain't. I don't believe it."

Sally Rose nodded. "Yes, I have, and I need to tell you about it."

# Chapter Twenty-Two

Sally Rose sipped the iced tea Ruth Ann brought her. They had moved to the side porch, out of the sight of nosy neighbors, where they watched the children play hide-and-seek in the yard.

"Ready or not, here I come!" sounded out as the girls and Benjamin ran between afternoon shadows and patches of sunlight escaping through the live oak branches.

"I don't mean to keep you from your chores, Ruth Ann." Sally Rose rocked slowly in the wicker rocker as she drew lines with her finger on the moisture of the glass.

"You don't worry none about that. Supper's on and everything else is done, except the laundry, and I'll take that home with me and do it there." Ruth Ann's voice was filled with compassion as she stood nearby, hands clasped in front. "Now, what's this terrible thing you done? This have somethin' to do with why you don't let that fine Mr. Hernandez see you no more?" Sally Rose lifted her gaze to the woman. "Please sit down, Ruth Ann. I can't talk to you looking up like this."

Ruth Ann glanced around, then settled into a nearby chair and started fanning herself with her apron.

"I don't know where to start."

"From the beginnin'?"

"The beginning." How far back should she go? Her birth? No, that wasn't the problem she faced right now. "Well, you know I came here from Cleveland, Ohio."

"Yes, ma'am. I heard that. Way up north."

She nodded. "I worked there at a boarding school called Miss Middleton's School for Young Ladies. The students were daughters of Cleveland's most wealthy people."

Ruth Ann studied Sally Rose. "You was a teacher there?"

Sally Rose lowered her gaze and wiped the wet glass with her skirt. "No. I was the companion to the elderly Mrs. Middleton, the mother of the lady who ran the school. I took care of her."

"That right? I thought you was a teacher."

"Well, that's where it gets complicated, I'm afraid. You see, I lived there all the time, seldom traveling the distance home to my family. While the elderly woman was resting, I had plenty of time to listen to the classes, as well as study on my own. I'm a quick learner, and soon I knew all the subjects well."

"So why'd you leave? Did you get in trouble?"

"No, no. Mrs. Middleton passed away." Tears filled Sally Rose's eyes. She still missed the lady who was so kind to her. "Her daughter was so distraught, she decided to close the school for a time, a year at least, to travel and get away."

"So you didn't have a job no more."

"That's right. I had hoped to get a job helping at the school."

"I don't understan' how you got here." Ruth Ann shook her head.

"When I found out about the school closing, I started reading the newspapers, looking at the classifieds. That's how I saw Mr. Powell's advertisement for a governess."

"So you tole them you was a teacher?" Ruth Ann sounded surprised.

"No, I didn't. The advertisement said a governess was needed who could teach children reading, writing, arithmetic, language, music—all the basic subjects. I knew all those, Ruth Ann, and I wanted to teach. I submitted my application with my knowledge of these things and gave Miss Middleton as a reference."

"And she didn't tell them you wasn't no teacher?"

"No, she didn't. She just confirmed my employment and gave me a high recommendation."

"So Mr. and Mrs. Powell, they thought you was a teacher at that school."

"Yes, apparently so. But I didn't realize that until I got here, and by that time, well, I couldn't bring myself to straighten it out."

"You was afraid they'd send you back."

Sally Rose nodded, sniffling "I suppose so. And I'd come so far ..."

"Well, looks to me like you know how to teach." Ruth Ann gazed out at the children running around. "The children, they're learnin' things."

"Oh, they are! They're very bright children."

"I don't see nuthin' then. And what this got to do with that nosy Mrs. Chapman?"

"She found out the truth about my credentials, and she's threatening to expose me."

"She did?" Ruth Ann shot a glare toward Mrs. Chapman's house. "She needs to keep her big nose out of other people's business!"

"So you see why I must leave."

"Leave? Go away? Why you want to do that?"

"She told me she'll tell everyone what a liar, a fraud, I am if I don't."

"So why don't you just tell the Powells yo'self?"

Sally Rose shook her head. "I can't. I know they'll be angry, hurt, and they'll fire me. I might as well leave of my own volition rather than wait for the upheaval the truth will cause."

"Maybe they won't. Maybe you don't know them too good. I know they like you, I can tell."

Her voice shook as she tried to talk. "I can't bear the disappointment, the embarrassment, the humiliation." Tears fell into her lap.

"And you don't want that Mr. Hernandez to know either, do you? You think he won't like you no more?"

Sally Rose jerked her head up. Yes, that was true, but not the whole truth. She exhaled a deep sigh before continuing and fixed Ruth Ann with her gaze.

"That's not all, Ruth Ann."

Ruth Ann cocked her head. "What else is it? You didn't kill nobody, did you?"

Sally Rose covered her mouth with her hand. "Goodness, no." She withdrew a handkerchief from her pocket and wiped her face, then wadded the cloth into a ball. "Ruth Ann, will you promise to keep this between us?"

"Yes, ma'am. I promise I won't tell nobody your business."

Sally Rose took a deep breath. "Ruth Ann, my parents were slaves before the war."

Ruth Ann's eyes grew round until the whites of her eyes showed. "They was? But . . ."

"They were Negro ... well, part Negro. My mama's daddy was her master. He got her mama with child, then sold the child, my mama, when she was a girl. My papa's father was French and his mama was a quadroon in New Orleans, so he was even more white. So you see, I'm part Negro too."

The woman shook her head and stared at Sally Rose. "You sho' don' look it. I thought you was white."

"Most people do. Not that I go around telling people I'm white, but I don't tell them I'm Negro either. They just assume I'm white because I look it."

Ruth Ann gasped. "And that's why you can't tell, ain't it? 'Cause if they knowed you was Negro, you couldn't teach those white children anymore. That's what the law say."

"I didn't know about the law, but since I've been here, I suspected as much." Sally Rose felt her eyes fill again. "I didn't know anything about that law before I came south. I didn't intend to mislead anyone; I just didn't see a reason to divulge otherwise either."

"And you can't tell Mr. Hernandez 'cause you think he won't like you because you're a Negro?"

Sally Rose dabbed her eyes, nodding.

"But what if you're wrong? What if they like you so much it don't matter? Like my husband loves me anyway, and I'm a Negro."

"But Ruth Ann, he already knew that. You didn't hide it from him. He can trust you."

"That's a fact. My, my, you do have a mess on your hands, don't you? We gots to pray hard about this. So don't you go runnin' off yet. God will tell us what to do, even if we don't see it yet." Ruth Ann stood and placed her hands on her hips as she looked down at Sally Rose. "You go upstairs and get yourself cleaned up for dinner. Mr. and Mrs. Powell will be home soon."

Sally Rose opened her mouth to protest, but Ruth Ann put up her hand.

"I'll get the children washed up for dinner when it's time. You go on now, and get to prayin'."

~

Bryce paced the floor in the law office. Finally, Frank put down his pen and lifted his glasses to peer up at him.

"Bryce, you'll wear the wood off the floors."

Bryce stopped and looked at Frank. "Why won't she see me?"

"You don't believe she's not been feeling well?"

"You told me yourself that she's well enough in the morning to resume her duties with the children, and that she's fine until after dinner. Just in time for my visits. She has to be avoiding me, and I have no idea why." Bryce raked his fingers through his hair.

"The two of you didn't have a disagreement about something?"

"No. In fact, we've been getting on splendidly. Or so I thought." The pacing began again.

"I can try to talk to her, but Ellen asked her already, and she insists she gets tired after dinner." Frank laid his glasses on the desk.

"No, I need to speak to her myself. Look into her eyes and see what's going on."

"Give her time. You never know what might ruffle a woman's feathers. Perhaps you did or said something she didn't like, and she's pouting over it."

"I honestly don't believe she's the pouting type."

Frank glanced at his pocket watch then stood and stretched. Reaching for his hat, he spoke over his shoulder. "Well, it's time for me to go home. Are you coming by this evening?"

"Yes. I'll try again. Maybe she's been miraculously cured. I want to see her before I leave for Cuba."

"Did you say there might be a connection between the problems I'm having at the store and Cuba?" Frank walked to the door and grasped the knob.

"Yes, I believe so, and I need to act soon. Of course, while I'm there I'll also visit my mother and perhaps my sisters' families."

"And when do you expect to leave?"

"As soon as I can tell Sally Rose goodbye."

# Chapter Twenty-Three

"Sally Rose, you haven't eaten a thing." Ellen nodded toward the plate across the table from her.

"I'm sorry. I'm not very hungry." Sally Rose had pushed her food around her plate since dinner began. All she could think about was whether to leave or stay, tell the Powells or not, before Mrs. Chapman exposed her.

"I'm getting worried about you. Perhaps you need to see Dr. Thompson."

"No, I don't think that'll be necessary." Sally Rose attempted a bite of potatoes, though swallowing it was a challenge with her tight throat.

"I insist. What if you have something the rest of us might get? You wouldn't want that, would you?"

"Of course not. I just think …"

A knock on the door cut off her sentence.

Sally Rose stifled a gasp behind her napkin. Bryce. He came early. She glanced from Mr. Powell to Ellen, wondering how to make her escape.

"Who could that be?" Ellen turned toward the hallway.

Mr. Powell tossed his napkin on the table and stood. "Excuse me. That must be Mr. Hobbs. I asked him to come by after dinner. We need to discuss a few things."

"Business, Frank?" Ellen's forehead pinched in the center. "Couldn't you have spoken with him at the store today?"

Her husband placed his hand on her shoulder. "It's all right, dear. Mr. Hobbs has been away so much during the day, we haven't seen each other to talk."

As Mr. Powell went to the door, the children asked to be excused as well.

Ellen nodded. "Very well then, if you're finished. But please don't disturb your father and Mr. Hobbs."

Albert Hobbs entered the foyer with his boisterous laugh.

"Am I late for dinner?"

Ellen moved to greet the man, her eyes wide. "I'm sorry. I didn't know you were joining us for dinner." She glanced at Mr. Powell with a raised eyebrow.

"Haha. Just foolin'. I just had dinner with Mary Etta. But it sure does smell good in here."

Sally Rose's stomach roiled. The man was so rude. At least she now had a better excuse for losing her appetite. As she pushed away from the table, she focused her attention on clearing the dishes. Anything to avoid eye contact with him.

"And how is Mary Etta?" Ellen, always the polite lady. Sally Rose admired her for keeping her poise around such a man.

"Oh, she's fine, except she can't get outside with all these things blooming. Her hay fever gives her fits."

"It can be a problem if you're sensitive to those things."

Maybe the hay fever would keep her inside long enough for Sally Rose to make things right.

The men moved into the parlor and settled into the two upholstered armchairs.

"Albert, would you like some coffee or tea?" Ellen stood in the doorway and looked from one man to the other.

"No thank you, ma'am." He scanned the room. "I don't suppose you have any brandy."

Mr. Powell answered, "I'm afraid not, Albert. We seldom have any spirits here."

"I see. Well, I guess I'll have to do without."

Sally Rose watched from the dining room across the hall as Mr. Hobbs pulled out a fat cigar. Ellen blanched.

Mr. Powell stepped in. "Albert, please don't light that in here. Ellen doesn't care for the odor in the house."

Mr. Hobbs looked at the cigar in his hand then shrugged and stuffed it back inside his coat pocket.

"Frank, perhaps you men would be more comfortable outside."

"Perhaps you're right, Ellen." Mr. Powell stood and turned to Mr. Hobbs. "Let's go to the side porch."

Sally Rose stayed in the dining room, hoping Mr. Hobbs wouldn't see her.

As he passed by the round table in the center of the parlor, Mr. Hobbs glanced down at some papers spread out on it. He paused and lifted one, studying it.

"Well, what have we here? Looks like the children have been working on their French lessons."

Sally Rose gasped, her heart skipping a beat. Why did she leave those papers out? Adele, who was helping clear the table, looked up. Putting down the bowl in her hand, she hurried to the parlor. Sally Rose followed her to the open doorway.

"That's mine." Adele pointed to the paper in Mr. Hobbs's hand. "I know the most words."

"I see. Hmm."

Adele pointed to the objects drawn in crayon. "*Papillon* – butterfly, *fleur rouge* – red flower, *poisson* – fish, *soleil* – sun." She crossed her arms and puffed out her chest.

"Very good," Mr. Hobbs replied. "I know some French myself."

Sally Rose stood breathless at the door. Mr. Hobbs glanced her way and gave her a crooked grin. "Good evening, Miss McFarlane. I'm admiring your work."

Her face heated, and beads of perspiration sprouted at her hairline. She swallowed and tried to nod her head but couldn't unlock the stare he fixed on her.

Mr. Hobbs looked over at Adele. "And what is the word for 'moon,' young lady? Do you know that?"

Adele frowned and shook her head. "I don't remember. Miss Sally, what is it?"

Sally Rose gulped and managed a soft reply. "*La lune.*"

Mr. Hobbs threw his head back and laughed. "That's right! Haven't you heard the song, 'Au Clair de la lune?' By the light of the moon? Perhaps Miss McFarlane can play it on the piano for us sometime." He started humming the song, loud and off-key.

Sally Rose thought she would sink through the floor. He must know she remembered what was said at the lighthouse. She could tell by the way he looked at her that he did, and he enjoyed taunting her about it.

Mr. Powell placed his hand on Mr. Hobbs's back. "Yes, I think we have heard that one, Albert. Let's leave the ladies and go outside now."

As Mr. Hobbs passed by Sally Rose, he gave her a wink. But not a flirtatious one. No, this wink looked more like a message that he knew … and a warning that she shouldn't.

When the men exited the house, they greeted someone. Through the open window, Sally Rose heard Bryce's voice.

"Ellen, I'm feeling a little light-headed again. Please excuse me." And she ran up to her room.

~

Her heart twisting, Sally Rose listened once more to Ellen making excuses to Bryce for her. She shook her head. He would be better off without her, better off forgetting her when she left. As tears filled her eyes, she remembered his. How she longed to gaze into his eyes again—those eyes that sometimes appeared fathomless, while at other times, like when he teased her, they twinkled.

She sighed. Why did she ever get so involved with him? She hadn't meant to, but the more time they spent together, the more she wanted to be with him. But it couldn't go on. There was no future for them, and it was best to end it now.

Hearing Mr. Hobbs laugh reminded her that the two men sat just below her window. She tiptoed over and strained to hear the conversation taking place on the side porch. Mr. Powell questioned Mr. Hobbs about the availability of some of the goods the store sold. Each question he posed was met with a guffaw from the other man, along with an excuse about how difficult the trade business was these days.

"What with all these tariffs they've got, there's more and more smuggling going on."

"So you think someone might be taking products from our shipments before they arrive?"

"I'm certain of it. I tell you, Frank, I have my hands full trying to keep up with all the ships out there."

And he was probably involved with the smugglers too. Sally Rose replayed the scenes from her dreams in her mind. Of course, that's what they were doing. Bryce was right. But could she trust her dreams? The words she overheard came back to her. Yes, they were planning a big smuggling job right before the head lighthouse keeper returned. The more she thought about Mr. Hobbs and his insolent attitude, the madder she got. He must be stopped. But how to get the information to Bryce without seeing him? She'd find a way to deliver it to him, if it was the last thing she did before leaving town.

~

First thing the next morning, Sally Rose hurried down to the kitchen and rushed in, breathless.

"I'm so relieved to find you here, Ruth Ann."

Ruth Ann looked up from the oven and grabbed the coffee pot and a cup. She filled the cup and handed it to Sally Rose.

"Glad to see you here too. So you decided to stay and tell them yourself?" Ruth Ann placed a hand on her hip and tilted her head.

"I'm not sure, but maybe. If I can work up my courage today, I'll tell them tonight."

"And if you don't?"

"I'll take the first train out in the morning."

Ruth Ann shook her head. "Well, I'll pray you get enough courage because I don't think you should leave."

Sally Rose sipped her coffee. "Perhaps you're right. But either choice is a difficult one."

"Papa says the right thing to do isn't always the easiest."

"I think my papa would say the same thing, if he were here," Sally Rose whispered into her cup.

Ruth Ann studied her. "So are you going to tell Mr. Hernandez the truth too?"

Sally Rose glanced up. "No. I don't think I can."

Shaking her head again, Ruth Ann walked over to the stove to stir the pot of grits. "That man needs to know the truth. It's not right for you to just run off and let him think you didn't care nothin' bout his feelings."

"I do care about his feelings! That's why I should go away. He needs to forget about me and find someone else."

"So if you leave and Mrs. Chapman talks about you, he'll think you're a liar too."

Sally Rose sighed. "I suppose so. And, well, I am. Sort of."

"Does Mrs. Chapman know you part-Negro?"

Sally Rose froze. "No, no, she doesn't know about that. No one here knows but you." She fixed an imploring gaze on the other woman. "Ruth Ann?"

"Don't you worry about me telling nobody. I won't tell nobody unless you say it's all right."

"Thank you." Sally Rose exhaled a deep breath. Then she remembered what she needed to tell Bryce, and her heart raced. "Ruth Ann, there is something Mr. Hernandez needs to know. But it's not about me."

Ruth Ann stopped stirring and put the lid on the pot, moving it to the edge of the burner. She faced Sally Rose with her head cocked and raised an eyebrow. "What's that?"

"Well, you see, I promised him I wouldn't tell anyone, but he's been working on something to catch some people in their wrongdoing, but nobody knows besides me and Mr. Powell."

"Miss Sally, your head must be swimmin' with all these secrets you keepin'."

Sally Rose wished Ruth Ann could call her by her surname like a friend would. "It has been, and I truly have had headaches trying to keep them all inside."

Ruth Ann moved to the wooden cutting board and began slicing oranges in half. "So what's this Mr. Hernandez needs to know? And how you gonna tell him if you don't let him see you?"

"Oh, I don't know. I can't figure that out." Sally Rose wrung her hands. "I was hoping you could get a message to him for me."

"So you gonna tell me?" Ruth Ann picked up a stainer and placed it over a bowl, then began squeezing the orange halves over it.

"Ruth Ann, you might be in danger like I am if the wrong people find out you know."

"Well, the way I sees it is like this: either you tell me or you tell him yourself. But if it's real important, you best tell him soon."

"All right. I'll tell you, so you can tell him if I leave first. That way, he'll know. But please be very careful, and make sure no one else is around when you tell him." Sally Rose then told Ruth Ann what she heard at the lighthouse. "Please don't tell anybody but Mr. Hernandez," she repeated. "I don't want you to get in trouble."

"I don't expect anybody would think you told the cook."

Sally Rose grimaced. "You're more than that to me, Ruth Ann. You're the only friend I've got."

Ruth Ann smiled then walked over to Sally Rose and put her arm around her shoulder and squeezed it. "Miss Sally, let me tell you somethin'."

Sally Rose tried to hold back her tears as she glanced sideways at the woman.

"The good Lord, He sent you here. He knew you wanted to be a teacher and that you'd be a good one. Of all people for you to work for, He sent you to Mr. and Mrs. Powell, the nicest people in town. It's no accident you're here and no mistake either. The way I sees it is you been sent here for a reason. Them kids needed you. And just maybe Mr. Hernandez does too."

Sally Rose sniffed. "But what about the lie? What about Mrs. Chapman?"

"That ole devil, he's always tryin' to mess up our lives, make us quit hopin.' But he's the biggest liar they is, that's what the good book says. You a strong woman or you wouldn't a come here by you'self in the first place. You gonna let that devil scare you away?"

Sally Rose straightened her spine and smiled at Ruth Ann. "No, I'm not. You're right. I'm not a weak person. I'll tell them the truth tonight after dinner."

"Tell *all* of them?"

"Yes, Ruth Ann ... *all* of them."

# Chapter Twenty-Four

The clock in the hallway chimed three times, and Sally Rose jerked upright in her chair.

"Miss Sally? Why are you jumping every time the clock chimes? Are you afraid of it?" Lucy peered over the top of the book she read while Tilly leaned against her shoulder.

"Oh, no. I don't know why it startled me." In fact, she was nervous as a mouse in a room full of cats. She'd been rehearsing her confession in her mind all day, hoping she'd be brave enough to deliver it correctly tonight. She planned to tell Mr. Powell and Ellen privately after dinner and prayed they would forgive her for being dishonest with them. But first, she needed to face Bryce. She'd tell him when he came by for their evening walk. Perhaps part of her jitters was due to the anticipation of being with him again.

"Can we go outside now?" Benjamin closed his book and jumped up.

"*May* we?" she corrected. Would he ever get that right?

"Huh?" Benjamin cocked his head at her. "Sure, you can come too, Miss Sally."

She chuckled and nodded. "Thank you, Benjamin, but I need to straighten up in here before your father gets home."

The children ran out the front door and around to the side yard, with Adele leading the way to the place where they usually drew the customary squares in the dirt. "Let's play hopscotch!" she suggested. Sally Rose watched from the porch and sighed. Oh, to be a child again, with nothing more serious to do than play a game. As she went back into the house, she glanced over toward Mrs. Chapman's. She would *not* let that woman run her off. She'd worked too hard to get where she was and would even risk embarrassment over the disgrace of running away. She would do the right thing, even if she suffered for telling the truth. Taking a deep breath, she lifted her head and prepared to meet her judgment.

~

At dinner, Ellen smiled at Sally Rose across the table. "You look like you feel better. I hope so."

"I am feeling better, thank you." But her appetite was gone. There was no room in her stomach with all the butterflies there. She glanced from Ellen to Mr. Powell. "I'd like to talk with both of you after dinner."

Mr. Powell stopped his fork mid-air to look at her. "Of course. Is there a problem?"

"Well, I hope not. I'd rather wait until later to explain." Sally Rose shifted her eyes toward the children to suggest the conversation wouldn't be suitable for them to hear.

"Oh, I see. Certainly, perhaps after the children go to bed, then."

"That would be best." Sally Rose nodded, wiping her sweaty palms across the napkin in her lap. "I'll help them get ready after dinner."

After they all finished eating, the children were excused to go upstairs, and Sally Rose followed. For the past several evenings, she'd stayed in her room at their bedtime. But tonight, she wanted to see them to bed. It was time to get out of her self-imposed prison.

As she helped Tilly get her bedclothes on, the little girl grinned up at her. "Will you read us a story, Miss Sally?"

"Yes, will you, Miss Sally?" Lucy begged.

Adele handed her *Little Women*.

"Can I go to my room and play with my soldiers?" Benjamin looked displeased with the choice of books.

"Yes, Benjamin, I suppose you can do that until your mother comes up to say good night."

Sally Rose sat on the bed, with the girls gathered around her, and started reading. She had gotten caught up in the story when she heard the front door close. Wonder who that was? She started to continue reading when it occurred to her that it was time for Bryce to come by.

"Girls, that's all for tonight." She closed the book and laid it down on the bedside table. "We'll read some more tomorrow night."

After she kissed each one good night, she went downstairs, expecting to see Bryce. As she reached the lower hallway, she glanced into the parlor where Mr. Powell sat reading the newspaper while Ellen worked on her crewel.

"Was someone at the door?"

"Yes, dear. Poor Mr. Hernandez. I told him you were upstairs as usual, but I do hate seeing him so disappointed. He might quit coming by. Is that what you want?" The needle poised in her hand, Ellen tilted her head at Sally Rose.

"No. I mean, I intended to see him tonight."

"You did? Dear me, I wish I had known."

"Are you ready to come share with us what's on your mind?" Mr. Powell lowered his paper to look over it at her.

"Not just yet. There's something else I need to do first." She ran upstairs, grabbed her shawl, then hurried back down and rushed out the front door. She had to catch up with Bryce before she lost her nerve.

The last glimmer of sunset was being consumed by black clouds as she hurried down the street. A gust of wind blew dust into her face, stinging her eyes. As she looked out beyond the houses, she saw the sky darkening over the water. Hopefully, she could catch up to him before the storm hit.

Rounding the corner, she saw Bryce down the street. She opened her mouth to call out to him, but he was too far away to hear her, so she quickened her pace.

Suddenly everything went dark. Scratchy material covered her head, and arms encircled her from behind.

She kicked and squirmed, but she couldn't free herself from the grip or the thick material that covered her. Strong hands lifted her off the ground and slung her over large shoulders.

"Help! Let me go!" She yelled with all her might but the heavy cloth smothered her words, and she struggled to breathe.

An unrecognizable male voice grunted, "Ain't no use puttin' up a fight, lady. You ain't gittin' away, 'cept on a boat!"

The last thing she heard was the deep rumble of thunder ... or was it the sound of someone laughing?

~

Bryce kicked a stone down the street on his way back to his room. It was no use. She just didn't want to see him. But why? What had he done? Couldn't she just tell him, give him an explanation? He had apparently misread her previous responses to mean she liked him, perhaps even cared for him. This is what he got for being interested in a woman again. He should've known he would only feel pain.

The next morning, when he went downstairs, Mr. Greene hailed him from the store.

"Mr. Hernandez! You got a telegram just now. I think it's important."

Bryce hurried inside and took the paper from Greene's hand.

"Come quickly. Father very ill. Mama."

Bryce looked up at the clerk. "When does the next steamship leave for Cuba?"

"Let me see." Greene ambled behind the counter to the schedule posted on the back wall. "Well, there's two different routes——one goes to Tampa and the other to Key West first."

"Which one's the most direct?" Could the man move any faster?

"Hmm ... That would be the one going straight to Key West. It overnights there then goes on to Havana. Takes about two days to get there, I believe."

"Then that's the one I want to take. When does the next one leave for Key West?"

"Oh, that'd be nine this morning. You better hurry if you want to catch it."

Bryce raced up the stairs to throw a few things in his bag then hurried back down. He stuck his head inside the store and called out to Mr. Greene.

"Please tell Mr. Powell I had to leave for Cuba right away. Family illness!"

"Yes, sir. Will do!" Mr. Greene waved a salute.

Bryce rushed out the door toward the dock where the steamship was boarding. He knew Frank would understand, but he had no idea what awaited him at home or when he'd be back. A pang of regret stabbed his heart as he reached the end of the pier. If only he'd had time to say goodbye to Sally Rose before he left.

# Chapter Twenty-Five

Someone was shaking her. Bright sunlight glared down in her face as she tried to open her eyes. Was that the sound of waves? Where was she? The hard, uneven surface she lay on was unyielding as she struggled to move. An overwhelming smell of fish penetrated her nostrils, making her stomach churn. Her clothes were wet, and the memory of a thunderstorm registered somewhere in her mind. She kicked a sodden wool blanket off her feet.

"Git up! No more sleepin' for you, lady!"

Sally Rose tried to sit up, but the constant motion fought against her. As she attempted to reach out and steady herself, she found her hands were tied together. She peered up at the voice, squinting to see its source. The sun behind him kept his features dark, and she didn't recognize the large shadow looming over her.

Shaking, she mustered the strength to get some words out. "Who are you? Why have you brought me here?"

Strong arms lifted her by the shoulders to a standing position. She glanced around and discovered she was in a boat. Her empty stomach roiled with the motion of the vessel, and she fought the queasiness while she sought her balance.

"Be quiet. Get up on the dock."

Sally Rose jerked her head in the direction the man pointed.

"Would you please untie me? I can't manage without the use of my hands."

"Hmm. All right." He pulled a shiny knife out of his back pocket and sliced through the rope around her hands.

She shivered at the sight of the metal so close to her. When the rope fell off, she rubbed the red stripes on her wrists where it had been, wincing at the rope splinters that had penetrated her skin.

"Go on! Git out! I ain't got all day. Gotta get this boat back."

As she glanced around her, she noted fishing net piled up on the side of the boat. No wonder she smelled fish. She turned to the dock and grabbed a post to pull herself out. As she stepped up, the man's large hand gave her derriere a push, almost sending her flat on her face against the hard planks. She struggled to her feet, gasping at the indignity. Turning around to give him a word about his impropriety, she noted another man standing nearby ... and froze. The assistant light-keeper stood with his arms crossed, watching her.

"Mr. Gray! Please tell me why I've been brought here. What is the reason for all this ... this rudeness?" She swept her arms out to include the man in the boat as he pushed off from the pier.

Mr. Gray pulled his scraggly beard and grinned. "Didn't you enjoy your boat ride? Your little nap? Why, *Miz* McFarlane, where are your manners? You didn't even tell the nice man 'thank you.'"

"*My* manners! Why, how dare you?" Her anger took over the fear she'd felt before, and she wanted to slap the man. "Mr. Powell will not let this affront go unheeded!"

Mr. Gray stepped forward and pointed a long, skinny finger in her face. "You can come off that high horse now. I heared you ain't a real schoolteacher no way. You think them folks back in town will care 'bout you once they find out you's a fake? Besides, I bet they think you've up and run away."

Her heart fell, and the weight of it pulled her down with it. He knew. So Mrs. Chapman must've told him or told Albert Hobbs, who shared the information. Did Mr. Powell and Ellen know yet? Oh, no! They weren't supposed to find out like this. What must they be thinking now?

"But why am I here?" Her voice, now weak, whimpered its way out.

"Why?" Mr. Gray leaned over and whispered. "Because it's almost a full moon."

Her eyes widened as his words penetrated her mind. She leaned away from him and the stale smell of his breath. He reached inside his coat and pulled out a gun, then pointed it at her. Her strength left her, numbing her hands and feet, and she fought dizziness.

"Start walking." He waved the gun toward the shore.

Somehow, she willed her feet to move. When they reached the end of the dock, he gave her back a shove. "Keep going. Up the hill."

Grasping her long skirt, she trudged up the sandy path. Where was he taking her? What would he do with her? She glanced at the woods around her. Maybe she could get away and hide.

Like he knew what she was thinking, Mr. Gray taunted, "Don't get no ideas 'bout gettin' away. Even if you did, you won't git off this island by yourself. It's a long swim back to Cedar Key."

Through the trees ahead, the lighthouse came into view. Mr. Gray marched her up to the house and around the rear where the kitchen building stood. He pointed to it with the gun.

"Go in."

Sally Rose complied and entered the small tabby kitchen and scanned the walls. A wood stove occupied one side, and a little table with two chairs sat below the only window. A pie safe rested against the opposite wall. Two pots hung on nails above the stove, reminding her of Ruth Ann.

"Sit over there." He waved with the gun.

She moved to one of the ladder-back chairs and sat. Her throat was parched, and she began to cough.

"Please. Could I have some water to drink?"

"All right." Mr. Gray walked over, pulled a length of rope from his pocket, and tied her to the chair.

"Is that really necessary?"

"Just makin' sure you don't go nowhere."

"You already told me I couldn't get away."

"Well, I don't have time to look for you if you decide to play hide-and-seek."

Through the window, Sally Rose watched Mr. Gray go to the well and draw out a bucket of water. When he returned, he plopped the pail on the floor so hard, water sloshed over the sides. Next he crossed over to the pie safe, then opened the doors and retrieved a tin cup, which he dipped in the bucket and handed to her.

Once her thirst was quenched, Mr. Gray sat down across from her and leaned the chair back against the wall. Pulling a can from his pocket, he pinched some snuff, then stuck it in his mouth. He stared at her while he drummed his fingers on the table.

She could hold her tongue no longer. "Mr. Gray, of what use am I to you? If you wanted me to leave town, why didn't you just put me on a train?"

"Ha! Well, if'n you woulda gone and left like you shoulda, you wouldn't be here. But you had to stick around and put your nose in other people's business."

"Sir, I am not interested in your business." She really wasn't, but she knew someone who was. But how could she tell him now? Why did she wait so long to decide?

"We just want to make sure you ain't."

"We?" No doubt who else he meant.

Mr. Gray grinned. "I believe you know Mr. Hobbs."

She flinched at the name. "What do you plan to do with me? How long will you keep me here?"

"Can't say. Hobbs has some ideas. He knows lots of folks in lots of places. Who knows where you may end up—that is, if we keep you alive?"

She shuddered. Was this what it felt like to be a slave? Her heart twisted, knowing her ancestors may have felt this same helplessness, this total lack of control over their future. There must be something she could do.

Mr. Gray interrupted her thoughts. "Well, 'fraid I can't stay and chat with you any longer. Got work to do in the lighthouse."

"But what am I to do here?"

"Sit and wait. Too bad I can't untie you and get you to cook for me, but I can't risk you runnin' off." Mr. Gray stood and stretched, then ambled out the door.

Wait? Patience was not one of her strengths. She had always been responsible for seeing that things got done—as the oldest child, as a companion, as a governess. How could she wait and do nothing? She stared out the window at the trees beyond the clearing. What were the children doing? Did they miss her? She missed them so much. And what about Bryce? What was he thinking now? *Lord, please don't let them hate me.*

# Chapter Twenty-Six

Bryce hurried down the gangplank when the ship reached Havana, hoping he wasn't too late. *Please let him still be alive.* After he hailed the nearest carriage for hire, he headed for the family plantation outside of town. What awaited him? Mamá would be distraught if Papá died before Bryce got back. He should have come sooner. Maybe he would've been here already when his stepfather fell ill.

The carriage bumped along the dirt road, seeming to take longer than he remembered before it reached the familiar turn. Rows of sugar cane on both sides led to the impressive hacienda he had called home most of his life. The fields weren't full of slaves as they had been when he was a boy. Instead, some hired laborers toiled the fields and waved to the carriage, eyeing it with curiosity as it rolled past.

He breathed a sigh of relief as the two-story white house with its red-tiled roof finally came into sight. When the carriage stopped, he jumped from the vehicle and paid the driver, then rushed inside the front gate. He spotted one of the house maids near the door. What was her name? Maria? Diana?

"Estella!" Had he remembered correctly?

She spun around, eyes wide, then hurried to admit him to the courtyard.

"Gracias!" The Spanish rolled off his tongue as if he'd never stopped speaking it. "Dónde está Mamá?"

"With the señor in their bedroom." The maid pointed toward the wing of the house where the bedrooms were.

"Gracias," he repeated, before hustling across the courtyard.

As he approached his parents' room, he saw his sister Teresa standing outside the door. She wasn't crying, which was a good sign.

"Bryce, I'm so glad you've come! Mamá has been very anxious to see you."

He hugged his sister and kissed her on the cheek, then drew back to study her face. "How serious is he?"

"He's much improved. We did not know if he would survive at first."

"Hijo!" Bryce's mother rushed from the room to engulf him in an embrace. She peered up at him with moist eyes. "You've come! Gracias a Dios! I'm so happy you received my message."

"How is he, Mamá? Teresa told me he was better." His mother seemed to have shrunk, and the once coal-black hair now showed streaks of gray in her customary chignon.

"We almost lost him." Mamá dabbed her eyes with a lace handkerchief. "Come, see." She grabbed his arm and pulled him inside. "Papá, Bryce is here."

The silver-haired man lying against a bank of pillows in the massive mahogany bed opened his eyes. A tiny smile crept across his face, and he lifted his hand from the bedcovers, motioning Bryce to come. He, too, looked ages older than before. Had Bryce been gone so long?

"Papá." Bryce leaned over the bedside, lifting his stepfather's hand to place a kiss on it. "I'm sorry to hear of your illness. I came as soon as I received the telegram from Mamá."

The senior Hernandez patted Bryce's hand. "You are a good son, even if I did have to reach death's door to see you again."

The words jabbed like a knife. Bryce ducked his head. "I was planning to visit soon, but a problem with my work prevented my coming." *Problems with a woman too.*

"Yes, son. There are always problems at work, aren't there?" He pointed to a chair nearby. "Sit. We must talk."

Bryce obeyed, dreading the conversation. He already knew what his stepfather would say, because the topic came up whenever Bryce visited.

"Son, this time I almost did not survive the spell. The doctor says my heart is bad and may not endure another attack."

Bryce studied the creases in the weathered face of the man who had raised him. He couldn't even remember his real father, who had died when he was only two years old. Nor could he remember living in Florida before his mother moved back to Cuba. This was the land where he grew up, and this was the father he'd known. It had been difficult to leave him, but after Anna Maria died, it was even more difficult to stay.

"Bryce, I need you to come home, run the plantation. You are my only son and the heir to my estate. It is time for you to take over—before I die."

Tears filled Bryce's eyes and trickled down his cheeks. As a boy, he'd ridden his pony alongside his father's stallion, mimicking the man's actions. At that time, he wanted nothing more than to be a plantation patrón like his stepfather. The workers had even called him "the little patrón," expecting him to follow the family tradition. No, he couldn't bear the thought of losing this dear man.

But life had changed since then. *He* had changed, perhaps becoming even more American now that he had returned to the land of his birth.

"What is your answer, son? Can I count on you to take my place?" The man stretched forward, his eyes searching his son's face for an answer.

"I could never take your place, Papá." Bryce wiped his damp face with the back of his jacket sleeve. His heart twisted as it was pulled in two directions.

"You are the only one who can. I've taught you everything I know about our business."

Bryce nodded. "I know you have, Papá. But what about Teresa and Sonia's husbands, Carlos and Roberto? They've worked beside you in the business for years. They're capable, aren't they?" Besides, they were the ones who had worked alongside Papá since Bryce had been gone. Was it fair for him to come back and take charge? Did he really want to do that?

"Yes, they're good men, but they know you are the rightful heir. I've never given either of them the impression that they will be in charge when I'm gone."

Bryce hesitated to answer. He counldn't say "no" and hurt his stepfather, but he wasn't ready to accept the man's wishes for his future. Bryce cleared his throat. "I must return to Florida first. There is unfinished business there I must take care of."

Was Sally Rose included in that unfinished business? The tightness in his chest answered his question. He still needed to finish the job Frank had hired him for, even if he couldn't make things right with her. Perhaps it was just as well. He doubted she would be interested in leaving Cedar Key to live in Cuba. Why was he thinking of marriage? Because he had wanted to marry her, but didn't realize it until now. Would it have made a difference if he had told her?

His stepfather nodded, then fell back against the pillows and closed his eyes.

"Your papá needs to rest now. What will you do, son?" Mamá's brow puckered as she moved to the bedside and stroked her husband's head.

Bryce gazed at the form of his stepfather lying on the bed, a carved crucifix hanging on the wall above. He wished he had this man's faith, solid as the bed on which he lay. Would it be any easier to make decisions if he did? He needed more time to think about his future, but how much time did he have? He couldn't give an answer yet.

"I have some people to see. I'll be back in time for dinner. Will Sonia be joining us?"

"Yes, with the children. They have grown so since you were last here." Mamá lifted an eyebrow. "Will you go to the company office and speak to Carlos and Roberto?"

"If I have time. They'll be at dinner too, won't they?"

"Of course, but perhaps you should discuss business with them elsewhere. Let us enjoy our family time tonight." She placed her hands on his arms and pleaded with her eyes. "When will you leave? Why are you in such a hurry, son? You have just arrived."

"I had not known Papá would be so improved, so I didn't know how long I'd be here. However, now that I see he is better, I must return to Florida soon to take care of some urgent matters, especially if I come back here permanently."

"If?" Mamá frowned and pursed her lips. "My son, how can you tell your Papá you will not?"

Bryce's gut wrenched as he left the house and strode to the stables. How indeed could he tell the man "no"?

~

"Here!" Mr. Gray tossed a fish on the table. "If you can cook, I'll untie you."

Sally Rose flinched and averted her gaze from the eyes of the fish staring up at her. She'd never been proficient at preparing fish, but the opportunity for her hands to be free was worth handling the slimy creature.

"Of course I can cook. But would you allow me to go to the privy first?"

Mr. Gray pulled his beard as if the question was of great significance.

"Please, sir. I promise I'll not run away." This was one promise she didn't intend to keep, however.

"Oh, all right." He strode over to the chair and untied the ropes from behind. Grabbing her by the arm, he jerked her up. "Come on."

"Ow!" Sally Rose cringed at the man's rough handling.

"Git on with ya'." He shoved her in the middle of her back toward a small shack down the path and stopped short of the door. "I'll be right here waitin' for you."

Sally Rose stole glances around her to assess her surroundings. Beyond the clearing, the woods reclaimed the hilly mountain with twisted tree trunks and dense undergrowth of jagged-edged palmettos. Even if she could get away, it would be difficult to get through the tangle without becoming trapped among the unforgiving brush. Perhaps there was another path she could find that would lead her away from the dock.

"Look out for the snakes!" Mr. Gray's warning was accompanied by obnoxious laughter.

She dropped her hand by her side, afraid to open the door, and shuddered. *Lord, please help me.* Taking a deep breath, she pulled the outhouse door open and inched inside. Afternoon sunlight crept under the walls where some of the boards didn't reach the ground displaying spider webs in every corner. Perhaps she could crawl out the back side and Mr. Gray wouldn't see her. She studied the boards and noticed they'd been gnawed. By what, though? Her eyes widened at the realization. Rats! She grabbed her skirt and glanced around, hoping she didn't have unwelcome company of any type.

"Hurry up in there. Don't make me come in and get you!"

Sally Rose sighed, giving up hope of escaping that way. She took care of business and opened the door, grateful for the fresh air. Mr. Gray leaned against a tree just a few feet away. He pushed away from it and crossed the distance to grab hold of her again.

"Sir, I am capable of walking on my own."

"Sure you are. But don't you try nothin', you hear?"

She walked back toward the kitchen, and when they reached the door, he shoved her back inside. "Now get busy. I'm hungry."

Sally Rose scanned the room for utensils. "I'll need a knife to clean this fish."

Mr. Gray reached into the sheath on his belt, grabbed the handle of his knife and pulled it out, pointing it at her. She gasped and drew back, eyes fixed on the glinting point. Would he use it on her?

A crooked grin crawled across his face, revealing his stained teeth. "Don't you worry. I won't cut you. Unless we need some bait for the gators." His laugh turned her stomach.

He laid the knife on the table beside the fish. "You ever clean a fish 'fore?"

She couldn't remember if she actually had or not, but she'd watch her papa and mama clean them years back. It couldn't be that difficult, and it'd be worth the trouble just to keep from being tied to the chair again. She picked up the knife in one hand and studied the fish. If it would just quit looking at her! She closed her eyes and raised the knife, but before she could bring it down on the fish's head, a hand surrounded hers on the knife.

"Hey! Watch out!" Mr. Gray jerked the knife away. "I'll do it. Don't want you ruining my dinner."

Sally Rose exhaled relief, then stepped back and watched the man make swift work of the fish. He scraped the discarded pile of fish head and guts into his hand and threw them outside. Within minutes, gulls appeared to fight over the morsels.

"There. Now you cook it. Think you know how to do that? You must be good for somethin'."

Sally Rose scrambled to get a frying pan off the hook. Then she found a bin with some cornmeal in it and covered the fish with the crumbs. A can of lard sat on the back of the stove. She scooped some out and threw it in the pan, while Gray lit the wood inside the stove. Maybe if she proved herself useful, she'd earn his trust, at least long enough to plan her escape.

She found some coffee in the pie safe and got some of the brew started. Then she took some more meal, mixed it with water, and formed hoecakes, thankful she remembered how her mother had made them. Of course, on the farm, they'd had plenty of milk, but she'd make do with what she could find. Hopefully, he'd be satisfied with what she cooked and allow her more freedom. Yet, even though her own stomach was empty, the thought of sharing a meal with this man repulsed her.

Mr. Gray returned to the table, leaning the chair back on two legs against the wall and gazing out the window. "Be gittin' dark soon. I'll have to get the light going in the lighthouse."

Dark? Where would she sleep? She glanced around the tiny space, imagining being curled up in a corner under that filthy blanket again and shuddered. Would Mr. Gray keep her locked in the kitchen all night?

"Will Mr. Hobbs be coming back?" What would happen to her when he did?

"No. Not tonight. Got to wrap up some things before the big night." He chuckled as his chair scraped the wall. "Didn't know you was sweet on Albert. I'll tell him you miss him."

She dropped the hot pan on the stove and flashed a glare at Mr. Gray. "I most certainly am not interested in Mr. Hobbs!"

Mr. Gray burst into raucous laughter, snorting loudly. "Well, now, for someone not interested in him, you shore ask a lot of questions 'bout him."

Sally Rose's face flushed as hot as the stove beside her. She bit her lip to keep from reacting to the man's taunts. Anger burned inside her chest and she fought the urge to throw the hot pan in the man's face. If she thought she could get away with it, she might try.

# Chapter Twenty-Seven

The ride to the Lopez plantation took over two hours—plenty of time for Bryce to contemplate his future. Back and forth he argued with himself about his choices. Did he *want* to come back to Cuba? Or did he *have* to? What if he gave up his law practice in the States and then regretted it?

As his horse crested a hill, he spotted the arched entrance to the Lopez property, with acres upon acres of sugar cane stretched out beyond. The family had been friends of his family for years, and Bryce had grown up with the three sons of Don José Lopez, the patriarch. Their business in rum production and beer brewing had become very successful, with exports all over the world.

Bryce turned his horse down the road to the distillery instead of heading toward the family mansion. The sign on the building advertised Ron de Villa, the family brand, with its distinguished trademark of a white stallion. He dismounted the horse and tied it to a hitching post, then entered the cavernous building. Spotting Eduardo Lopez standing near a copper vat, Bryce waved his arm.

Eduardo broke off his conversation with the worker beside him and grinned broadly, then strode toward Bryce. Wearing a loose white blouse tucked into his white pants, Eduardo's olive skin looked bronze. "Amigo! What brings you here? Have you come back to run Hernandez plantation?"

Bryce shook the hand offered. "Not yet. I came because Papá had a heart attack."

"I heard about his illness. How is your papá doing? Is he recovered?"

"He is much better, thank you, but still weak."

"And you, Bryce. How are you?"

Eduardo had known Anna Maria, as well as how Bryce had grieved for her. In fact, they had once competed for her attention until Bryce won her affection and married her. Bryce had never understood why she chose him over Eduardo, who was the more handsome, with his wavy black hair and swarthy skin that made his teeth flash like pearls. He smiled to himself, remembering Anna Maria's words that she couldn't marry a man who thought he was more beautiful than his wife.

"I'm doing well," Bryce said. "I'm a lawyer in Cedar Key, Florida."

"Cedar Key?" Eduardo rubbed his smooth chin. "I believe we do business with a company in Cedar Key. In fact, we have a large shipment going there soon."

"That's what I'm here to discuss with you."

Eduardo raised an eyebrow. "Yes? Well, then, come to my office."

Bryce followed Eduardo to a small house beside the distillery. Inside the well-appointed room, his host strode to a carafe on the desk and poured a glass of amber liquid. He turned and offered it to Bryce.

"Try our latest rum? It's the purest made."

"No, thank you. I'm afraid I'm too hot for spirits, but I'll take some water if you have any."

"Only water, my friend? If you insist, you can have some that's still cool, fresh from the well." Eduardo motioned to a table by the wall with a crystal pitcher and glasses." Help yourself."

Bryce readily accepted the opportunity to quench his thirst after such a long dusty ride.

Eduardo dropped into a leather chair behind a massive carved desk and propped his feet up, displaying ornately detailed leather boots. He gestured to the two padded leather chairs in front of the desk. "Please sit." Taking a sip from the glass, he exhaled. "Ah.

It's perfect." Then his eyebrows pinched together, and he got more serious. "You wanted to discuss a customer of ours?"

Bryce sat down and placed his glass on the small table between his and the other chair. "Yes. Are you familiar with Powell and Hobbs Mercantile?"

"Of course. One of our best customers. I believe they ship our rum across Florida on the rail line from Cedar Key to the Atlantic, then off to ports along the east coast."

"Hmm. And who have you dealt with?" Bryce took in the well-appointed office with its tasteful furnishings and rich tapestry rug, far more elaborate than the law office back in Cedar Key. Light streamed through tall windows that overlooked the vast plantation and beckoned memories of a past life.

"Mr. Hobbs. He's been here a couple of times. Man has no concept of manners, but he's a shrewd businessman. Dealt with him in New Orleans too."

"I see."

"Bryce, what is your interest in this company? Do you know Mr. Hobbs?"

"Yes. His partner, Mr. Powell, is also my law partner. Eduardo, I have reason to believe Mr. Hobbs is involved in smuggling. What he buys from you is not coming through the port, so no taxes are being paid on it." Bryce rested his hand on the desk and sat forward, lowering his voice. "I believe it's being off-loaded elsewhere before it gets to Cedar Key. Mr. Powell is not making the profit Mr. Hobbs is making, although Mr. Hobbs uses the mercantile to appear legitimate."

"You don't say. So, do you want me to stop the next shipment he's ordered? It's going out in a few days."

"Did you say it's a large shipment?"

"The largest one yet. His business must be very good." Eduardo set his feet down and leaned on his elbows, his hands clasped beneath his chin. "I don't wish to get into trouble with your government, especially the customs agents."

"Eduardo, you'll never guess who the customs agent is at Cedar Key."

Eduardo's eyes widened as realization hit. "Not Mr. Hobbs!"

Bryce nodded. "One and the same, I'm afraid."

"How convenient. Now I understand. I'll stop doing business with him immediately!"

Bryce held up his hand motioning Eduardo to wait. "No, not yet. We need to catch him red-handed. Tell me when your shipment is to arrive at Cedar Key."

"The end of the week. It should leave in two days."

"Good. Go ahead and ship the merchandise. That'll give me time to get back and be there when it arrives."

"But how will you know where the merchandise is going, if it's being off-loaded before it gets to Cedar Key?"

"I have a very good idea." Bryce stood and shook his friend's hand. "Thank you very much for helping me, Eduardo. I must get back to the hacienda."

"I'm glad to know I can be of assistance." Eduardo came around the desk to escort Bryce out the door. "Don't let it be so long before you come back, old friend." Eduardo patted him on the back.

"It won't be, I assure you." As he turned to walk out the heavy wooden door, Bryce added, "Perhaps I'll even be your neighbor someday."

Eduardo placed his hands on his hips and cocked his head. "Yes? Then I look forward to welcoming you home."

~

By the time Bryce returned to his parents' hacienda, the pieces of the puzzle were coming together. Hobbs had been using the mercantile as a front for his smuggling business, and since he was the customs agent inspecting ships before they reached the port, he could get away with it. It seemed he started out merely adjusting the inventory at the store, but he had branched out into full-fledged smuggling since then. Gray was obviously in cahoots with him, which made the island where the lighthouse was the perfect place to hide goods. And they could use the dock to rendezvous with other ships to take the merchandise elsewhere. When the main lighthouse keeper took a leave of absence, Gray had been given free rein on the island. Now that the keeper was coming back, they had one last chance to make a major exchange. And it would be soon.

When Bryce entered the house, he was met by the sound of children's laughter as his nieces and nephews chased each other around the fountain in the courtyard.

"André'! Carlito! Maria! Elena!" His sisters tried to corral the children, their voices overlapping each other. "Come say hello to your Tío Bryce!"

The children swarmed him as Bryce bent down on one knee to envelop them in his arms. He ruffled the coal black hair of the boys and warmed in the glow of the little girls' round, dark eyes.

"My, my! How big you've all gotten!"

The children beamed their pleasure and boasted of their growth simultaneously. Their fathers stepped forward to greet Bryce as he stood. He shook each of their hands and nodded.

"How are you, Carlos, Roberto?"

"Good. Glad you could come." Roberto patted Bryce on the back as they walked toward the dining room.

"The business? Is it doing well?" Bryce glanced from one brother-in-law to the other.

Carlos shrugged, then nodded. "Yes, good. Not so profitable now that we have to pay our laborers, but we've got a good crop this year. We make do with less labor these days." Since slavery had ended in Cuba, many of the plantation owners had struggled with paying their labor. Some had even refused until the government stepped in to force them.

"Come now, we will not speak of business during dinner." Mamá ushered the family into the room. She sat at one end of the table opposite the empty chair where Papá usually sat.

A lump formed in Bryce's throat seeing the absence of his father at the table. He must recover and resume his customary place at the head of the table. What would happen if Papá did not recover? No doubt Bryce would be expected to return to take his place in the family business.

Mamá waited until everyone at the table quieted. In her role as family matriarch, she appeared regal, sitting straight with chin raised as she surveyed her brood. She scanned the expectant faces, then took a deep breath before speaking. "We will see Papá after dinner. His nurse is taking him something to eat. He's not had much appetite, but he must eat and get stronger."

If determination alone could make Papá well, his mother had enough for all of them.

After dinner, Bryce pulled his mother aside. "Mamá, I need to ask you about my father's family."

"Your father's family? You mean Tía Consuelo and Tío Miguel? What about them?"

"No, Mamá. I need to know about my real father, my American father. Wasn't his last name McFarlane?"

"Sí, yes. His name was Donovan McFarlane."

"Do you remember his mother's name? My grandmother?"

A warm smile crossed his mother's face. "Oh, yes. Her name was Sally. Sally McFarlane. A very nice lady. Why do you want to know?"

Bryce's pulse quickened. Didn't Sally Rose say she'd been named after Granny Sally? Could it be the same person? "Just curious. I met someone with a similar name and wondered if we could be related. Did my father have any brothers or sisters?"

"No. He was the only child who lived to be an adult." Bryce eased out a breath.

"So I wouldn't have any cousins?"

His mother tilted her head at him. "Not through your father's family. But your grandfather had a brother who lived in Florida too. You might have cousins on that side of the family."

"I see." Surely he wasn't related to Sally Rose. After all, she was from Ohio. What an unusual coincidence, and thankfully so.

"Who is she?" Mamá peered up at him, placing her hand on his arm.

"She?"

"You're thinking of someone, someone you care about. I know that look."

Heat crept up Bryce's neck into his face. He never could hide things from his mother. She knew him too well.

"I am. There's a woman in Cedar Key, a governess, I'm quite attracted to. We've spent some time together."

"And how does she feel about you?"

"I don't think she likes me. I thought she had grown fond of me as I have her, but she refuses to see me anymore, and I have no idea why."

His mother squeezed his arm and studied his face. "You've been a gentleman, sí?"

"Yes, of course. As far as I know, I've done nothing to offend her."

"Then there's another reason, son. A reason that has nothing to do with you."

Bryce stared at his mother. How did she know these things?

"What can I do?"

"Do you love her?"

"Yes, Mama, I believe I do." Was he admitting feelings for Sally Rose to his mother that he hadn't admitted to himself? "But . . ."

"Bryce, Anna Maria has been gone for five years. It's time for you to love another. She would want you to. Who knows if God did not bring you both to Cedar Key to meet? You must tell the woman you love her. Whatever it is that's bothering her can be defeated by love."

"But what if she won't see me? How can I tell her?"

"You will find a way if you really care about her."

Bryce nodded. And he knew what he must do. As soon as he returned to Cedar Key, he'd go tell Sally Rose he loved her, even if he had to take up residence on the Powell's front porch. She'd have to come out sometime.

# Chapter Twenty-Eight

Sally Rose stared out the window of her kitchen prison as the shadows lengthened, then blended into a dark jungle of gloomy shapes. Sweat dampened her hair and clothes in the stuffy room, the only air coming through the open window. She sighed as tears trickled down her cheek. What would happen to her? Could she have prevented this?

If only she hadn't been keeping so many secrets—about what she heard, about who she was. But she'd been too proud, too unwilling to give up her position for the truth. Was God punishing her for not telling them? She dropped her head and stared at her hands, tied together again. Mr. Gray didn't trust her either. Why should he? Why should anyone? *Lord, I'm so sorry. Please forgive me. Please help me!*

She imagined the faces of Mr. Powell and Ellen when Mrs. Chapman told them of her deception. Such upright people, they would be shocked to find out. And what would they tell the children? Her heart was wrung out from the guilt she carried. If she lived, would she ever see them again? Could she face them?

The chain rattled on the door as Mr. Gray unlocked it and shoved it open.

Sally Rose jerked upright and squinted to see the man in the waning light. Was he going to take her someplace else?

"Here. You can sleep on this." Mr. Gray tossed a musty wool blanket against the wall.

"You expect me to sleep in here?"

"Oh, excuse me, ma'am. Our guest room is full." The man emitted a sinister laugh." Well, I suppose you could share my bed, if you want."

Her stomach tightened into a knot. "I'd prefer to stay here." She restrained herself to mutter a response, instead of screaming at the repulsive man. "Am I supposed to sleep with my wrists tied together?"

Mr. Gray glanced around the room as if to find the answer. When his gaze landed on the window, he nodded at it. "Reckon you'll have to. Just in case you got any plans to climb out that window."

That idea sounded like a good one, but where would she go if she got out? Hide until she could hail a passing ship? "What good would climbing out the window do me.?"

"None. I just don't have time to look for you if you go missing. Mr. Hobbs would be pretty mad, and he might do something drastic."

*Feed her to the gators.* She shuddered at the memory of her dream. Somehow, she had to stay alive.

"Or I could just nail this here window shut." Her captor strode over to the window and examined it.

"Please don't. It's so hot in here anyway. You don't have to worry about me getting out." Would he believe her?

"All right. I'll keep the window open, but your hands will stay tied." He grabbed the coffee pot and a tin cup and headed to the door. Looking over his shoulder, he grinned. "Watch out for snakes crawlin' in the window." He snorted a laugh as he turned back to the door. "See you in the mornin'." The door closed behind him, and the sound of the chain reminded her she was still a prisoner.

~

Bryce leaned over and hugged his mother, then kissed her cheek. "I won't be gone long, Mamá."

The little woman looked up at him and pointed her finger at his chest. "You will promise, son?"

Bryce nodded. "I promise. I hope to be finished with my business back in Florida in a couple of weeks."

"And you will return for good?"

He stared at the passengers boarding the ship. "I'm not certain. I know you want me to say 'yes,' but I don't want to make a promise I can't keep."

Mamá took his hand and held it to her chest. "I will pray God will give you wisdom. You'll pray for that too?"

Should he lie to her or tell her he didn't pray anymore? No, that would be too upsetting for her. Her son, a pagan? Perhaps not. Perhaps he just doubted God had any interest in his life. He would keep that doubt to himself as well. He nodded to appease her.

"And you'll pray for my safe trip too, Mamá?" If God listened to anyone, it was his mother, who kept her rosary tucked into her skirt pocket at all times.

"Of course, son. And I'll pray for the safety of the young lady you are returning to in Florida."

Bryce tilted his head and quirked an eyebrow at his mother. "Her safety? Why?"

"Because if God wants the two of you together, he'll need to keep her safe for you."

A shot of alarm raced through his body. Her safety? He'd forgotten she was afraid of Hobbs and Gray. And he had left town, left her unprotected and vulnerable to them. His mother had no idea how profound her statement was. He had to get back soon. Before it was too late. Too late to catch the men in their crime. But hopefully, not too late for him and Sally Rose.

~

Moonlight shone through the trees, giving sinister new characteristics to the woods beyond the clearing. Sally Rose strained to hear the sounds outside her confines. Crickets chirped and frogs croaked in a cacophony of noise. "Who? Who?" an owl nearby hooted. Was he taunting her, asking her to identify herself to the world? Somewhere in the distance, she heard the sound of waves lapping the shore, a sound which might have been peaceful at another time in another place.

She leaned close to the window to catch any breeze that might materialize. As she watched, creatures skittered across the ground and ran up trees. What sort of animals were they? Not squirrels at this time of the night. With a jolt, she realized they were rats. She backed away from the window. Would they come inside? Out of the corner of her eye, something slithered down a tree and crawled toward the kitchen.

Sally Rose raised her tied-together hands and pulled down on the window, hoping to close it before anything could get in. Her heart raced as she yanked on the frame, her eyes searching all around. The window wouldn't budge, and she couldn't move it. Out of breath, she panicked. What could she do?

*Make noise.* The idea came out of nowhere, but she thought she remembered hearing animals were usually more afraid of you than vice versa. She would try to scare the creatures away. But how? She ran over to the stove and, with both hands, grabbed a large metal spoon hanging on the wall above, then snatched a pan out of the pie safe. She returned to the window and turned the pan upside down on the window sill. Taking the spoon, she started banging on the upturned pan.

Shadows scurried across the clearing away from the building. It worked. She exhaled a deep sigh of relief. But how could she sleep? She glanced over at the blanket on the floor, yearning to stretch out on it. No matter how uncomfortable it was, she was so tired, she could sleep anywhere ... but not yet. Not knowing some creature might come in the window and join her in her makeshift bed. She had to stay awake. At least until daylight appeared.

# Chapter Twenty-Nine

Bryce paced the deck of the ship as he deliberated his next steps. He'd need to get help to catch Hobbs and Gray in the act. He'd already sent a telegram to Frank, advising him of his return date, but he'd had to be careful in the wording so Mr. Greene wouldn't accidentally tip off Hobbs. When the ship reached Key West, he asked directions to the customs office. He strode down the street until he saw the shingle and pushed open the door. A leathery-skinned, white-haired fellow with a bushy white mustache raised an eyebrow as he looked up from a desk covered in stacks of paper.

"Can I help you, sir?"

"Are you the customs collector here?" Bryce spied a nameplate hidden under some paperwork, but couldn't make out the name.

"I am. Thaddeus Thomas. And whom might you be sir?" The man stood and offered his hand.

"Bryce Hernandez. I need your help breaking up a smuggling operation out of Cedar Key."

"Cedar Key?" Mr. Thomas put his thumbs in his vest and rocked back on his heels. "There's an agent there already. You should speak to him about the matter."

"Are you familiar with Albert Hobbs?" What if this man was also involved?

"Not well. I believe he took over the position a couple of years back. I been here over ten years and don't have time to visit other places." He tilted his head and eyed Bryce. "Smuggling, you say? We have plenty of that in these parts. Those thieves are hard to catch, but I'd sure love to get rid of them, especially the big ones."

"This is a large enterprise, from what I have discovered. Apparently, Mr. Hobbs is in league with the criminals."

Mr. Thomas's eyes bulged and his mouth dropped open. "You have proof of this? That's a mighty strong accusation."

"Yes, sir, I do." Bryce rested both his palms on the desk as he fixed his gaze on the official. "We have an opportunity to catch them this week, but we must make haste and get support. I don't know how many people we'll have to deal with besides the two men leading the operation. Can you help round up some lawmen to meet me in Cedar Key?"

"I can, and I will. Heck, I'll go with you and get the Deputy Collector to cover for me here until I get back." The man walked to a hat rack, where he retrieved his coat and hat. "Let's go see Sam Jackson, the treasury agent here, and see what he suggests. I know he'll want to be involved too."

Bryce accompanied him down the block to another office where they met Mr. Jackson, and Bryce explained the situation. Before leaving for lunch, the agent telegraphed his counterpart in Tampa, requesting his help. Then the three men sat down in the corner of a restaurant and devised a plan.

They agreed to converge in Cedar Key and rendezvous on the island of Atsenie Otie under the guise of businessmen calling on the pencil factory, away from the watchful eye of Hobbs. Jackson would alert agents in the Fernandina and St. Augustine areas, who would arrive by train, while other lawmen would pose as fishermen, giving them access to boats.

Time was of the utmost importance. Eduardo expected the shipment of rum to reach Cedar Key in three days. Bryce would be back in two, if the weather cooperated. Mr. Thomas accompanied him on the ship as promised. The customs officer had brought a nautical chart of the Cedar Key area, so they could study the region, especially Seahorse Key, where Bryce suspected the exchange of goods to take place.

After several hours of planning and discussing on deck, Bryce bid Mr. Thomas goodnight but wasn't ready for bed himself. Instead he stayed on deck, keeping a wary eye on the sky. This was the time of year a hurricane might appear, but a storm now would be devastating to their plans. He needed to sleep, but how could he? If he wasn't thinking about how to catch Hobbs and Gray, he was thinking about Sally Rose.

He blew out a breath and leaned on the ship railing. When was the last time he'd seen her? It seemed like such a long time, but it had been just over a week. Yet each day without seeing her dragged by. Over and over he recalled the times they'd spent together, conversations they'd had, looking for a clue to her withdrawal from him. He knew she was afraid of Hobbs and Gray, but was she afraid of him too? Had he given her any reason to mistrust him? He'd only wanted her to remember what she heard, but now it didn't matter. Had he pressured her about it too much?

A disturbing thought made him start. What if he didn't have time to see her before joining the other men to catch the smugglers? He really wanted to talk with her first. But there might not be time. He pounded the railing with his fist, startling the couple standing a few feet away. Apparently, he'd interrupted a romantic moment. They shot him a glare then stepped farther away.

Why couldn't this ship move any faster? It was so frustrating to wait. So much was out of his control. He just couldn't stand still and do nothing. As he started pacing again, he realized that was the main problem. He could only do so much, and he had to leave the rest up to ... fate? His conscience niggled him with another answer. God? *All right, God, since you've got more control than I have, you'll have to make sure everything happens at the right time.*

Did that constitute a prayer? His mother probably wouldn't think so.

~

A loud squawk shook Sally Rose out of her sleep. She raised her head from the table where it had fallen sometime during the night, resting next to the upturned pan. Her arms were stretched out alongside it, still holding the spoon, her hands and face itching from mosquito bites. As her eyes adjusted to the dim light, she peered out the window as dawn lifted the dark mask off the trees. The sound of heavy wings flapping alerted her to the flight of a large heron, the author of the sound that had awakened her.

The sky was still gray, the island engulfed in fog. Moisture dripped from the Spanish moss that hung from the trees, adding weight to the fatigue she felt from a restless night. She stood and stretched out her back, stiff from sitting in the hard chair so long. There were no sounds coming from the lighthouse. Mr. Gray must be asleep now, having stayed up to maintain the light.

She glanced at the blanket on the floor. Now she could sleep too, without fear of some creature invading the space. Her stomach grumbled, but hunger was not something she cared about anymore. She shuffled over to the blanket, ready to collapse. Picking it up, she shook it out then folded it to create a small amount of padding against the hard floor. She lay down and allowed her body to relax.

As she closed her eyes, she thought about all the people she knew who might care about what happened to her. Would the Powells be concerned? Or did they think she was a liar, someone not to be trusted? She hoped Ellen would be more understanding, but what if she was too hurt by Mrs. Chapman's revelation? And the children … Did they miss her, or had they been told she was a bad person? Of course, her family would care, but they were so far away.

Then there was Bryce. She knew he cared, or he wouldn't have come to see her every day, even when she refused to see him. But now, he too must believe she was untrustworthy and not worth his time. Her heart ached as pain wrenched it. Oh, how she wished things could be different. Even if she'd told him the truth about not really being a teacher, they still couldn't have a future with her Negro blood. Tears seeped out of the corners of her eyes and dropped onto the blanket.

As her conversation with Ruth Ann replayed in her mind, she was comforted that at least one person knew the truth. And that one person had not judged her—in fact, still liked her. Sally Rose had seen the concern in her eyes, felt the warmth of her company. And Ruth Ann would pray for her safety, of that Sally Rose was certain. Maybe God would listen to her prayers. He surely wouldn't listen to a liar's.

~

"Albert will be here tomorrow."

Sally Rose felt her stomach lurch. She had barely tolerated Mr. Gray as one day dragged into another, but just the thought of Mr. Hobbs seeing her in her desperate condition made her ill. She was weak from lack of food but had no appetite. If no one else cared for her, why should she?

So far Mr. Gray had left her alone most of the time. Other than having her cook for him, he'd kept her locked up in the kitchen. At least once a day, he allowed her to go to the well and use some water to rinse off. Without the privacy to bathe, the water did little to cleanse yet provided some relief from the heat. Every night, she resumed her pot-banging, convinced it was her only means to keep the unwanted vermin away.

"Why would I be happy to see him? Will he let me go?" She knew the answer, yet had to ask.

"Well, he just might have some news about where you're going."

"Where I'm going? What do you mean?"

"Don't you want to take a nice long trip?" Mr. Gray grabbed the coffeepot as he did every night and headed to the door, chuckling. "Good night, Miz McFarlane. See you in the mornin'."

She listened to the bolt on the door slamming into place, like someone sealing a tomb. She dragged herself back to her position by the window, ready to resume her battle. Mr. Gray's words echoed through her mind. Mr. Hobbs would arrive tomorrow; then what? All she could do was wait and find out.

# Chapter Thirty

After a stop in Tampa, the ship took another day to reach Cedar Key. As soon as the ship tied up to the wharf, Bryce and Mr. Thomas headed down the dock to the law office. Frank jumped to his feet as the men entered.

"Bryce! Welcome back!" Frank extended his hand and turned to the other man.

"Frank, this is Mr. Thaddeus Thomas, Customs Collector for Key West."

Mr. Thomas nodded and shook hands. "Pleased to meet you, sir."

"Sit down, sit down." Frank pulled up another chair so both men could sit across from his desk, then he sat back down in his chair. "Bryce, I got your telegram, but it didn't say much. How is your father?"

"Much better, thank you. You understand why I couldn't reveal more information on the telegraph with Mr. Greene receiving it. He might have said something to Albert that would hinder our plans."

"Yes, of course. Well, what have you found out? I'm very anxious to hear."

"It seems Hobbs and Gray have been smuggling rum from Havana."

Frank fell back in his chair. "So that's what he's been up to. And you're sure about this?"

"I am." Bryce nodded. "They're getting it from the Villa family, some old friends of mine."

"So what are they doing with this rum?"

"My bet is they have a partner in New Orleans who's taking it off their hands. We think they're making the exchange at the lighthouse dock."

"That's logical, I assume, while the head keeper is away. But he'll be back soon, I understand. Then what?"

"Then they'll get away or change their methods. At any rate, they'll be harder to catch once the keeper returns." Bryce left his chair to retrieve a glass of water. He raised the pitcher for the others to see as an offer. Mr. Thomas lifted his hand, then faced Frank. "That's why we need to move quickly."

"Immediately." Bryce handed Mr. Thomas a glass and sat back down. "We believe the exchange will happen either tonight or tomorrow night."

Frank searched the men's faces. "How are we going to catch them?"

"I've contacted agents all over the state and other lawmen as well. They'll all be coming into town today. We're meeting over at Atsenie Otie this afternoon to set up the surveillance." Mr. Thomas emptied the glass, then set it down. "I certainly hope we can catch the crooks."

"What can I do to help?" Frank glanced from one man to the other.

"Sir, we'll need to procure some fishing boats. I trust you have some acquaintances who can oblige."

"Yes, I know several people who have boats. I'll offer to pay for the use. What should I tell them?"

"Tell them you have some clients coming into town who want to go fishing." Mr. Thomas laughed out loud. "That's the truth, isn't it?"

Frank chuckled. "I suppose you could say we're trying to catch some very big fish, yes."

Mr. Thomas slapped the arms of his chair then stood. "Well, if you gentlemen can show me the way to the nearest hotel, I'd like to freshen up before our meeting later."

"I'll take you to the Bettelini, just down the street." Bryce rose to follow him then turned back to Frank. "Before we go over to the island today, I'd like to see Sally Rose. I trust she's been well since I've been gone."

A cloud passed over Frank's face. "I'm afraid I have some rather bad news, Bryce." He glanced over at Mr. Thomas. "We'll discuss it when you return."

A rock sank in the pit of Bryce's stomach. "Bad news? She's ill?"

"No, Bryce. She's gone."

~

Sally Rose woke to the sound of light rain hitting the roof. The sky strained to show daylight through dense clouds. She stood and stretched, then headed to the blanket as she had done every day. As she knelt on the blanket to pray, she remembered Mr. Gray's words last night that Mr. Hobbs was coming today. She did not want to face him, did not want to find out what else he had in store for her. She had to get away. Something inside her urged her to try again.

She got up and went to the door and pulled. *Please, open this time.* But she only heard the rattling of the chain outside holding it shut. She turned around and fell back against it, sighing. Was there nothing she could do? Her gaze landed on the open window, and a spark of hope lit in her chest. The window was open at the top. If it was open at the bottom, she could squeeze through.

She had to push the window up, but how could she manage with her hands tied and her long skirt? Memories of climbing trees with her brothers and sisters sparked a ray of hope in her heart. Why, she could out-climb them all when she was younger.

She needed her hands free, and Mr. Gray had taken the knife with him. She glanced around the room, searching for something that could cut, and then stared back at the window. Broken glass would work. She returned to the window, grabbed the spoon, and then, holding it with both hands, beat on the glass. Tap. Tap. It would take more than that to break the window. But would the noise awaken Mr. Gray?

*"Girl, youse can do anythin' yo' put yo' mine' to."*
*Yes, Papa, I can, and I will.*

The memory of her father's words deepened her resolve. She needed to escape—and she would. She pounded harder on the glass. Her arms ached from the awkward position, but that didn't matter. She'd never wanted anything as much as her freedom at the moment. A crack appeared, running in several directions. She stopped and listened for the sound of the light keeper's approach.

Even the birds were quiet, their calls muffled by the dense mist. Her heart thumping against her chest, she hit the center of the crack harder until pieces of glass fell out. She dropped the spoon and raised her hands so the rope on her wrists touched the ragged glass that remained in the window, and then began to saw against it.

Sweat ran down her face as she rubbed the rope back and forth against the sharp edge, her heart racing. Finally, a piece of rope broke through, releasing one hand. She'd leave the rest of the rope on the other hand for now. Returning to the worn blanket, she tore off a piece, then wrapped a shard of glass in it and placed it in her skirt pocket in case she needed a weapon to defend herself. Then she went back to the window and pushed up with all her might.

The window budged then gave way as she shoved it up. She brushed off pieces of glass from the window sill with the blanket. Then pulling her skirt up and tucking it into her waist, she crouched down and bent her body to fit in the window opening. She threw one leg over the sill as if mounting a horse, then the other leg followed, and she dropped down to the hard sand. Freedom. Now she had to keep from being caught again.

She made a dash for the outhouse and ran directly into a large spider web between two trees. She fought the urge to scream as she battled the sticky strands that clung to her face and hair. She reached the outhouse panting, then opened the door and waved it back and forth to make sure anything that had taken up residence in it during the night would leave. Once inside, she considered her options.

Where would she go? She had to hide from Mr. Gray to avoid recapture. What would he do when he discovered her gone? One thing she knew for sure—he wouldn't be pleased. Nor would Mr. Hobbs when he got there. She shuddered. What would his reaction be? She didn't want to find out.

There must be some place to hide, some place where, hopefully, she could see boats on the water and perhaps signal one for help. She couldn't use the usual path to the water, though. She'd have to go through the undergrowth and the woods instead. And the possibility she'd encounter snakes was another danger. Which was the lesser of the evils?

She chose the snakes.

Sally Rose left the outhouse and pushed through the dense undergrowth, her skirt snagging on the ragged palmetto. Mosquitoes droned around her face, and she slapped at them constantly. Which way was she headed? North? South? East? West? It didn't matter, as long as she went down, where the water would be, and didn't leave any tracks for someone to follow. But as long as she walked on the leaf-covered ground instead of the sand, they shouldn't be able to see where she'd gone.

As she pushed a branch out of her face, she stepped forward and hit something hard, losing her balance. She fell flat-faced onto the ground, knocking the air out of her lungs. What did she trip over? She pushed up to her knees, looked back, and gasped. A small footstone poked out of the ground. The headstone lay a few feet away. Beside it was another footstone and a somewhat larger headstone. She bent over and peered at the words engraved on the stones.

"Joseph Crevasse Born March 19, 1809 Died March 26, 1874." The smaller one read "Timothy Crevasse Born March 13, 1852 Died September 13, 1869." Father and son? How did they die?

Her nerves tingled all the way to the ends of her hair. Afraid of what she might see, she shot a glance in the other direction, and her breath caught. Four more headstones stood in a row. She had fallen in the cemetery, a place of death. Was this an omen? Was she doomed to the same fate?

*God, please no. Not here, not now.*

She scrambled to her feet. She had to get out of here, had to get off this island. She plunged back into the undergrowth, glad to realize she was going downhill.

Something rustled in the bushes nearby. She froze and listened. Was it a snake? More rustling, then a squirrel scurried across the ground and up a tree. She blew out a deep breath and kept going. Finally, she caught a glimpse of sparkling blue through the trees. Water! Thank God. She rushed ahead, tripped over some tree roots, and stumbled down the hill until her feet were deep in sand. Just beyond the next tree, the beach began.

She stepped out of the woods into the open and glanced around. All she could see was water, sand, driftwood, and seashells. Where was the dock? She needed to find it to get her bearings but didn't want to be seen. Maybe if she stayed close to the tree line, she could walk around the island until she found it. But first, she wanted to rinse off some of the dirt and debris she'd accumulated.

At the water's edge, she stooped and put her hands in the refreshing water, letting it filter through her fingers and soothe her sore wrists. The rope was still attached to one wrist, but she withdrew the glass from her pocket and sawed it off, letting the water soften the cord. Her skin tingled as the saltwater licked her cuts and scrapes. She cupped her hands and splashed her face, relishing the rinse. *Thank you, Lord.*

The sun peeped out of the cloud cover as the rain stopped. Soon it would be hot again and she'd be exposed. She stood and wiped her hands, then staggered back through the sand toward the trees. Surely she'd find a good hiding place where she could keep a wary eye for signs of Mr. Gray. Fatigue attacked her limbs and made each step a great effort. If only she could rest a little while. Her mind dizzy and dull, she could no longer think clearly. Ahead, she spotted a tree stretching its branches out toward the beach as palmettos clustered around its base. As she drew closer, she saw a space between the base of the tree and the shrubs, just enough room to lie down and not be seen. She fit herself into the area and collapsed on the ground. A warm breeze blew off the water as the waves lapped the shore. If she could just close her eyes a few minutes . . .

# Chapter Thirty-One

"Gone? She left town?" Bryce had held himself together while he escorted Mr. Thomas to the hotel, but now he stood in front of Frank's desk, his hands uplifted, grasping for answers.

"I'm afraid so. You'd better sit down." Frank pointed to the chair behind Bryce.

"But what happened? Why did she leave?" Bryce plopped down and raked his hair with his fingers. If only he'd returned sooner.

Frank shook his head. "I'm not completely certain. You remember Mary Etta Chapman?"

Bryce nodded. Yes, the gaudy woman who lived across the street from the Powells. "What does Sally Rose's leaving have to do with her?"

"About four days ago, Sally Rose left the house in a hurry and didn't come back. Ellen and I didn't realize it until the next morning when she didn't come downstairs. We thought you and she had had a lengthy discussion, and then she came in after we went to bed."

"Why would you think she was with me? She's been refusing to see me for almost two weeks."

"Well, because it was shortly after you came by the house that she left. When she found out you had called and we had sent you away, as we'd been doing, she looked anxious and hurried out."

"She was coming to see me?" Bryce's pulse quickened.

"So we thought. Until Mary Etta came by the next day and told us some rather unsettling news."

Bryce leaned forward, his elbow on the desk, his chin resting on his hand. "What did she say?"

"Apparently, Mary Etta has a friend in Cleveland. As you know, that's where Sally Rose worked, at the private school before she came here."

"Yes, I know." Bryce's chest was so tight, he had trouble taking a breath.

"Well, it seems that Sally Rose—that is, Miss McFarlane—wasn't honest with us about her employment there."

"You mean she didn't work at the school?"

"Oh, she worked at the school all right. However, she wasn't a teacher. She was a companion to the elderly mother of the school headmistress."

Bryce fell back in the chair, puffing out his cheeks and blowing out the air. She had lied? How could she do that? He didn't believe she was capable of being dishonest.

"So you think she ran away before the truth came out?" The muscles in Bryce's jaw tightened.

"That's what Mary Etta thinks. She had confronted Sally Rose with the truth and asked her to tell us about it. Apparently, she couldn't face us."

Bryce shook his head from side to side as he gazed up at the ceiling. "Do you really believe she ran away?"

"Bryce, I don't know what or whom to believe." Frank's shoulders slumped, as he shook his head. "Apparently, I'm not a very good judge of character after all. First, I get mixed up with Hobbs, this situation with Miss McFarlane."

How could he put her name in the same breath with that lying crook? Bryce's heart stopped as a thought flashed through his mind. She couldn't possibly be working with the man, could she? No, it wasn't possible. She was terrified of him, and that was no lie.

He sat forward in his chair. "Have you considered another explanation? Sally Rose confided in me that she'd overheard a conversation between Hobbs and Gray spoken in French when she went out to the lighthouse. She couldn't remember exactly what they said because she was preoccupied with finding Benjamin at the time. However, she said that when the men realized she could speak French, they began to act strangely toward her, even menacing."

Frank's eyebrows knit together. "Why didn't you tell me this before?"

"She asked me not to. Said she didn't want you and Ellen to be worried."

"So perhaps she heard something that would prove their guilt."

"She thought that was a possibility. She tried very hard to remember the words they spoke." Bryce stood and strode across the room, studying the bare wooden floor, a sharp contrast to Eduardo's office. "You say she ran out after me?"

"It appeared that way."

"If it was after dinner when I usually come by, then it was late in the day, almost dark." She must have really been anxious to tell him something. Had she remembered?

"Yes, as a matter of fact, a thunderstorm blew up after she left, and we decided she was waiting for it to abate before she came back."

"Did you check with the ticket agent at the train station to see if she took the train out of town?"

"Yes, I did. But he didn't remember selling her one. However, his memory and his eyesight aren't too good."

Bryce stroked his chin. She couldn't have just vanished. Where would she have gone? An idea startled his thoughts and his heart began to race.

"What if…"

"What if what, Bryce? What are you thinking?"

"What if she was taken against her will?"

Frank's eyes widened. "Who would do something like that?"

"Hobbs? Or someone working for him?"

Frank's mouth dropped open. "Oh, my. Do you think Hobbs would resort to such callous behavior?"

"Maybe." Bryce plopped back down in the chair. Had he abandoned Sally Rose and left her in danger? "If he decided Sally Rose was too much of a threat to his underhanded dealings."

Frank stared up at the ceiling, like the answer would come from above. Then he sighed and looked at Bryce. "I do hope you're wrong."

"Frank, I believe Hobbs is capable of anything." His gut clenched at the reality of his statement.

"Surely you don't think he would harm her."

Bryce's jaw twitched as he peered at Frank's face. "You must tell me. Is there *anything* else peculiar about her disappearance?"

Frank nodded. "There is. She didn't take a bag—left her things behind. I questioned that, but Mary Etta was so convincing, and I suppose I was just too shocked to believe otherwise."

Bryce lowered his head, clenching his fists.

"There's something else, Bryce. Ruth Ann, our housekeeper's daughter, said she didn't believe Miss McFarlane ran away either."

Bryce raised his head, an eyebrow lifted. "Really? Why?"

"Ruth Ann told us she needs to tell you something Miss McFarlane told her. She's been most anxious since both you and Miss McFarlane left. She won't tell us, though. Said Miss McFarlane specifically wanted you to hear it. We assumed it was of a personal nature."

"Where is Ruth Ann? I must speak to her at once."

"I believe she's at our house. She's been helping out since her mother hurt her back."

Bryce almost knocked over the chair as he stood. "Then I'll go there now."

"You do that, Bryce. We need to get to the bottom of this." Frank rose from his chair, and reached for his hat. "Wait, I'll follow you out. I need to get down to the dock and procure some boats."

"Fine. I'll meet you back here at three."

Bryce practically ran all the way to the Powell home, his head spinning. Where did Sally Rose go? Did she leave of her own free will, or was she forced? Was she in danger?

When he reached the house, he leaped up the steps to the porch and knocked on the door.

Ellen Powell opened the door and her eyes widened when she saw him. A mixture of emotions swam through her eyes. Regret? Sadness? Confusion? She put her hand to her forehead.

"Mr. Hernandez. Good to see you. How is your father?"

"Better, thank you. Mrs. Powell, I heard about Sally Rose's disappearance."

Ellen glanced sideways toward the parlor then put her finger to her lips. "Let's talk on the veranda." She stepped out and pulled the door closed behind her. "I'd rather not discuss this in front of the children. They've been very upset about the circumstances."

Bryce looked intently into Ellen's eyes. "Mrs. Powell, I don't believe Sally Rose ran away."

"I don't want to believe it either, but where is she? And what of the lie about her teaching at the school?" Ellen twisted the handkerchief in her hands as she let her gaze drift toward the yard, her eyes misting over. "I really trusted her."

"I don't know how to explain it, but I'm sure that if we could hear her side of the story, it'd make sense. However, we must find her first, and I fear she may be in danger."

Ellen's hand flew to her mouth. "Danger? Oh dear, I hope not. But what kind of danger?" She searched his face for an answer.

"I really don't have time to tell you about it now, but I promise, you'll be told later. Right now, though, I need to speak to Ruth Ann. Is she here?"

Ellen raised her eyebrows. "Ruth Ann? Why, I believe she's in the kitchen." Ellen nodded toward the outbuilding. "Would you like me to get her for you?"

"No, thank you. I'll go see her myself. Please excuse me." Bryce descended the veranda steps and headed to the kitchen. He knocked on the door frame to keep from alarming the woman standing at the stove with her back to him. He cleared his throat. "Excuse me."

Ruth Ann spun around, eyes round as the pot on the stove. "Oh, Lord, you're here!" She dropped the wooden spoon in the pot she was stirring and wiped her hands on her apron before crossing the room to him. "Mr. Hernandez, I'm real worried about Miss Sally. She told me some stuff to make your hair curl, and I'm afraid she's in terrible trouble!"

Bryce clasped her hands together in his, trying to calm her. "It's all right; I'm here. Tell me what she said. Please. I have reason to believe she's in danger too."

Ruth Ann told him about the fears Sally Rose had concerning Hobbs. She told him Sally Rose had remembered the words she heard at the lighthouse and what they were.

"She said you needed to know, that it was real important for you. Is that right? What do it mean?"

"It means the men I'm trying to catch were planning to do their business during the night of the full moon. But I don't understand why she told you."

"She told me to tell you in case somethin' happened to her. But when somethin' did, you was gone!" Ruth Ann patted the sweat around her bandana with the edge of her apron.

"Did she also tell you the truth about her work at the school?"

"Yes, sir, she did. She felt real bad about that. She never meant to tell a lie. When she answered the ad for governess, she said she could teach children 'cause she'd learned all the things Mr. and Mrs. Powell wanted her to teach. But she never told nobody she had been a teacher at that school up North. They just thought it themselves, and she was afraid she'd lose her job if she told them different. She's really a good person and she didn't want to let Powells down."

"So you don't think she ran away, like Mrs. Chapman claims?"

Ruth Ann shook her head from side to side. "No, sir, I don'! That Mrs. Chapman's a mean lady, and she tried to scare Miss Sally away. And she almost did, but Miss Sally told me she was gonna tell everybody the truth that night she turned up missin'."

Bryce put his hand on her arm and studied her face. "She did? She told you that?"

"Yes, sir." She hung her head, shaking it. "Somethin' don't feel right about all this, Mr. Hernandez. 'Cause she was gonna make sure you knew too."

"I'm afraid you're right, Ruth Ann. Thank you for telling me. It's a good thing she confided in you." He wondered why Sally Rose chose Ruth Ann as a confidante, but perhaps she didn't want to burden Ellen or Frank. As he watched the Negro woman, he saw a glimmer of something else in her eyes—genuine concern. Ruth Ann really cared about Sally Rose, which was one thing they had in common.

"Mr. Hernandez, I hopes you can find her before it's too late. She's been gone for days now, poor woman." Ruth Ann grabbed the edge of her apron and wiped her eyes. "I been prayin' for her every day. She was so scared. I hope nobody's done nothing to hurt her."

He patted her on the shoulder. "I think I know where she is, Ruth Ann. I promise you, I'll find her."

"You has to, Mr. Hernandez. You has to."

# Chapter Thirty-Two

Sally Rose awoke to buzzing in her ears. As she swatted at the flying insect, she tried to open her eyes and discovered her face half-covered in sand. She sat up and shook her head to dislodge the grit, then used the back of her hand to clear it from her eyes and mouth.

She paused and listened for a sign of Mr. Gray. How long had she been sleeping? She squinted at the bright sun above and gauged the time of day. Straight up, so it must be near noon, and he must be awake by now. And aware that she was gone. Was he at this moment combing the island in search of her? She unfolded her legs, stood, and glanced around at her surroundings.

The dreary morning had turned into a bright, summer day, the kind she would enjoy under other circumstances. A great blue heron strolled along the edge of the beach, his eyes fixed on something in the water. A memory of the children's voices haunted her. *Look, Miss Sally! We saw one of those in the bird book!*

Her heart twisted with the knowledge that she couldn't share the moment with the children. Could never teach them again. Suddenly the bird plunged his sharp beak into the water and came up with a fish it had speared, then began the process of working the fish down his elongated neck. Sally Rose gawked at the quickness of the bird to catch its prey.

She flinched. Something had bitten her. She jerked her hand off the tree beside her. Red ants? Shoving aside palmetto fronds, she rushed to the water and leaned over, swishing her hands to rinse off of the painful pests.

Satisfied she'd washed them away, she straightened and shook out her dress, hoping no other varmints were attached to her. Sally Rose exhaled a deep breath. What next? If this were *Treasure Island*, Benjamin's favorite book, it would be an adventure. She shook her head as tears filled her eyes. Everything reminded her of the children.

What was that on the water? Was it a boat? It was! This was her chance to get help! She waved her hand to get its attention. The boat appeared to come toward her. Excitement bubbled out as she waved both hands, then a shock of alarm rippled through her. She lowered her arms. What if Mr. Hobbs was in the boat? The boat came closer. Her entire body shook.

She turned and ran into the trees as fast as she could, tripping over pieces of driftwood and the wet bottom of her skirt. But what if it wasn't Mr. Hobbs and instead her only opportunity to be rescued? Her heart pounded against her ribs as she looked back and watched the boat approach. Now she was certain it was heading for the island but not directly towards her. The dock must be to her right, around the curve of the beach. Crouching down amongst the palmettoes, she strained to see who was on it. Mr. Hobbs. Her breath caught. Had he seen her?

How far was the dock? She heard voices as if people were yelling at each other. No doubt Mr. Gray had informed Mr. Hobbs of her escape. Soon they'd be looking for her. And if she'd been seen, they knew where to look. She had to change her location. She moved out of the trees and ran down the beach in the opposite direction from where the dock must be. What was ahead? Where would she be able to hide? She didn't know where she was going. All she could do was run—and pray.

~

About twenty men huddled together on the island of Atsena Otie, away from the noise of the Faber Pencil Company around the bend. Bryce handed out maps as he spoke.

"The wharf is on the eastern side of the island. Hobbs and Gray will be there waiting to make the exchange, so we need to position ourselves out of sight but close enough to move in quickly."

Mr. Thomas took one of the maps and laid it out on the ground then squatted next to it. With a stick, he pointed to the map. "Mr. Jackson, you take your men and anchor out here. Look like you're fishing." Mr. Thomas looked up to his right at another man. "Mr. Murphy, you place your boat over here to the southeast of the island." Mr. Thomas turned his attention to the tall man next to Mr. Murphy. "Mr. Walker, you'll pass the island and anchor to the north. Does everyone have binoculars?"

Several men lifted their hands, while others displayed their binoculars. Mr. Thomas nodded, then rose and stepped aside as Bryce stepped forward. "Mr. Thomas and I, plus Sheriff Rogers and his deputies, will approach the island from the south, where we'll beach the boat and go ashore. We'll hide out in the brush where we can keep our eyes on the dock."

"So how do we know when to move in? What's the signal?" Mr. Walker glanced from Bryce to Mr. Thomas for an answer.

"When we move in to make the arrests, we'll shoot a flare. At that time, everyone pulls up anchor and gets to the wharf as soon as possible. A revenue cutter is on its way and will be in position to pursue the larger vessels involved. If you see any other boats attempting to get away, pursue them yourselves. We need to catch all involved." Mr. Thomas scanned the circle of lawmen. "Keep your eyes open and be alert. These men are dangerous."

Heads nodded and men grunted, then Mr. Murphy stepped forward. "Sirs, let us pray for protection from the Almighty." As the men bowed, he offered a prayer for their safety and success for their mission.

"Amen," the group chorused.

Bryce breathed a bit easier. At least someone knew how to speak to God. They needed all the help they could get. Sally Rose needed prayers too, but Bryce wouldn't ask the man to pray for her. Ruth Ann was doing that. *God, if you're listening to me, please answer Ruth Ann's prayers and take care of Sally Rose.* Maybe that was one prayer God would listen to.

~

Her sides hurt as she tried to catch her breath. She couldn't run anymore. She had to rest. Leaning against a tree, Sally Rose wrapped her arms around her middle, gasping for air. Her feet ached. She longed to remove her wet boots and tend to her blisters. How long had she been running? She had splashed through tidal pools and scampered over washed-up seaweed as she tried to increase the distance between herself and the dock.

A branch snapped then familiar voices followed. Sally Rose held her breath, afraid to move.

"She can't get too far." Mr. Gray's voice sounded above her. "She won't get off the island."

"Maybe not. But she can hide," Mr. Hobbs said. "And if she decides to reappear at the wrong time, it could mean trouble."

"You sure you saw her?"

"Yes, man! How many women do you think are running around this island anyway?"

"Maybe we should go back to that beach where you spotted her. Might be some tracks if the tide hasn't washed them away."

"Right. We have to find her before dark. And when we do, we'll make sure she can't get away again."

Sally Rose crouched low beside the tree, hoping they couldn't see her from their position. The voices trailed off into the distance, away from her.

She released a long sigh. Good. She'd eluded them. She stood and scanned the area. The shoreline curved around away from her, not revealing what lay on the other side. What if there were alligators? The huge alligator hide in the store flashed through her mind and weakened her knees. How would she defend herself?

She took a look over her shoulder. There was no turning back. She knew what was behind her. She had to keep moving forward. Taking a deep breath, she glanced skyward. *Lord, are You there? Do You care? Please help me.*

# Chapter Thirty-Three

She rounded the curve then came to a dead stop. The sand had ended; in its place, a marsh blended into the shore. Either she had to walk through the wet reeds, which hid the depth of the water, or climb up into the woods and make her way through them. She studied the dark water. What kind of creatures lived among those reeds? No. She wasn't that brave. She turned toward the tree line and scrambled through, trying to gain a footing in the uneven ground.

Cooler temperature from the shade was a brief respite from the hot sun, but soon bugs swarmed her sweat-soaked hairline. Whatever had become of her bonnet? She had worn one when she left the house that evening to catch up with Bryce. It must've fallen off when her kidnappers had taken her. Now she had no protection against the biting insects. Yet, maybe she did. She reached down and lifted her skirt and tore off a long strip of her underskirt. Then she wrapped it around her head until she'd created a turban. Just like Mama used to wear. Like Ruth Ann wore. She was comforted by the connection to these two strong women. If only she had their strength.

The progress was much slower as she maneuvered over and around roots and branches, grasping whatever she could to maintain her balance on the slippery incline. The shadows deepened. Soon it would be dark. Where would she go when it was nighttime? *Keep moving. Don't stop.* She pushed herself ahead. She could no longer see the water, having moved uphill to solid land.

She forged ahead until she spotted a clearing through the trees. Where was she? She edged to the open space and looked out. The cleared-out area ran from the top of the hill to the bottom. To her right and downhill, she glimpsed the water. When she looked to the left, she gasped. She could see the top of the lighthouse. Hadn't she been moving away from it? Her heart sank, and so did her hope. Across the clearing, the woods thickened. If she could just get across without being seen . . . She had to try. She sucked in her breath and sprinted across the clearing into the trees.

She plunged into the woods until she could see no farther. Then she stopped and leaned against a tree, struggling to catch her breath. What was that noise above her? Sounded like a guttural cooing. And large wings flapping. What kind of birds were up there?

She put her hand on the tree and peered up, noticing several large nests in the tree limbs. Then the tree moved under her hand. She screamed and jerked her hand from a snake crawling up the trunk. She couldn't breathe, but willed her feet to step back.

Two hands gripped her arms and pulled her away. Mr. Gray's voice breathed into her ear. "Gotcha. You ain't gittin' away this time."

He dragged her out into the moonlit clearing. Mr. Hobbs stood waiting, his face hard and cold. Sally Rose saw no sign of the flirtatious humor he usually showed. She choked back tears. Her escape had failed.

"You've been quite a lot of trouble, Miss McFarlane. Don't know why I've put up with you so long." Mr. Hobbs motioned to Mr. Gray. "Put her in the underground cistern, and make sure she can't get out."

~

Bryce fixed his gaze on the island of Seahorse Key as the boat sliced through the waves, the only sound the splash of the oars as they slapped the water. Clenching and unclenching his fists, he couldn't wait to get his hands on Hobbs. His stomach tensed at the thought of the detestable man harming Sally Rose. What must she be going through? He turned his face toward the full moon rising in the nighttime sky, its brilliance illuminating the world beneath. This had to be the night.

"Hope they can't see our boats in this bright moonlight." Mr. Thomas spoke behind him.

"There are lots of boats out here." Bryce waved his arm over the water. "Why should they suspect anything?"

"Well, that revenue cutter is a big boat to hide. If they see it, they'll run."

Bryce grimaced, his back to the man. Mr. Thomas didn't need to tell him what could go wrong. He was well aware of the risks. "The cutter is out of their line of vision and won't move in until they see the signal."

"Hope we catch 'em. These smugglers are mighty wary folks."

Another fact of which he was acutely aware. That's why they were being very careful.

"Shh." Bryce placed his finger in front of his mouth and whispered over his shoulder. "No more talking now. Our voices will carry over the water. Quit rowing and let her drift in with the current. Just use the oars to keep us from moving toward the wharf."

The boat floated on the waves until it reached shallow water, thumping on the sandy bottom a few feet from shore. Bryce and the five other men aboard hopped over the side and dragged the boat up on the beach. Bryce led the lawmen as they crept along the curving beach until the wharf came into view.

Bryce raised his hand to bring the men to a halt. They dropped to a crouching position and pulled out their binoculars. Fixing his sights on the men on the wharf, Bryce gritted his teeth when he recognized Hobbs with the glowing ember of a cigar stuck in his mouth. The taller man beside him must be Gray. The two men looked out from the dock as if waiting for someone.

An occasional bellow of laughter carried through the air. Bryce's blood boiled. How could the man be so nonchalant when Sally Rose might be in danger?

Thomas tapped Bryce on the shoulder and pointed. Bryce turned his head. A boat approached from the south.

"Over there! Another boat." Thomas whispered behind him, and Bryce fixed his binoculars on the boat approaching from the west. Both boats appeared to be heading for the wharf. Hobbs and Gray moved to the edge as if to meet them. When the boats reached the dock, a man climbed out of each and shook hands with Hobbs and Gray.

"Get ready to move in." Bryce spoke to the others in a low voice. "Is the flare set?"

Mr. Thomas showed him the flare gun aimed toward the sky.

"We have to wait until they start unloading, or they'll run."

Bryce tensed his muscles in anticipation. Finally a crewman from one ship began unloading crates onto the dock. Hobbs bent over and watched as one of the men opened the crate. When Hobbs nodded his head, a man from the other ship loaded the crates onto his ship.

"Now!"

Mr. Thomas fired the flare as Bryce and the other lawmen rushed toward the wharf, pistols raised. The men on the dock whirled around, and pandemonium broke out as they scampered in all directions. Those who had arrived on ships jumped back in and untied as fast as they could.

Hobbs drew his gun and started firing at the men rushing the dock. The lawmen returned fire. Gray went down when a shot hit his shoulder. Bryce's mind was a blur of rage as he ran, barely noticing the events around him as other boats arrived to capture those trying to escape. Nor did he see the revenue cutter approach and block the wharf. Instead, he headed straight for Hobbs, whose gun was aimed directly at him. Before Hobbs could pull the trigger, however, a bullet hit him in the arm and he dropped the gun.

Bryce charged at Hobbs, tackling him to the ground, then flipped the man over on his stomach and pulled his arms behind his back. Hobbs shouted and cursed. "What's the meaning of this? I'm conducting government business! How dare you interfere?"

"Is that right, Mr. Hobbs? Then why are you conducting your business at night?" Bryce twisted a rope around the man's wrists. "Where is she?"

Hobbs spat. "Where is who, Mr. Hernandez? Have you lost your lady friend?"

Bryce yanked the man's arms tighter, and the man cried out in pain. "Don't play the fool, Hobbs. I know you took her. What have you done with her?"

Hobbs grunted a laugh. "I'm afraid I can't help you find *Miz* McFarlane."

Bryce balled up his fist and knocked the guy out.

# Chapter Thirty-Four

She trembled from the damp chill inside the cavern as she listened to the dripping of water. Was this the way her life would end? Tears flooded her face, and her stomach clenched in agony. Would they come back for her or just leave her there? To rot. To die.

*God, no. Please, no!*

She slid down against the wet wall, too tired to stand anymore. Too tired to fight. If only she had another chance. A chance to tell everyone the truth. She sobbed. An image of Bryce's face entered her mind. *Oh, Bryce, I'm so sorry. I should have been honest with you. I should have told you what I really was, who I really am. I should have told you I love you.* She choked, sobbing silently.

*Lord, please forgive me for not being honest, for lying. Please let Bryce, Ellen, Frank, and the children know I didn't mean to hurt anyone. If You see fit to save me from this pit, I promise I'll tell the truth. I'll never lie about anything again. And please tell Papa I'm sorry I let him down.*

A calm settled over her, and her eyes grew accustomed to the darkness. She strained to see her surroundings, barely making out the stone walls around her. The space was perhaps three feet wide and about seven feet deep. A glimmer of light slipped through the crack in the floor above and reflected glistening wet walls. Thank

God, it hadn't rained much lately, or the cistern would have water in it instead of the tiny puddle at her feet.

She stood on tiptoe and stretched, pushing against the lid that covered the opening inside the house. She shoved and shoved until her arms ached, but the lid wouldn't budge. Exhausted, she let her arms drop. At least it was cool in here, unlike outside. And there were no bugs, at least not the buzzing kind. Out of the corner of her eye, she detected movement. So there were bugs after all. A large cockroach skittered across the side wall. She wrapped her arms around herself and moved away. A shudder quaked her body.

Were those holes in the wall? She squinted to look. Yes, holes as big as her fist were scattered at random on the wall. That must be how the bugs got in. What else could get in through them? She jerked her head to look around and make sure she had no other unwelcome company. Where did the holes go? Did they come up somewhere outside? If they did, at least she had some air. But if they didn't, if they only went underground, then . . . would she suffocate? Is that how she would die?

Her heart raced and she looked back up to the closed lid. Was any air getting in? She hated being confined this way. Even the kitchen was bearable with its lone window. But the pit that was her prison now closed around her, threatening to choke the life out of her. She closed her eyes. *Lord, please be with me. If I must die, please let me die in peace.*

~

Bryce rushed back down the dock. Was she here? Why'd he have to knock Hobbs out? Maybe he would have told Bryce something. He couldn't help it, though. Bryce despised the man and had run out of patience. Besides, he'd wanted to punch him for a long time.

The moonlight shone on an object on the beach between the dock and the path. Bryce rushed over to pick it up. A lady's bonnet. It was hers, he was sure of it. So she was here. He didn't know the island well other than what Frank had told him. Bryce rushed over to Gray and grabbed him by the neck. "Where is she, Gray?"

Gray moaned as he held his shoulder. "Up there." He tried to motion with his head.

"Where? In the lighthouse?"

Gray nodded then collapsed.

Bryce sprinted off the dock to the path. She had to be all right.

"Mr. Hernandez, do you need any help?" One of the agents called out.

Not taking time to answer, he charged up the path.

When he reached the crest of the hill, panting, he scanned the clearing and saw several buildings—the main house with the light coming through the center of the roof, the kitchen, outhouse, and another small shed that must be the fuel shed. Gray had indicated the lighthouse, so Bryce raced inside the front door and up the steps to the light room. No sign of her. He walked around the gallery outside the light room and searched the area below and around the lighthouse, but nothing looked unusual.

His gut tightened as he fought dark images of her fate. He ran back down the steps, yelling her name. "Sally Rose! Sally Rose!"

No response. She must be here. He sensed it. He walked into the two rooms on either side of the hallway. In the parlor, he saw no sign of her. Across the hall was the bedroom. She wasn't in there either. He stood and ran his fingers through his hair. Where could she be? Something beside the foot of the bed caught his attention.

He leaned down and picked up the strip of white cloth. Where did this come from? The material felt like part of a woman's chemise. His stomach churned at the implications the fabric aroused. No. Please no. He walked back out to the porch and scanned the grounds. Perhaps she was in one of the other buildings. He hurried to the kitchen, rushed in, and found it empty. The outhouse and fuel house were too. Was he too late?

As he strode back to the lighthouse and stepped onto the porch, he gazed up at the full moon. *All right, Lord. I can't do this by myself. I need Your help. I'm sorry I've been so stubborn. I give up. Please forgive me for being angry at You about Anna Maria. You've given me another chance, and I thank You for it. Please take care of Sally Rose, and help me find her.* Tears streaked his face as he bowed his head.

~

A scratching noise made Sally Rose open her eyes. Had she dozed off? She fixed her gaze in the direction of the sound and froze at the sight of a rat, just two feet away. As she sucked in her breath, movement from her right jerked her glance sideways. A snake crawled out of one of the holes, slithering toward the rat. She swooned but forced herself to maintain consciousness. A snake, a rat. Was this her punishment for the lies? The snake slithered toward the rat. Sally Rose couldn't breathe. Suddenly, the snake attacked the rat, swallowing it in a huge gulp. Sally Rose screamed at the top of her lungs.

~

Bryce jerked his head up. A scream. And it came from inside the house. He rushed back in. The sound was muffled, like it came from a closet, but he didn't see any.

He searched the rooms again. *Oh, God, where is she? Is she hurt?* Another scream, definitely from the bedroom area. He raced back into the room and pulled the bed away from the wall. Then he saw it. A square metal cover in the floor.

He scrambled over to it, knelt down, and pulled the lid up. "Sally Rose!"

A beloved, dirt-streaked, wide-eyed face peered up at him.

"Here. Give me your hands." He reached down into the hole and grabbed her arms, pulling her up until she could sit on the floor to pull her legs out. Then she collapsed against his chest as he embraced her.

"Thank you ... for finding me," she murmured with a tired voice.

"No, thank God for finding you."

# Chapter Thirty-Five

"I'm Mr. Bryce fighting the pirates!" Benjamin swung a stick through the air, fending off imaginary foes in the yard.

Bryce and Sally Rose watched from the settee on the side veranda and laughed at the boy's antics. She appreciated Ellen and Mr. Powell giving them some time alone. She'd been waiting for the right time to tell him about her background.

"It was very nice of Ellen to let me come back."

"Nonsense. She and Frank never wanted you to leave. You've been a good teacher to the children." Bryce gazed at the three siblings racing around the yard.

"Everyone's been so good to forgive me for not telling the truth about my experience." Sally Rose gazed down at her hands in her lap. Thank God, the unsightly cuts and scrapes were healing.

Bryce reached over and patted her arm. "We can put that behind us now, along with the rest of this whole sordid affair. Mr. Hobbs and Mr. Gray are behind bars, and you can get back to teaching—if that's what you want to do."

"If?" Sally Rose turned to face him. "Of course I want to continue my teaching, now that I know the Powells will let me." She tilted her head. "What else would I do?"

Bryce sighed and took her hand in his, then gazed into her face. "What if someone asked you to go somewhere else? Some place that might be in another country?"

Sally Rose's breath caught. Was he about to propose? He couldn't, not yet. Not before she told him the whole truth. And once he heard it, he might reconsider proposing to her.

"Bryce, I have to tell you something." Could she tell him? She had to. She'd promised God, no matter what the consequences.

"No, I need to tell you something first." He stroked her fingers, sending heat waves up her arm to her face. "When I was in Cuba, I couldn't get you out of my mind. I realized then how much I love you. And when I came back and you were missing, I was terrified I'd lost you. Forever. I don't want to lose you again."

Her heart squeezed. *Lord, help me.* "Bryce, please don't say anymore before I tell you what I need to say."

His forehead creased, and a painful look flashed through his eyes. "What is it? Have I misjudged your feelings toward me? I thought you cared for me too."

Sally Rose hated to think she might hurt him. That depth of his eyes had haunted her since their first meeting, and she couldn't bear the thought of causing him more pain than he'd already suffered, first with the loss of his wife and child, then with her dishonesty. This was so difficult.

"Oh, Bryce, I do care for you!" She leaned toward him, taking his hand in both of hers. That's why I have to tell you this now, before you say anymore."

Bryce blew out a deep breath through a clenched jaw. "All right, Sally Rose, if it's that important. Say what you must say."

She studied his large hand enveloping hers, then straightened and faced him. "Bryce, I need to tell you about my family."

He angled his head. "Your family in Ohio?"

"Yes. Well, you see, they haven't always lived in Ohio. I was actually born in Florida."

He leaned forward, eyebrows raised. "Where in Florida?"

"Apalachicola."

His eyes widened. "Are you going to tell me we're cousins?"

She jerked back. "Why would you say that?"

"Oh, you don't know, do you? My given name was McFarlane too."

"It was? But you're from Cuba, aren't you?"

"No. Well, yes. I mean, I wasn't *born* there. I was born in Apalachicola too. My father was a McFarlane, but he died of yellow fever when I was two years old. My mother took me and moved back to Cuba where she was from. When she married again, she married Juan Hernandez, my stepfather, who gave me his name."

An old photograph flashed through her mind. So that was him, the child in the picture on Granny Sally's dresser. He was her grandson. Her head began to swim and she grasped the side of the settee.

"I knew I'd seen your face before. Granny Sally kept a picture of you, your mother, and your father on her dresser. You still have the same eyes." Her voice was just above a whisper.

"We're related, aren't we? I can tell you're surprised."

All she could do was shake her head. "No. No, we're not."

"Oh. I thought you might have been named for my grandmother, Sally McFarlane."

"I was."

He shook his head. "I don't understand."

She sighed then fixed her gaze on his face. "My mother's name is Bessie. She was Sally McFarlane's slave before your grandmother freed her."

Bryce's mouth dropped open, and he started rubbing his chin with his hand. His expression darkened. "Your father wasn't . . ."

Realizing his meaning, she jumped. "Oh, no. My father was also a freed slave."

Bryce's shoulders relaxed. "I see."

"It's confusing, I know. You see, your cousin Kate McFarlane hid on her father's ship when the war started, and Pensacola evacuated. When he found her, he took her to your grandmother's house in Apalachicola. He left his freed slave there to help. That was John, my father. He and my mother fell in love and married and had me. But Aunt Kate—I always called her that—married a Union sailor from Ohio, so the whole family moved to Ohio, away from the war. So, my name isn't really McFarlane. It's just the name my parents went by, like slaves used to do."

Bryce collapsed back against the settee, staring out at the trees.

Sally Rose's eyes filled with tears. "So you see, that's why we can't be together."

He jerked his head to look at her. "Why? We're not related."

"Bryce, I'm part Negro."

He leaned toward her, his eyes piercing hers with his gaze. "Sally Rose, I don't care what kind of blood you have running through your veins. I fell in love with *you*."

"But you know there are laws against whites and Negroes—together." Tears trickled down her cheeks.

"I'm a lawyer, remember?" He reached up with his thumb and traced a tear down her face. "Listen to me. I love you. I fought for you before, and I'll do it again."

He *had* fought for her, hadn't he? He really did love her anyway. Her heart swelled with such joy it could burst.

"So, Sally Rose McFarlane, would you do me the honor of being my wife? But don't say yes unless you love me too."

"Yes, Bryce, I do love you. And I'd be honored to be your wife."

He stood, reached out his hand, and pulled her up next to him. As she fell into his embrace, she saw Ruth Ann standing in the doorway of the kitchen with a big smile across her face.

## THE END

Don't miss Book One of Coastal Lights Legacy, ***Rebel Light.***

# Acknowledgements

One of the benefits of writing historical fiction is being able to research such interesting places. Cedar Key, Florida, is one of those places. The little coastal town still has many of the buildings mentioned in Revealing Light, though they may have changed names since 1883. The present-day Island Hotel and Restaurant occupy the place of a former mercantile and hotel, which is where Frank Powell and Albert Hobbs co-owned their business. I loved seeing the original woodwork and counters in the old hotel.

While I was in Cedar Key, I stayed at the Cedar Key Bed and Breakfast. This home was built in 1880 and was the residence for the superintendent of the Eagle Mill Pencil Factory. In Revealing Light, it was the home of Frank and Ellen Powell and their four children, as well as Sally Rose McFarlane, their governess. If you are fortunate enough to stay in the B & B as I was, you'll be able to imagine the Powell family there sitting on the porch or the children playing in the lovely side yard. I want to thank Alice Phillips-Oakley, the owner of the home, for all her hospitality, information and willingness to help me.

I also visited the Cedar Key Historical Museum run by the Cedar Key Historical Society just around the corner from the B & B, where accommodating docents filled me in on much of Cedar Key's history.

Of course, one of the biggest highlights for this lighthouse fan was being able to go to the Cedar Key Lighthouse. I have Dr. Harvey B. Lillywhite, professor at the University of Florida, to thank for making that trip possible while he was director of the Seahorse Key Marine Lab. Seahorse Key, where the lighthouse stands, is leased by the University of Florida for their marine biology school and houses ten to fifteen students at the lighthouse several weeks at a time for marine study. The island is also a bird sanctuary, and at certain times of the year when the birds are nesting, visitors are not allowed. Dr. Lillywhite made an exception for me to do my research and arranged for the island caretaker to take me out to the island for a brief visit. Bronco, the caretaker, was my boat captain and a great source of information about the island. He was the one who suggested the cistern as a place to keep Sally Rose out of sight. When he showed me the secret door that hid its location inside the house, I could almost see Sally Rose down in it!

I must also thank my editors—Kathi Macias and my wonderful editor/critique partner Sarah Tipton. Sarah worked hard and fast to help me make my deadline and really assisted me in polishing the story.

Last but certainly not least, I thank my dear husband Chuck for allowing me to go on my research trip even though he couldn't go with me at the time, and also for being my final proofer to make sure any errors were cleared.

And above all, I thank God for giving me such interesting stories to write!

## REBEL LIGHT

She ran away from the war only to find herself in the middle of it. Who will protect her now?

It's 1861, Florida has seceded from the Union, and residents of Pensacola evacuate inland to escape the impending war. But Kate McFarlane's impulsive act of rebellion changes her life and that of many others in ways she never expected.

As a result, Kate finds herself with an eccentric aunt in an unfamiliar place. Lieutenant Clay Harris, a handsome Confederate officer, offers a chance for romance, but his actions make Kate question his character. When a hurricane brings an injured shipwrecked sailor from the Union blockade to her aunt's house, Kate fights attraction to the man while hiding him from Clay. She's determined to warn her sea captain father about the blockade, but needs someone to help her. Who can she trust - her ally or her enemy?

"Rebel Light by Marilyn Turk is an absolutely delightful yet compelling read. If you like Civil War stories, romance, and heart-pounding action, you will love this book!" ---
Kathi Macias, award-winning writer of more than 50 books, including Red Ink, Golden Scrolls Novel of the Year.

## REDEEMING LIGHT

Cora Miller, a recent widow, moves to St. Augustine in 1875 with her young daughter Emily to start life over as a single mother. She opens a fine millinery shop to court the tastes of the wealthy and become part of the town's social elite. She succeeds in gaining the hat business of tourists Pamela Worthington and her daughter Judith, as well as, the attention of their family friend, extravagant Sterling Cunningham. But aloof Daniel Worthington, Pamela's son, is more interested in the Indian captives recently brought to the fort.

Daniel Worthington has escorted his mother and sister to St. Augustine. Their trip has coincided with the arrival of Plains Indians being brought to Fort Marion as prisoners. He is sympathetic to the plight of the Indians and seeks to help them learn to communicate through art. Daniel believes Cora Miller is only concerned with unimportant frivolities, but when he sees her with a benevolence group at the fort, his opinion begins to change.

Just when Cora's business is picking up, jewelry from her wealthy customers begins to disappear and then mysteriously reappear in Cora's shop. What will happen to her when she is accused of theft? Will her reputation and future be ruined? Or will someone else step up in her defense?

Discussion Questions for Revealing Light

1. Sally Rose lives with two lies, neither of which she told intentionally. Have you ever let people think something is true that isn't, rather than tell them the truth?

2. Jim Crow laws were written by southern states to separate whites from Negroes (the word used for former slaves at that time) after the Union occupation was over. Did you know about them?

3. Bryce was torn between what his parents wanted him to do and what he wanted to do. Have you ever been in that position? What would you have done?

4. Bryce wanted peace and quiet after the turbulence of union strikes in Pittsburgh, but trouble seemed to find him. Can you think of a time you tried to get away from something, but it seemed to follow you?

5. Mary Etta Chapman was a nosy busybody and jealous of Sally Rose. What do you think should have been done about her? Have you ever known a "Mary Etta"?

6. Sally Rose had always wanted to be a teacher. When she was hired by the Powells, do you think she should have told them she hadn't ever been one? What do you think would have happened to her job if she had?

7. Ellen Powell has a very demanding mother-in-law. Who do you identify with – Ellen or Mother Powell?

8. Bryce quit going to church and praying when his wife died in childbirth along with their child because he blamed God for their deaths. Do you know anyone like that?

9. Have you ever had a Faber pencil? What did you think about learning cedar was harvested in the United States, then sent to Germany for the lead?

10. Albert Hobbs was a deceitful man, but jovial and outgoing. Have you ever known any "Alberts"?

11. Bryce's mother always kept him in her prayers. Do you think her prayers made a difference in his life?

12. Sally Rose's relationship with Ruth Ann helped Sally Rose have the courage to trust in the Lord and confess her

deception. Has someone you trust ever advised you to make the right decision. What was the outcome?

Made in the USA
Coppell, TX
05 August 2020